SOMEONE
IS
LYING

Jenny grew up in Shropshire thinking that authors were rock stars and that she needed to get a real job. After being made redundant she decided to write a book, then another, then another and at some point writing became her real job. SOMEONE IS LYING is her fifth book and she is now unemployable in any other field.

Praise for **The Night She Died**:

'*The Night She Died* is a gripping and hugely enjoyable book. As their lies weave a trap for the characters, the twists come at a pace that will make your head spin. I was hooked from the start' Jane Casey

'Utterly fabulous. Hooked all the way through, from one chapter to the next.' Rebecca Bradley

'Blackhurst's excellent writing keeps the tension high right through to the final page' Rachel Abbott

'*The Night She Died* is expertly pl___ __ __ __ y captivating and wonderfully

'Hooked from the first page and kept me guessing right up until the end.' Claire Douglas, *Sunday Times* Top 10 bestselling author of *The Sisters*, *Local Girl Missing* and *Last Seen Alive*.

'A fiendishly twisting mystery I finished almost in one sitting. Jenny Blackhurst is the new queen of the psychological thriller.' Mason Cross

'*The Night She Died* is a rollercoaster ride you'll love' Lucy Dawson

'This talented writer knows a thing or two about her craft.' Amanda Jennings

'This book has been read under desks in lecture theatres, on the school run, on trains . . . #obsessed!' C.R. Myers

Praise for **The Foster Child**:

'From the get-go *The Foster Child* twists and turns and creeps you out and has you wanting to scream "Behind you!"' *Weekend Sport*

'An eerie story that will keep you guessing' *Daily Mirror*

'I absolutely loved it and the ending certainly took me by surprise! Jenny has an incredible talent for taking the reader inside the minds of her characters and for delivering a heart-stopping twist!' Kathryn Croft, author of *The Girl With No Past*

'Deep, dark and disturbing . . . *The Foster Child* is a book that will stay with me. I loved it' Liz Lawler, author of *Don't Wake Up*

'A perfect blend of psychological intrigue and downright creepiness. I was thrilled, chilled, terrified and enthralled. This deserves to be a huge hit' SJI Holliday, author of *Black Wood*

'Completely engrossed, I devoured this in two sittings and couldn't turn the pages fast enough. An exhilarating read' Nina Pottell

Praise for **Before I Let You In**:

'An unnerving psychological thriller with a stonking final twist' *Sunday Mirror*

'Compelling, disturbing and thoroughly enjoyable' Sharon Bolton, author of *Little Black Lies*

'I loved it. Jenny is an evil genius' Lisa Hall, author of *Between You and Me*

'An outstanding and original thriller with . . . an explosive conclusion' B. A. Paris, author of *Behind Closed Doors*

'[A] captivating, twisty and satisfying tale . . . I can't wait to see what Blackhurst comes up with next' SJI Holliday, author of *The Damsel Fly*

'Gripping and relatable. I loved it' Helen Fitzgerald, author of *The Cry*

'A gripping clever book. I loved it and didn't want it to end' Claire Douglas, author of *Local Girl Missing*

'Such a clever twist, I really enjoyed it' Claire McGowan, author of *Blood Tide*

'A superb thriller. Compelling and thoroughly gripping. Highly recommended' Luca Veste, author of *Dead Gone*

'Brilliant. A dark psychological thriller that will have you looking suspiciously at your own friends' Mason Cross, author of *The Killing Season*

'A fantastic, twisted story' Adam Hamdy, author of *Pendulum*

'A fabulously addictive read with an amazing twist!' Sibel Hodge, author of *Look Behind You*

'Brilliantly done!' Gillian McAllister, author of *Everything but the Truth*

'A chillingly cautionary tale . . . that will linger in your mind long after you've turned the final page' Lucy Dawson, author of *You Sent Me a Letter*

'This novel is genuinely unsettling . . . A nuanced and gripping read' Catherine Ryan Howard, author of *Distress Signals*

Praise for **How I Lost You**:

'Utterly gripping – brilliant debut!' Clare Mackintosh, author of *I Let You Go*

'As twisted as a mountain road, Blackhurst's fast-moving and unputdownable debut will keep you glued to your seat' Alex Marwood

'A thrill' *Shropshire Star*

'It's unsettling, unforgettable and you won't want to put it down' *Essentials*

Also by Jenny Blackhurst and available from Headline

How I Lost You
Before I Let You In
The Foster Child
The Night She Died

SOMEONE
IS
LYING

Jenny Blackhurst

HEADLINE

First published in paperback in 2019 by
HEADLINE PUBLISHING GROUP

1

Cataloguing in Publication Data is available from the British Library

ISBN 978 1 4722 5369 9

Typeset in Meridien by Palimpsest Book Production Ltd,
Falkirk, Stirlingshire

Printed and bound in Great Britain by
Clays Ltd, Elcograf S.p.A.

MIX
Paper from
responsible sources
FSC® C104740

Headline's policy is to use papers that are natural, renewable and recyclable
products and made from wood grown in sustainable forests. The logging
and manufacturing processes are expected to conform to the
environmental regulations of the country of origin.

HEADLINE PUBLISHING GROUP
An Hachette UK Company
Carmelite House
50 Victoria Embankment
London EC4Y 0DZ

www.headline.co.uk
www.hachette.co.uk

To my gorgeous nephew Nyjah;
your smile is worth a thousand words.

Prologue

Erica

No one had expected the Facebook post, yet just minutes after it appeared everyone had seen it and they all had something to say. That's the way things were in our community. Good news travels fast, but bad news? Usain Bolt had nothing on scandal in Severn Oaks.

The first post didn't name names, but in a way, I suppose that was worse. Everyone knew who they were talking about, but those six had to front it out, pretend they had no idea it was them, and wait. Wait for the next episode, wait to see if they would be named as a murder suspect by that pitchy, nasal voice. A suspect in *my* murder, as it happens. Because although I'd love to say that reports of my death have been greatly exaggerated, the fall was unfortunately the end of the story for me. But for the Severn Oaks Six, as they would later become known, it was only the beginning.

Every story has to have a hero. And that hero has to want something.

Well, this is my story . . . so what do I want?

I want everybody to know the truth.

Because someone is lying.

1

When the alarm sounded at 5:45 a.m. on Monday 20th August, Felicity Goldman counted down from five, heaved herself out of bed and crossed the room to switch it off. Downing the bottle of water she had placed on the dressing table the night before, she popped two vitamins and headed downstairs for her regular twenty-five-minute exercise routine. Exercise done, she showered and dressed; by 6:30 she was ready for meditation and positive thinking. The children's alarms would go off at seven, and breakfast would be on the kitchen table waiting for them.

Routine was everything to Felicity. She had absorbed all of the books on productivity and personal development she could find, her 'miracle morning' taken from the minds of some of the most successful people on the planet, and there was little room for deviation. The children would be fed and teeth brushed by 7:20, dressed and ready to leave the house by 7:50. In the car on the way to school, they would talk about their goals for the day and any impediments they may face, as well as implementing a plan to overcome them. Every morning the same as the last – you could build an empire on a solid routine, and

Felicity was the queen of hers. Not that anyone ever noticed.

No, the thing that defined Felicity to the rest of the women in Severn Oaks was not a something at all, but the lack of a something. A husband. With her long blonde hair, athletic figure – she could be seen running the estate every day, twice some days – and fresh face, you would be forgiven for thinking that Felicity would be the luckiest in love, with a dashingly attractive husband who showered her with gifts and screwed her on every available surface in their four-bedroomed detached, but you'd be wrong. Felicity was very much single, and as long as she'd lived in Severn Oaks had been a mystery to the other women. None of them knew what had happened to Mollie and Amalie's father. No one except Erica, of course.

After dropping the kids at Little Owls at precisely 8 a.m. – something none of the other mothers saw, as they herded their offspring through the school gates at ten to nine – Felicity would stop at the Starbucks just outside the entrance to Severn Oaks and order a flat white before returning to her home office, which was located at the back of the house and therefore not visible from any angle.

The 20th of August started no differently than any other Monday; despite it being the middle of the summer holidays, Mollie and Amalie went to holiday club, and Felicity kept to her routine. As she walked the twins into Little Owls, she was greeted with a warm smile from Jemma, the lead co-ordinator. 'Morning, Miss Goldman,' she gushed, oblivious to the eye roll Felicity gave her at being referred to as 'Miss'. She'd filled in every form and replied to every email as 'Ms', corrected the over-enthusiastic teenager once a week for the three years the twins had been attending holiday club, and still, she was *Miss Goldman*. 'Will you be at the community picnic later?'

4

'Wouldn't miss it.' Felicity smiled, glancing at her smart-watch. She had only four minutes to complete drop-off before she would have to sacrifice her flat white – and if there was one thing she hated, it was a break from routine. Jemma gave her a conspiratorial smile – assuming, of course, that Felicity would have forgotten all about the picnic and that her morning would now consist of a last-minute dash to Waitrose for her promised contribution of cupcakes. Jemma had no way of knowing that Felicity's perfect home-made cupcakes had been baked the evening before, cooled for sixty minutes and iced with a steady and creative hand.

'And all set for the trip?'

All set was an exaggeration. Felicity had been waiting for the girls' trip since the moment she'd agreed to go along to help out. Her business meant the world to her, but only half as much as her children. She'd worked herself into the ground for the last four years, missing so many vital moments in the twins' lives, always telling herself that she was doing it for them. She'd ignored the fact that what they wanted was for her to be just like the other mums who arrived an hour early to get front-row seats for their school plays and didn't run in at the last minute and stand at the back. Mollie and Amalie had teamed up to beg her to come along on their class trip and she'd moved heaven and earth to make sure that day was free in her diary – pure, unadulterated mum time – and now she was looking forward to it more than they were.

'Very much so. The girls can't wait until Mummy comes to holiday club for the day, can you? Come on, kisses!' She kissed each twin twice, fixed the bow in Amalie's hair and was out of the door by 8:05 a.m. on the dot.

'Flat white to take out. I threw in a muffin – a treat for our regulars.'

The barista smiled, pleased with himself for remembering the order she made literally every day, this time with a blueberry muffin next to it.

'Thank you.' Felicity smiled. It hadn't escaped her notice how cute he was, or how he always gave her special attention, making conversation; once she thought he'd even winked at her.

'No problem. You live in Severn Oaks, right?'

'How do you know that?'

'I have a friend who lives there. Tristan Patterson?'

Felicity frowned. 'Patterson? Wait, yeah, I know his mum, Janet? He drives a yellow car?'

'Yeah, that's him.'

'Right, well, I don't know Tristan but his mum is lovely.'

There was an awkward pause while Felicity tried to figure out where he was going with this conversation. Was he going to ask her out? That could be awkward.

'Well, you're probably in a rush. Have a nice day.'

Felicity let out a relieved breath and tossed the muffin in the bin outside as she left.

2

The community picnic was a staple at Severndale Primary. It had been running so long that, had Erica not reminded them every year that it was her idea, they might have forgotten completely. She'd always hoped that if anything tragic should happen to her, they would continue her legacy – in her name, of course – and surprisingly it had been Karla Kaplan who had brought up the issue at the first PTA meeting after her death.

'I think we should have a tribute to Erica,' she'd announced, to much murmuring of agreement.

Amazing how generous a guilty conscience will make you.

Severndale Primary was the school of choice for parents who wanted their children to have a decent education without the cost of going private. People assumed that those who lived in Severn Oaks – the gated community within Severndale Parish – could afford private education and were 'slumming it' for political reasons, but in truth the only ones with an extra twenty-five grand to spare were Karla and Marcus, and their children were never going to be sent to private school – not with their 'brand' being famous for being so down-to-earth. That was the reason Karla – Cheshire's answer to Martha Stewart – had told everyone who would listen that she'd turned down *Real Housewives of Cheshire* twice; that and the fact that they might have found out that she orders takeout every other night and throws beans on toast at her children the other evenings. Hardly Earth Mother, you might conclude.

Miranda Davenport swung her white Kia Sportage into the space marked 'taxis and buses only' and engaged the handbrake. Technically, she knew she wasn't supposed to leave the car here, but she always showed up after the school bus had gone so she didn't see any harm. And there weren't going to be any buses in the school holidays, so today was definitely fine. The on-street parking was always rammed, and if she parked up at the community centre she'd be forced into conversation with one of the other mums. Eurgh. No one really minded her being there – or they'd never told her not to park there, at any rate.

'Stand there,' Miranda instructed her eldest child, Logan, repositioning him so that he blocked the boot of her car from the eyes of any passers-by. 'Just wait a minute, Charity, there's a goo— No, I said wait! Close that door!' Shaking her head and muttering 'forgoodnesssake' under her breath, she tore open the plastic covering and gingerly began transferring Luxury Belgian Chocolate Cupcakes from the circular plastic tray into a large, square Tupperware container that had MIRANDA DAVENPORT printed in capital letters on the side in black Sharpie.

'They look better in that black thing,' Logan pointed out, glancing over his shoulder. 'They look like you made them yourself in that tub.'

Miranda smiled. 'You just watch out for that nosy cow Mary-Beth King.'

Cupcakes safely transferred, Miranda lifted the tub out of

the boot, nearly slamming into Felicity Goldman who was carrying her own Tupperware tub full of delicious-looking cakes. Miranda gave them a pointed look. 'They look very nice, Felicity. Nothing beats a bit of home cooking, eh?' She gave a conspiratorial smile that Felicity didn't return. 'Where are the girls?'

'I'm just going to grab them from Owls,' Felicity replied. 'I've been working this morning.'

'Aw . . .' Miranda gave what she hoped was a sympathetic smile. 'Poor things. My kids would go mad if I put them in school during the holidays.'

'Yes, well, I'm in a rush, actually,' Felicity said, sidestepping Miranda and leaving her behind completely.

Miranda shook her head. Some people only wanted to be hostile. Really, she didn't understand some of the other mothers at this school, acting like they were better than everyone else.

'Miranda! Just the person. I was hoping I'd catch you here.'

Steph, the school secretary, had a way of appearing as if from nowhere – she was particularly good at using the trick when it came to getting donations out of people. 'Here, let me hold those while you help Charity out.' She took the tub of cupcakes and inhaled deeply – exactly why, Miranda had no idea, because all she'd be able to smell was plastic. 'These look amazing,' she beamed, her round cheeks fixed in a smile.

'What was it you wanted, Steph?' *Might as well get it over with.*

Steph's smile faltered. 'Well, I was just wondering if you'd be running for Parent Governor this year? You did such a great job filling in after Erica, well, after Erica last year and—'

And no one else wants it, Miranda thought. *Not now that*

Erica's dead. She plastered on a smile. 'Of course! You can count on me.'

The minute she'd said it she wished she hadn't. Two months of running a campaign against whichever other poor sods Steph had roped in to make it look like Miranda wasn't a shoo-in. She wasn't sure she could be bothered. And yet there was that part of her that so desperately wanted to be everything to everyone: Chair of the PTA, Parent Governor, Parish Counsellor. Hell, she'd even tried to start a Neighbourhood Watch, but no one in Severn Oaks could be bothered. Speaking of which, she was going to have to find time to talk to them all about the CCTV issue; it had been at least six months since she'd raised it last. Perhaps she could hire Felicity to run this campaign for her – her job was PR, after all, and it would leave Miranda time for all the other things she couldn't stop saying yes to. She thought about how Felicity had snubbed her only moments before. On second thoughts, perhaps she'd hire one of her rivals.

Over at the cake stall Felicity had handed over her distinctly medium-sized tub of cakes and was making civil small talk with Cynthia, who was running the stand, when Miranda sashayed over with her gigantic box.

'You've got the right idea, Felicity,' Miranda remarked, looking at the box still in Cynthia's hands. 'I wish I'd thought to buy mine. So much easier than home cooking. They look *wonderful.*'

Felicity opened her mouth to speak but Miranda, having delivered her killer blow, had already placed her tub on the table and walked away, Charity skipping ahead and Logan following behind with a confused look plastered on his face.

3

'I thought you said the other dads were going to be here.' Marcus Kaplan spoke through gritted teeth and nodded at Miranda Davenport, who was hovering around the cake stall looking overly pleased with herself. His wife, Karla, her phone jammed to one ear, gave Miranda a wave and a beaming smile that disintegrated the moment the other woman was out of sight. 'You said Alex had taken the afternoon off. I only came because—'

'Hiya, it's Karla. Just checking in on the *Real Housewives* pitch – crossing my fingers! Let me know as soon as you hear, okay? Thanks, bye bye.' She swiped to end the call. 'She's not answering. I bet it's a no *again*. Do you know I heard that Martin Houseman's wife is going to be joining them next season? What does she do? Nothing! She's just a housewife.'

'I thought that was the point?'

'Funny. What were you moaning about, anyway?'

'You said the dads would be coming to the picnic.'

'Oh, yeah, I thought they would be.' Karla lied with such ease that it was hard to see why she and Erica hadn't been better friends when she was alive. 'Besides, if I have to be here, I don't see why you shouldn't be. I did the last two school events on my own while you were swanning around the country on your book tour, you're lucky I didn't make you do this one by yourself.'

'What, and let me loose with all of our respectable neighbours? You wouldn't dare.'

Marcus Kaplan, a self-made millionaire, was the resident celebrity of Severn Oaks. His internationally best-selling self-help books *Unleash the Power of YOU*, *YOU are all you need*, and *Destroying the old YOU* had sold over ten million copies each, been *Sunday Times* and *New York Times* number ones and won numerous awards that currently lined the walls of his forty-foot garden office. Marcus travelled the world to coach some of the biggest celebrities, government officials – he'd even given advice to the President of the United States. His three-day conferences pulled in thousands of people, all wanting to change their life for the better. Miranda had tried to watch one of his YouTube videos once and there had been so many F-bombs that she'd turned off after less than ten minutes.

'Do you blame me? After Mary-Beth's last barbecue she had to explain to Teddy what a heroin addict was. Just because *our* kids are streetwise, Marcus, it doesn't mean you can just shoot your mouth off in front of everyone else's.'

Ah yes. The thing about Marcus Kaplan, the part of his story that really made him the talk of Severn Oaks, was the drugs. You see, in order to be able to tell people how to turn your life around, it helps if you have been where they have been – hit rock bottom, as they say. And Marcus Kaplan knew all about rock bottom. If you read any of Marcus's books, you'll find that the entire first three chapters are dedicated to his abusive childhood and his descent into heroin addiction, how he narrowly escaped death and prison and turned his *whole life on its head* by using his YOU principles to become a millionaire life coach to the stars. If he can do it, so can YOU.

'Mary-Beth saw the funny side,' Marcus grinned, and Karla relented, shaking her head. That was the thing with their relationship, the thing that most people didn't know. People assumed the hand holding and the face stroking and their inability to tear their gaze away from one another was part of the circus act that came with being the Kaplans, but the truth was they were devoted to one another in the true sense of Till Death Do Us Part. Whose death was another question.

'Felicity!' Karla waved her arm in the air and her friend, looking relieved to see her, crossed the field, the twins running ahead.

'Girls! Slow down, or you'll fall!'

Mollie and Amalie flung themselves at Karla and Marcus. Karla gave Amalie a tight squeeze then passed her to Marcus who had hoisted Mollie onto his back.

'You two!' Felicity said, shaking her head. 'Poor Marcus.'

'Oh, it's fine – at least they are lighter than my two,' Marcus said as both five-year-old girls clung to his neck. 'Not that Brandon has asked for a piggyback in some time.'

'I take it Bran isn't here?' Felicity asked, glancing around.

Karla snorted.

'What, spend time with his family? No, he could think of about fifty better things to do. Zach's over at the football stand – he'll be there all afternoon. Why doesn't Uncle Marcus take you girls for cakes?'

The girls cheered and Marcus bounced up and down a few times. 'You ladies don't want cake?'

'Not for me,' Felicity said. 'Besides, Miranda's over there. Do you know, she just basically called me a crap mother for putting my girls in Owls during the holidays? Said they would grow up to hate me or something.'

'She did *not*?' Karla scowled. 'If I was one of her kids, I'd be begging to be in school all year round.'

Felicity smiled. 'True. I do feel bad, though. I mean, it's their summer holidays and they are stuck in childcare.'

'They love Owls,' Karla replied, linking Felicity's arm and pulling her over to a picnic blanket all set up on the grass. 'Here, this is us. Anyway, my kids much preferred childcare to being with me. You'd just be stressed and thinking of all the work you should be doing, and they would be bored within hours. At least at Owls they are surrounded by kids and that annoyingly perky girl – what's her name . . . Jemma? Is she still there?'

'Yes,' Felicity sighed. 'You're right, it's just . . . when Miranda said that, I felt like the worst mum ever.'

'Ignore her. Women like that make it their mission to make other mums feel crap.'

'I think you're right,' Felicity replied. 'When I handed over the home-made cakes I'd spent all bloody night on she told everyone they were store-bought.'

'*Ignore her.* You're the only one of us without wrinkles – you don't need that kind of stress in your life, believe me.'

Felicity pulled a face. 'I'll try, but she's difficult to avoid.'

'Too true,' Karla groaned. 'She's coming over here now.'

'Afternoon, ladies!' Miranda walked towards them, beaming. 'Marcus said you were sitting over here. Mind if I join you?'

4

'Mary-Beth not coming to join us?'

'She said she would,' Karla said, rifling through her bag for her sunglasses. 'When I saw her on the gate. She looked like she was regretting saying she'd do it, to be honest. I almost stopped to help.'

'Almost?' Felicity grinned.

Karla pushed her glasses up her nose. 'I didn't want to leave Marcus on his own, did I?'

'I'm surprised she came at all,' Miranda mused.

They'd all told Mary-Beth that they would understand if she decided to opt out of this year's picnic, that she might feel like it was just too difficult to come alone, to see someone else manning the cake stall or handing out the medals to the winners of the three-legged race. In fact, no one had even bothered to organise the three-legged race this year – they were too busy lazing around the grass, enjoying the sunshine. Erica would have turned in her grave. But Mary-Beth had insisted that she was fine, that she'd be there. Now she seemed to have had a change of heart.

'Maybe she had to rush off to work?' Felicity said.

Mary-Beth loved her job at the local estate agents, helping

to match people with their dream homes. 'The most important thing you can buy and I'm right there with them,' she'd say.

'She said she'd got the day off for it,' Karla replied. 'I think she felt like she should, for Erica.'

'Poor thing,' Felicity said. She pulled a twin onto her lap and began lathering her in suncream. 'She's still grieving. These last ten months have been so hard on her.'

'On all of us,' Miranda pointed out, ruffling her red hair. 'We all loved Erica.'

To her credit, Karla refrained from rolling her eyes. She had never really understood why Mary-Beth loved Erica so much – the two of them were like chalk and cheese. Mary-Beth kept to herself, was quietly spoken and only ever contributed to a conversation when she had something diplomatic to say. Erica, on the other hand, had a smart mouth and couldn't help but use it. There was always something cutting and sarcastic lurking on the tip of her tongue. While other women thought of their glorious comebacks hours after an argument, while they were lying in the bath replaying every clever thing they could have said – but wouldn't have, even if they'd thought about it – Erica was the one who had a litany of put-downs ready and waiting. Sometimes she was disappointed if she didn't get to use them.

Not only that but Mary-Beth was always so generous, not just with her money, although she gave just as much as the Kaplans without feeling the need to take a full-page ad in the *Chester Herald*. No, Mary-Beth was generous from her understated, un-highlighted head down to her un-manicured toes. She would let you have from her whatever you needed, be it money, time, sage advice, or her husband.

'Can I nick a bit of that suncream, Fliss? Bran has his dad's skin, but Zach burns in the rain.'

Felicity tossed the bottle over to Karla, who scanned the field for her youngest son, made sure everyone saw that she'd *tried* to find him, then slumped back down in defeat.

Miranda's phone buzzed, and she made a show of picking it up to examine it.

'Oh, suncream time for mine too.' She smiled at the other women. 'I'd better go and get it out of the car.'

'Just use mine,' Felicity said. 'Save you going back to the car.'

'Oh,' Miranda looked at the bottle appraisingly. 'Factor fifty, is it?'

'Of course.' Felicity raised her eyebrows.

Miranda took the bottle from Karla's outstretched hand. 'Thank you, that will save me a trip.'

None of the other women had any idea that Miranda had left her children's suncream somewhere at home, having been entirely unable to find it that morning, or that the beep from her phone had been a news-in-brief update rather than a 'reapply suncream' alarm. She called Charity over, safe in the knowledge that as far as anyone knew, she was completely in control.

'Alex working today?' Felicity asked in a forced casual tone.

Karla looked at her with raised eyebrows – Felicity knew full well that Miranda's husband avoided these things like the plague.

'Marcus said he was hoping he'd be here.'

'No, he's working, as always,' Miranda grumbled. 'I'd place a bet that he'd take extra shifts rather than go to a school event.'

'Has he been working a lot recently then?' Felicity pushed.

Karla glowered at her. 'Is he going with the blokes to that Thai place they were on about next week?' she interjected, trying to swing the subject onto safer ground.

Both women ignored her.

'Not any more than usual.' Miranda's smile was pinched.

'It's just that I've seen him coming back late a few times recently . . .'

Miranda looked like she'd just drunk one of Felicity's chia seed smoothies.

'Well, it's very nice of you to be so concerned about my husband's work habits. As it happens, he's worked late a few nights to make up for some time he took off with *me*. He'll be touched you've been keeping an eye on his comings and goings.'

Felicity laughed, unfazed by Miranda's discomfort. 'It's a small community – everyone sees everything, remember? I hope he's not *working* too hard.'

The emphasis on the word 'working' hammered home Felicity's point – Miranda had failed to hide how insecure she was about her husband's fidelity, and Felicity wasn't going to let her get away with her offhand jibe about home-made cakes. Whether Miranda would let her get away with her comments about Alex's comings and goings, they would have to wait and see. Because less than ten minutes later something happened to make them all forget their petty war of words.

5

It was twelve fifteen when the first post went up, and by twelve thirty it had been shared by over forty people. A large portion of those people were the mums at the picnic, thumbing through their phones while their offspring jumped up and down mindlessly on the bouncy castle, or uploading photos of Martha and Sophia, stupid grins plastered on their faces, as proof they were picnic-attending, children-pleasing, 'hands-on' mums. One mum showed another, who turned to the next. *What does it mean, do you think? Is this some kind of joke? Who would say these things?* People took screenshots before the school's web administrator had a chance to react, and before long the number of views had risen to fifty, then sixty. Record numbers for the school Facebook page, which parents were always pretending not to have seen as they scrolled past updates about bingo nights and school discos in favour of their neighbours' disputes about on-street parking.

Miranda rarely ever used Facebook. Instagram was so much better for showing your life through a sunshine filter, little snapshots of a Level Ten life when the reality was much nearer a Four or Five. On Instagram, you couldn't see the last-minute dash to the shops for a forgotten picnic, just the 'after' picture of your children enjoying Asda pre-made sandwiches decanted into a sparkling clean lunchbox: #lovinglife #winning.

Karla was lying on the grass, her long tanned legs stretched out and her bare feet resting in her husband's crotch. Her cropped denim cut-offs were so short that the pockets were visible below the ripped edges, and her black 'Born to fly' eagle T-shirt had ridden up revealing a flat, golden stomach that showed no sign of the two children who had resided there.

'Does she have to dress like that?' Miranda muttered to Felicity, surveying Karla from under her sunglasses. 'I mean, there are children present. Young, impressionable boys. What must Brandon and Zachary think? Their friends' tongues are practically on the floor at the sight of their mother!'

'I'm pretty sure Zach is too young to notice,' Felicity replied. 'And Bran wouldn't be caught dead at a community picnic. Besides, I think she looks amazing. If the twins hadn't completely ruined my stomach and my legs weren't white enough to blind somebody I'd be flaunting it all too.'

'Yes, well . . .' Miranda made an unimpressed noise in the back of her throat. 'I think it's inappropriate.'

Karla rolled over and pulled down her glasses. She raised two perfectly plucked eyebrows. 'Problem, Miranda?'

Miranda gave a sharp laugh like the tinkle of breaking glass. 'No problem, sweetie. I was just saying how nice it is that we can do this in memory of poor Erica—'

'Jesus, fuck!'

All eyes spun towards Marcus but rather than apologise for his outburst he handed his phone to Karla, whose face went slack.

'Bloody hell,' she muttered, her brows knotting into a frown. 'Is this on the school page?'

'Yep,' Marcus replied. 'It's been up over fifteen minutes. Don't they have an administrator approving their posts?'

'I've told Steph about this a million times,' Felicity replied. 'But what do I know? I'm just a bloody social media manager. What does it say?'

'See for yourself.' Karla scanned the field and tossed Marcus's phone to Felicity. 'Where's Mary-Beth?'

Felicity's eyes travelled down the post and she sucked in her breath. 'Bloody hell, that's not funny.'

'I doubt Mary-Beth will think so either,' Karla said. 'But I can't see her anywhere. Should I ring her?'

'What is it?' Miranda trilled, looking at Felicity. 'What's going on?'

'I'm going to go and find her.' Karla ignored Miranda and pulled on her black leather sandals, desperately trying to poke the straps through the buckles.

'For God's sake, will one of you tell me what's going on?' Miranda snapped.

Felicity handed the phone to her without saying a word.

Miranda read the post and made a small gurgling sound in her throat. 'Who posted this? It just says "Andy".'

'Click on the name . . .' Felicity pointed to the screen. 'That's the profile. Click on it. Oh, for God's sake, Miranda, pass it here!' She grabbed the phone from Miranda and clicked around, shoving it back at her with a tut of exasperation. 'It's no use, the profile is private. "To see what Andy shares with friends send him a friend request."'

Miranda seemed to have frozen to the spot, her mouth hanging open dumbly. And no wonder – after all, she knew precisely who the post was about. And soon, so would everyone else.

'Has anyone seen Mary-Beth King?' Karla asked, moving through the crowd of mums herding their children from stall to stall.

'Karla, hey!' Cynthia Elcock, Poppy's mum, grabbed her

21

arm. 'Have you seen what someone's posted on the school Facebook page? Is it some kind of joke, does anyone know?'

'If it is, it's a pretty sick one.' Karla grimaced. 'Have you seen Mary-Beth? She'll be devastated if she sees this, she and Erica were so close.'

'No, sorry, I haven't seen her all day.' Cynthia shook her head. 'What is the world coming to when people think things like this are funny?'

'God knows who thinks this is funny.'

Karla pulled out her own phone and looked around. Dozens of people were doing the same, passing their own phones to their friends, pointing at the screens. She logged in to Facebook and checked again. It was still there, now with comments underneath popping up every few seconds.

SOMEONE IS LYING

THE MURDER OF ERICA SPENCER

A stunning new podcast called *The Truth About Erica* looks at the events of 28th October 2017 when, while at a Halloween Party, local hero Erica was believed to have fallen from a tree house and died, as a result of too much alcohol.

I know better.

This podcast brings to light new and never-heard evidence that will cast doubt on everything you think you know about this 'tragic accident' and expose a murderer living in the prestigious gated community of Severn Oaks. I introduce the six people with the most to gain from Erica's death, and over the coming weeks I will expose the shocking secrets they are hiding from you all.

Who killed Erica Spencer?

Tune in tomorrow to find out more.

4 comments 42 shares
👍 Like   💬 Comment   ↪ Share

Savannah Hepworth
Who is this? Why are you doing this?

Annalise Rodgers
Do you realise Erica's family can see this?
Haven't they been through enough?

Gary Holding
REPORTED TO FB AND THE SCHOOL. DISGUSTING.

Francis Carter
I wonder who the six people are?

6

'Did you find her?' Miranda heard Felicity ask as Karla arrived back at the group.

Felicity had gathered together all of the children while Marcus and Miranda had stared at each other dumbly, neither knowing what to do or say. Karla shook her head.

Because despite their differences, Erica had been one of them. Okay, she loved to know what was going on in everyone's lives, had an acerbic sense of humour and was always the first to take over whenever anything needed organising, but those attributes didn't mean she didn't have good qualities as well. She was naturally good at organising things, and she never complained about doing the bulk of the work when money needed raising or costumes making. Even the community picnic lacked its usual fanfare this year because she wasn't at the helm – much as it pained Miranda to admit it. And her death had devastated her husband, Jack, and her two children, Max and Emily, and had left the small community of Severn Oaks and the wider town of Severndale stunned with grief. Ten months on, no one – least of all the people present at that Halloween Party – wanted the details of her death dragged up again.

The phone pressed to Felicity's ear rang and rang. She cut it off.

'No one is at the school. I thought teachers were *always* in school during the holidays? I have Steph's number – should I call her, do you think? I'm certain she'd have access to the school Facebook page.'

'She's the administrator,' Miranda agreed. 'And she obviously hasn't seen it, or she'd have taken it down by now. Perhaps you could give her a call.'

But they both knew it was too late. Damage limitation doesn't work in primary schools – the one way to ensure information spread fast was to make it gossip-worthy. That was why no one had turned up to buy Easter egg hunt tickets in 2016 – until Erica told everyone that Phoebe Miller and Mr Randall, the PE teacher, were in the habit of using the annexe to meet up for extra-marital activity. Probably on the exact day for which she was selling tickets. In that very annexe! Funny how many people detoured from their usual route to their cars – and how many bought Easter egg hunt tickets, so they wouldn't look like shameless gossip seekers.

And now here was Erica again – not spreading the rumours, this time, but the subject of them. And so many people had seen the post that, even if it were removed now, there would be talk of nothing else for the rest of the day, probably longer.

'Why was she a local hero?' Felicity asked.

'She saved someone from the river a few years ago. Didn't you know that?'

Felicity shook her head. 'I haven't lived here as long as you, remember?'

'True, I'm just surprised she didn't find some way to slip it into the conversation. She usually did. Erica loved to play the hero.' Karla lowered her voice. 'I heard she was shagging him, but she forgets that bit when she tells everyone.'

'What do you think they mean, *the six people with the most to gain from Erica's death*?' Miranda asked suddenly, as though she had just remembered the others were there. 'Do you think they mean us?'

'Of course not,' Karla snapped. 'Sorry, fucksake, this is ridiculous.'

Miranda didn't even have the energy to admonish Karla for her language around her children. Her entire head hurt, an ache at the back, a pounding at the front – it was the beginning of the mother of all migraines, and she just needed to get home and lie down. As she glanced up she saw a group of six mums huddled together whispering. Two of them were glancing in their direction – both heads turned away as they saw her look over.

'I'm sorry,' she mumbled. 'Does anyone have any water? I just need to, I can't . . .'

'Migraine?' Karla, who was usually rolling her eyes at Miranda, or shaking her head when she thought the other woman wasn't looking, seemed to understand instantly. 'You go. I'll take Charity and Logan back to ours for a bit, Zach can shoot some hoops with Logan and Charity can do some arts and crafts. I need to get out of here and call my agent.'

Miranda nodded. Usually, she'd insist on being at any play date with the Kaplans – their parenting was too laissez-faire for her liking – but she felt like all the energy had been sucked out of her with a straw. 'Thank you. I'll send Alex over for them as soon as he gets home.'

'Are you okay to drive, Miranda?' Marcus asked, genuine concern on his face. 'I can run you home in your car and Karla can take the kids in ours?'

'I'm fine, thanks. And thanks again for taking the kids. You two be good, okay? Daddy will pick you up in a short while.'

SOMEONE IS LYING

She barely even waited for her children to reply before turning and stumbling through the staring crowds towards her car, where she sat in the front seat of her Kia Sportage gripping the wheel so tightly her knuckles were white.

7

Mary-Beth King leaned against the back door, panting to catch her breath, her chest wracked with sobs. She wiped her sleeve across her face, tears and snot streaking across the arm of her jumper. She let her weak legs give way and slid down onto the floor of the utility room, rested her head against the cold tumble drier. She couldn't get the noises to stop, the piercing scream, the sickening thud of a body hitting the floor. Thank God the kids were at her mum's – she felt like she might be losing her mind.

She needed to speak to someone. She should call the police, that was the only thing left to do, the only right thing to do. She could call Karla, or perhaps Felicity, but that would be it – they would make her go to the police, and there would be no way back.

Peter.

She was going to have to tell her husband everything.

Would he leave her? Possibly. But he was the only person who might not. Who might not make her go to the police and confess, who might not leave her to face this alone, who might not turn his back on her.

He was the only person who might help her.

8

'*Police say there will be no further investigation into the death of thirty-seven-year-old Erica Spencer from Severndale . . .*'

'Turn that shit off, will you, please?' Karla aimed the plastic fly swatter across the expansive granite surface at her son.

Brandon scowled. 'Don't you think it's in our best interest to know about this?' He pointed to the Alexa speaker on the kitchen windowsill, where the podcaster's nasal voice continued. 'He's talking about something that happened in our community. Nothing exciting ever happens here.'

'What happened to Erica was not exciting. It was a tragic accident,' Marcus replied, scooping pasta up with his fork and pointing it at his eldest son. 'Which happened at *our* party – or have you forgotten? In the tree house we had to have torn down because your mother was so upset. And this guy is exploiting her family's grief for salacious entertainment and personal gain.'

'And only a real asshole would do that,' Brandon retorted.

Karla dropped her serving spoon into the Le Creuset.

'Shit!' She plucked the tomato-soaked spoon out and wiped it on a tea towel. 'Brandon Kaplan, you apologise to your father! And don't ever let me hear you use that kind of language at my table again.'

Marcus shook his head. 'It's okay, sweetheart,' he raised his eyebrows at Brandon. 'I've never *exploited* anyone for what we have,' he gestured around at the solid oak kitchen, the wide AGA overflowing with pots and pans, Brandon's iPad flung carelessly next to the sink, 'and I don't see you complaining about living here, or spending the money my salacious entertainment makes.'

'Alexa, stop,' Brandon muttered grudgingly, and the unidentifiable voice ceased abruptly.

'Thank you,' Karla said, knowing he would be straight up to his room to listen to the rest once dinner was over. 'The only way to protest people like that is to ignore them completely. If he has no listeners by this time next week, his show will be over, and Erica can rest in peace like she deserves.'

'Are you kidding?' ten-year-old Zachary scoffed. 'Everyone in school is going to be listening to it. This time next week, it'll be bigger than *Serial*. Do you really think he's going to name who killed her at the end?'

'How many times?' Karla sighed, pulling a stool up to the island. 'No one killed her. Erica drank too much and fell out of that tree house – a tragedy, but an accident.'

'You can plead Peterson as much as you like, but you know how much a small town loves a story,' Bran said. 'And people from my school already take the piss out of this place all the time—'

'Your mum told you to watch your language at the table,' Marcus chided.

Karla looked at her eldest son curiously. 'Why do people at your school take the mick out of this place?' she asked. 'You mean,' she gestured around, 'this place as in Severn Oaks?'

Brandon shrugged. 'Yeah. 'Cause it's posh and everyone is so up their own arses. Present company excepted, of course.'

'Your school is hardly the Bronx, Bran.'

'Nah, but the other kids don't have to lock themselves away as if they're scared they might get infected by the normal folk outside, do they? They joke that one day we'll make our own schools and grow our own foods and we'll never have to leave.' He grinned. 'Laura calls it the Cult of Kaplan, you know, 'cause we're in the big house in the middle. With all our disciples around us.'

'Laura sounds like a charmer,' Karla retorted, gearing up to ask him more questions on how the outsiders talked about those 'inside the walls', but Marcus spoke instead.

'Who do you think it is?'

'I thought we were forgetting the whole thing,' Karla reprimanded. 'Don't feed the trolls and all that.'

'I think it's got to be someone who lives here,' replied Brandon, ignoring his mother.

Against her better judgement, Karla couldn't help herself. 'That didn't sound like anyone from Severn Oaks.'

Brandon laughed. 'Well, it's not his real voice, is it? What, did you think his name was really Andy Noon too?'

'What are you on about, not his real voice?'

'He's playing it through voice distortion software,' Brandon explained. 'And I'm saying "he" but you know it could be a woman, right? It could be *anyone*.'

'It could be me . . .' Zachary joked in his best spooky voice.

'So what, he – or she, sorry – might not be as old as they sound, either?'

'Nope.'

'And—' The house phone started ringing.

'Saved by the bell.' Brandon tossed his fork onto his plate. 'Can I go?'

Karla dismissed him with a wave of her hand and reached over to pick up the phone.

'Kaplan residence?'

'Karla, have you heard it?' Felicity's voice was a hush, as though she were afraid someone might be listening in.

'The stupid podcast thing? Bran just had it on in the kitchen, but I made him turn it off. I hope you're not worrying yourself about this, Fliss. Erica has been gone nearly a year. The police investigated at the time, they determined there was nothing suspicious about her death. If you start stressing yourself about this now you'll— Wait there . . . Can I call you back?' She laid down the phone as Brandon walked back into the kitchen, his face slack and pale.

'What is it?' Marcus asked, jumping off his stool and crossing the floor to his son. 'What's wrong?'

'Laura just texted,' Brandon half whispered, all sense of excitement and gossip gone now. 'She listened to the podcast . . .'

'Oh, for God's sake, Bran, I told you—'

'He's named you two,' Brandon muttered, looking down at his feet. 'He says you two are suspects in Erica Spencer's murder.'

The phone began to ring again.

9

'Police say there will be no further investigation into the death of thirty-seven-year-old Erica Spencer from Severndale, Cheshire. Mrs Spencer fell to her death at a Halloween party inside the exclusive gated community known as Severn Oaks, but an inquest has concluded that a mixture of drink and the wrong footwear were to blame for the mother of two's death . . .'

I'm Andy Noon, and you're listening to the first episode of The Truth About Erica. *What you heard there was a news report following a short inquest into Erica Spencer's death, a death that the police closed as accidental. Yet I'm going to tell you a tale of lies, revenge and deception that ended in a Halloween murder here inside the gated community of Severn Oaks, Cheshire.*

On the 28th of October 2017, Erica Spencer, a resident of Severn Oaks for six years, woke up thinking that her day would be like any other. That she would do the food shop, buy the finishing touches for an outfit she was looking forward to wearing to the party that evening, spend time with her friends, then fall into bed with her husband, Jack. She had no idea that one of the smiling faces she greeted that morning would, by that evening, become her murderer.

For those of you who don't know, Severn Oaks is the place everyone aspires to live, where neighbour loves neighbour, where everybody knows your name and where nobody can penetrate our peaceful existence. It is a safe space – the money and status that pulsate within these walls protect us from the dangers of the big, bad outside world. But what if the danger has been inside the walls all along? On the 28th of October, Erica Spencer would find out.

Let's talk about Erica. She and Jack had been happily married for nearly seventeen years. In fact, it was their anniversary plans that consumed Erica's thoughts on the day of her death. Would they go to a restaurant or take a holiday? Who would look after the children? The couple have two children together, Max and Emily – Max was nearly sixteen at the time of his mother's death, and Emily just seven. Emily attends the local primary school, while Max is in the sixth form.

Although she had no paid employment, Erica was always busy. She dedicated her time and effort to giving back to the community, volunteering at the local library, running the PTA, volunteering as a parent governor at the school Emily attended, and organising events. Their sizeable home in Severn Oaks reigns from the top of the bank, looking down on the other houses that sit humbly at her feet, twelve other houses in total. A small, tight-knit community – or so they would have you believe.

So how did Erica Spencer end up lying sprawled on the grass beneath a large oak tree in Severn Oaks, her neck snapped in two places? Were the head injuries she sustained truly 'consistent with a fall' as the coroner concluded? Or were they inflicted before the fall? Did Erica need to be silenced? If so, by whom?

Who would want this philanthropic mother of two dead? What really happened that night? And how many of the Halloween party guests know the truth about Erica?

SOMEONE IS LYING

In this podcast I'll be looking at the six people with the most to hide about the night Erica Spencer died and discussing how each and every one of them had a motive to murder the woman who, in 2015, was named a local hero for saving a young man from drowning. We will meet a fresh-faced businesswoman with a reputation and a secret to protect; the new alpha female who slid seamlessly in to fill the gap Erica left in our community; the local celebrity couple who are not all they seem; a best friend who is a little too good to be true; and her husband, who features heavily in Erica's diary. A diary I just happen to have exclusive access to.

Six suspects, six podcasts and a murder. I'll see you the same time next week when we discuss how Erica Spencer died and focus on the first of the Severn Oaks Six.

10

'A fresh-faced businesswoman with a reputation and a secret to protect? I *know* you all talk about whether I've had cosmetic surgery behind my back. The beeping beeper is mocking me! Who else the flip could it be, Karla?'

'The beeping beeper? The flip?'

'I'm putting Amalie to bed. She's like a bad language sponge, the other day her teacher told her she'd made a mess in the toy area and Amalie asked her what the bloody hell she expected her to do about it. Are you coming over? Are you not freaking out about this?' Felicity wedged the mobile between her cheek and shoulder as she held up teddies one by one for Amalie to inspect.

'Not that one.' Her daughter shook her head.

'But you have this one every night, see—'

'*Not* that one.'

Felicity tried another – Benji Bear, or some other idiotic name. Felicity could remember the exact moment she bought one each for the twins because it was the first time she'd almost said 'fuck me' in a soft toy shop. She'd never realised you needed a mortgage to buy a couple of bears, especially considering you had to do half the work by stuffing and dressing them yourself.

'*No*. He's stupid.'

Stupid. Nearly fifty quid's worth of stuffing and pink tutus and poor, cross-dressing Benji had been relegated to *stupid*.

'Well, I mean it's not the nicest thing that can happen on a Tuesday evening but what am I supposed to do? We had a journalist call us the minute it had aired – we hadn't even heard it ourselves. Marcus is on the phone to his lawyer now so we'll just have to see what he says. I'm sure we can get this thing taken down by tomorrow, and hopefully no one has even listened to it. Maybe no one will think it's you if you screw your face up a few times, see if you can get some wrinkles like the rest of us.'

'Funny!' Felicity held up a dilapidated elephant, and Amalie shook her head. 'I can't help my *naturally* youthful complexion.'

'I'll have that one,' Amalie announced, pointing to the first toy her mother had offered her.

Felicity sighed. Mollie had been fast asleep nearly twenty-five minutes ago, her eyes closing the minute she laid her head down like a baby Annabell. How could twins be so different?

There was no way Felicity believed that Karla wasn't freaking out about the effect this might have on her career. Which Felicity supposed she should be worrying about too – after all, Karla was the most lucrative client her PR business had – but all she could worry about right at this moment was her own reputation.

'Natural, right,' said Karla sweetly. 'That's what I told Miranda. I said maybe she should set an alarm to drink algae every forty-five minutes and plunge her face into ice water

– perhaps then she'd be described as fresh-faced. Do you think she's heard it?'

'I'm more concerned about Mary-Beth. Have you even heard from her? Why would she disappear from the picnic yesterday? And now this awful podcast is talking about Erica's best friend knowing something. What do you think she knows?'

'She doesn't know anything,' Karla said, but her voice cracked a little. 'Do you really think that if she knew what happened to Erica she wouldn't have gone to the police straight away? Mary-Beth is straight as a ruler. She could have pushed Erica from the window of a fifty-storey building and she'd have a written and signed confession ready by the time the police arrived.'

Felicity leaned down to kiss the top of Amalie's head, almost dropping the mobile phone on her in the process. Amalie gave her a look that clearly said *If you think it's going to be that easy, you're crazy.*

'I know. I know. You're right.'

'I know I am. We can't start doubting each other. There will be enough people doing that for us.'

'I thought you said no one will have listened to it?' Felicity took her place at the top of the stairs and groaned. 'This is going to be all over Severndale by tomorrow, I just know it. My business can't afford a scandal, Karla. It's just getting to the point where I don't have to worry about where my next client is coming from. How can I run a brand management company if my name is linked to some-one's death?'

'You're worrying over nothing.' Karla's voice was soothing, but Felicity sensed something behind it, something that told her even Karla didn't believe the words she was saying. 'This isn't going to have any effect at all. I promise you.'

Amalie shouting her name cut short any reply Felicity

could have given. She sighed. 'I hope you're right. I have to go. Speak tomorrow?'

'Of course. Try not to worry, Fliss. I'm not.'

Karla placed the phone back in its cradle and let out a breath.

'She okay?' Marcus asked, placing a hand on his wife's shoulder.

'I hope so,' Karla replied. 'She's in charge of my brand management – if she goes to pieces, I'm screwed. Did you call your lawyer?'

'No, not yet. I've been trying Jack for the last twenty minutes. He's not answering. I'm going to go and knock on the door, check he's okay.'

'Yeah, poor thing, you're right.' Karla nodded and looked slightly ashamed of herself. 'We can talk to lawyers and agents in the morning. Jack is more important right now.'

'Mum,' Zachary's voice came from behind her. 'I've been thinking, about this podcast—'

'Oh, for God's sake, Zach,' she snapped. 'Why is everyone so obsessed with this stupid thing? It's just some idiot with nothing better to do than cause drama. Go and play in your room, okay?'

Zach's blue eyes blinked twice, and he nodded, taken aback at his mother's sharp tone. 'Yeah, okay,' he mumbled, nodding. 'Fine. Whatever.'

'You need to calm down,' Marcus murmured gently as a crestfallen Zach trudged past him up the stairs.

'I know, I'll go and say sorry to Zach. I shouldn't take it out on him.'

Marcus pulled her in close to his chest and wrapped his arms around her shoulders. 'It's like you just told Felicity – this is just someone's idea of a sick joke, it'll all blow over when people realise he knows nothing.'

'And what if it doesn't?' Karla looked up at her husband

– the man she had protected for all of their marriage, the man whose fame and reputation had made their life possible. She wouldn't – no, she couldn't – lose it all now. She had worked too hard to create the life they now shared, their perfect home, their fame, the success. Karla Kaplan knew all too well what it was like to never feel good enough. Now she had it all, and she would do anything she could to protect it.

Just like she had ten months ago.

'What if it doesn't go away, Marcus?' she repeated, looking up into her husband's sky-blue eyes, the perfect mirror image of their youngest son's – only Zachary's were innocent and trusting, while Marcus's eyes held the knowledge of what the world could be like for them if he was wrong. 'Who is he? Andy Noon, who is he? What if he does know something? What if he knows *everything*?'

Marcus laid a gentle kiss on top of his wife's head. If her fears were true then their money, their fame, nothing they had would save them from what was coming. And he didn't know how to tell her that, so he said nothing at all.

11

'Mummy? Can I just put this message in the cross?'

Miranda sighed and waved a hand in the general direction of her daughter (who was watching YouTube videos on her phone), her head not emerging from the bottom drawer in the kitchen where she was currently searching out the sticky notes she'd written the PTA bank details down on. You see, despite Miranda being Erica's natural successor, she really wasn't. Natural, that is. In fact, the only thing Miranda had going for her was her ability to think on her feet. Take, for instance, the time she had forgotten to dress Charity up for 'My Hero' day at school. Upon seeing the other mums turn up with mini firemen and nurses, and Charity in her uniform as always, Miranda had whipped off her blouse in the back of the car, pulled out her make-up bag and fashioned little Charity as her chosen hero – Mummy, of course. How everyone had coo'd at the little angel swamped in Mummy's flowery blouse, as Miranda kept her emergency jacket zipped up to the neck in the middle of spring. Yes, Miranda's ability to think on her feet had helped her practically get away with murder.

Until last night, it seemed. Last night and that man with

the voice like nails scraping down a chalkboard, sermonising about an angelic version of Erica that no one Miranda knew would even recognise.

'What time are we going to Poppy's house?' Charity appeared again in the doorway.

'Oh bugger, I forgot you had that play date thing arranged this morning. Quick, darling, get dressed in one of your nice dresses, and we'll go. LOGAN! Get some shoes on, we have to drop your sister off at the Elcocks'.'

Ignoring the groans of annoyance from her son, Miranda slipped on her pumps and looked around for her car keys. How did everything go missing in this house?

'Ready, Mummy!' Charity pirouetted proudly into the room wearing her best dress and ballet pumps.

Miranda smiled. 'You look beautiful, sweetie. I just have to find my keys and . . . LOGAN, ARE YOU READY YET?'

'Your keys are in the fruit bowl.' Charity pointed to the table where her bunch of keys were indeed perched on top of what Miranda was confident were out-of-date apples.

'Thank you, honey. Come on, into the car . . . YOU HAVE FIVE SECONDS, LOGAN, OR I'M LEAVING WITHOUT YOU AND CHANGING THE WIFI PASSWORD.'

Logan appeared reluctantly, his head still buried in his tablet. Miranda smiled. Out of the house in less than an hour – not too shabby.

Predictably, Logan opted to stay in the car while Miranda took Charity to the door of the Elcock's. The two girls had been friends practically since they were born, much to Miranda's consternation. Trust Charity to pick the daughter of the local gossip brigade as her best friend.

Miranda rang the doorbell and waited. When the door finally opened, Cynthia stood behind it looking red-faced and confused.

'Miranda, hey.' She smiled without looking happy and scanned the street. 'Didn't you get my message? Only it said on Facebook you'd read it . . .'

Miranda shook her head, confused. 'I haven't checked my phone this morning.'

'I told you, Mummy,' Charity piped up. 'That I was putting it in the cross. I was trying to watch YouTube, and the circle was in the way.'

Miranda laughed. 'Ah, that would be it then. What did it say?'

Cynthia chewed on her lip. 'Just that it was best if Charity didn't come over today. Poppy didn't sleep very well and—'

Predictably, as is always the way when trying to lie to a fellow mother, Cynthia's daughter chose that moment to yell from inside the house.

'MUUUUM? Can me and Amy get some ice cream later?'

Miranda cleared her throat. 'If Poppy isn't very well then why is Amy here?'

'Well, her mum didn't get the message either, and she had come so far, and Poppy was feeling a bit brighter so . . .'

'Glad to hear it.' Miranda plastered on a smile. 'So it's fine for Charity to come in too, yes?'

'Of course.' Cynthia looked defeated and stepped to one side. 'Come on in, sweetheart.'

'What time shall I collect her this afternoon?'

Cynthia glanced up and down the street again, and Miranda fought the urge to ask if she was waiting for the police to swoop in and arrest her. The words from the podcast she'd barely managed to make it through floated back to her. *The new alpha female who slid seamlessly in to fill the gap Erica left in our community.* Was this how it was going to be from now on? Women she had known for years not wanting her to stand outside their houses in case anyone saw them talking to her?

'I can drop her back at yours if you'd like?' Cynthia's voice was so casual that Miranda could have grabbed her by the neck and strangled the life out of her on the front porch.

'No, actually Cynthia, I wouldn't fucking like. I will turn up here whenever you're ready for me to pick my daughter up, and if you try and pull this shit on me again, I'll turn up covered in blood playing that fucking podcast at full blast on the car radio. See what your neighbours say then.'

As she stalked down the path, leaving an open-mouthed Cynthia staring after her, Miranda had to admit that after all these years it felt good to finally drop a carefully placed F-bomb or two.

12

Felicity jammed her finger on the buzzer for the third time, her foot impatiently tapping against the floor. At her feet, the twins fought incessantly about which colour bow was best, and she felt as though if she missed her coffee the day would be nothing short of ruined. Screw it, the way she felt she was stopping for her coffee if it put her off schedule or not. The idea actually felt quite free—

'Morning, girls!'

The door swung open, and Felicity made no attempt to hide the impatience in her voice as she said, 'Oh, it is still morning then?' She laughed, as if she was joking.

'Sorry,' Jemma muttered, without looking at her. 'We're rushed off our feet.'

'No bother, you're here now. Can I just run through with you the plans for next Wednesday while I'm here?' Felicity whipped out her planner and turned to the page marked 'Girls' Day Trip (yay!)'.

'Um, yeah, about the trip . . .' Jemma sucked on her bottom lip and pretended to look over Felicity's shoulder at the children playing. 'There's, um, there's been a bit of a mix-up. You see we have plenty of volunteers, so we don't actually need you to come any more.'

Felicity froze, planner mid-air. 'What do you mean, "don't actually need me to come"? I've planned a full week's meetings and appointments around taking Wednesday off. It's the first trip I've been able to volunteer on since the girls started coming here.'

'I know.' Jemma looked uncomfortable, her eyes finding a spot on the wall and sticking to it. 'And I'm sorry, Miss Goldman, really I am, but all the volunteer spots are gone.'

'So tell someone else they can't go,' Felicity demanded. 'What about Chloe's mum? She goes every single time. Tell her to stay at home and get her hair done or something – God knows, she needs it.'

Jemma sighed. 'I'm just telling you what I've been told. I'm sure you understand. Look, I have to go – we're short-staffed today.'

Felicity glanced at her watch and gave a groan.

'Fine,' she muttered, blinking furiously to rid her eyes of the tears that threatened to spill down her cheeks, and turning her back on the young girl before she could see.

The coffee shop was quieter than usual – Felicity supposed there had to be some benefits of being in the post-9 a.m. crowd. The woman in front of her grappled with a pushchair while balancing a baby on her hip, as a toddler – probably around four – sat at her feet ripping a napkin into pieces. Behind the vast glass cake cabinet, two baristas chatted animatedly.

'I listened to it twice. Do you think—' The whoosh of the milk steamer blocked out the end of the sentence.

'—at all. I mean, who is this guy? How does he know more than the police anyway? Come to think of it, if he has real evidence why hasn't he—' Felicity strained to hear snatches of the conversation as the two young girls walked back and forth to the counter, mugs clattered, and the coffee machine sprang into life.

'—he will? Like at the end of the podcast or something. What I want to know is why he didn't name her husband as a suspect. I mean, the husband is *always* a suspect, right?'

'Unless the podcast guy *is* the husband? He wouldn't put himself in the frame, would he? Maybe he's trying to deflect attention . . . '

Felicity cringed, thinking of the run-in with Jemma at the holiday club, suddenly feeling certain it had something to do with last night's podcast. A local businesswoman – well, she knew very well that she was the only 'businesswoman' who lived within the walls of Severn Oaks, unless you could count Kelsie Major's Avon catalogues as a business. Was that why they didn't want her on the trip? Had someone complained? Perhaps there wasn't a tick box on the risk assessment for 'risk of murderer in volunteer pool'.

Felicity sank down into one of the seats in the corner, farthest away from the girls talking about the podcast. She didn't feel like going back to Severn Oaks yet, she just wanted to forget all about it, but everywhere she went people had been listening. Severndale was a small place, Severn Oaks even smaller. She wondered how Karla was coping – if she thought the reference to her was thinly veiled, it was nothing compared to the guy practically calling out Karla and Marcus by name. Cheshire had its fair share of celebrities, of course, with the Real Housewives and footballers by the score, but only two of them resided inside the walls of Severn Oaks. And what had he said about Mary-Beth? *A best friend who is a little too good to be true.* And her husband – Peter, obviously – featuring heavily in Erica's diary. And why was Erica keeping a diary about them anyway? The lives of the Severn Oaks residents hardly seemed the most thrilling; occasionally the men would all gather at one of the houses to watch the odd football match, maybe they talked about something interesting but Felicity doubted it. Maybe the barista and her friend were on to something when they said it could be Jack – Erica's husband would be best placed to find her scrawlings on the comings and goings of her neighbours. But surely that was crazy. Jack was just an ordinary guy, a nice guy – not the type of person who would start something like this. Felicity sighed. It was too much to even think about.

Was this how it was going to be from now on? Constantly wondering who knew what about her life? And what had Erica written about her in that goddamn diary of hers? Then there was the best friend's husband who featured heavily in Erica's log. So what had she written about Peter?

Pulling out her phone, she dialled Mary-Beth's number. She had been oddly silent throughout this whole thing – it was unusual for her not to have contacted at least one of them since the post appeared two days ago. Karla had managed to get hold of Steph – the school administrator – who had promptly removed all trace of the post from Facebook, but that apparently hadn't stopped people finding out. Mary-Beth must know.

The phone rang and rang with no answer. Why wasn't she answering?

She slammed the phone down on the table, ignoring the stares of the customers around her. Did they already know who she was? Felicity imagined them going back to their friends or husbands, telling them how that woman from Severn Oaks had been acting so suspiciously in the café that morning.

Felicity jumped as the phone buzzed in her hand, but it wasn't Mary-Beth returning her call, it was Karla.

'What's up?'

Karla never called her in the day – she knew that Felicity

wouldn't take personal calls unless it was from the holiday club. So if she needed something, she would email – the only way to get added into Felicity's busy schedule.

'Sorry, Fliss,' Karla's voice was urgent. 'I know you're working, but I had to talk to someone. I'm going crazy sitting here thinking about this whole Erica thing. Will you come over?'

'I thought you said not to worry? That your lawyer—'

'I know what I said, but it's easier said than done, isn't it? Marcus spoke to our lawyer last night, and he said that until this guy names us, or says something that specifically points to the two of us being implicated in an actual crime, there's nothing we can do, and to try and do something at this stage would make us look like we have something to hide.'

'That's the problem, though, isn't it?' Felicity replied, biting the inside of her lip. 'We do.'

13

Miranda's delight at being a badass lasted all the way to the end of the street before she pulled over and crumpled against the steering wheel. What the fuck had just happened? Why would Cynthia lie to her face? Why didn't she want Charity at her house?

Or, more accurately, *Miranda* at her house. Because that's what that little show had been about, hadn't it? The alpha mum who had slid seamlessly into Erica's place – well, they all knew who that was referring to. There was no way she could go back to that house, despite how insistent she'd been that she would. Alex would just have to go and get Charity after work, presuming he wasn't working late again. Her cheeks burned as she thought of Felicity's smug face when she'd insinuated that her husband might be doing something other than working when he wasn't home until 8 p.m. some nights. She knew what they all thought of him, the mischievous joker with the wandering eye. If they had a Severn Oaks Yearbook, Alex's name would be under 'most likely to cheat on his wife'. And yet Miranda had never managed to find even the smallest shred of evidence that he'd strayed, despite checking his phone, emails and every photo in his iCloud storage. Once she'd found a phone hidden in the cloakroom that she'd spent an hour charging, in tears, only to find out it was an old one *she'd* given to Logan about three years ago to play games on.

The houses in Severn Oaks were mainly four-bedroomed detached. There was a row of three-bed terraces in the far corner, but as none of them had children . . . Or did number six have a new baby? – Miranda had never really noticed. Erica used to do all the welcome calls, she'd have known. She'd have known its name and birth date too. And, of course, there was Karla and Marcus's five-bed in the middle of the court, with its huge expanse of a garden and a conspic-uous space where the offending tree-house used to be. Miranda and Alex occupied the third house in on the left, with a perfect view of Erica, Mary-Beth next door and Felicity, as well as everyone who drove in. Miranda often thought Erica would have loved her vantage point, although the Spencers' house was up the bank slightly and therefore best placed to look down on the other houses and their inhabit-ants. All the better to see you with. But it was Miranda, now, who could keep an eye on the comings and goings, and so it was Miranda who saw Karla and Felicity drive back into Severn Oaks, in separate cars but at exactly the same time, and pull up Karla's never-ending driveway. They dis-appeared from view then, but she could imagine them getting out, going into Karla's state-of-the-art kitchen and pouring themselves wine, sitting at the breakfast bar picking at cheeses while they gossiped.

Miranda longed for a friendship like that, but she'd never met anyone she just gelled with in that way. Mary-Beth had Erica – well, she'd *had* Erica. Miranda had hoped that perhaps now Mary-Beth was as lonely as she was they would become better friends. They had plenty in common, children the same age, husbands who couldn't keep their eyes or hands to themselves. But Mary-Beth hadn't been interested in replacing Erica. In fact, in the last ten months, she hadn't been interested in socialising with any of them at all. It was almost as if she blamed them for Erica's death, by virtue of them all being present on the night it happened. Or perhaps she was trying not to let slip secrets of her own – according to the podcast, she had as many as the rest of them.

She was debating calling Mary-Beth, under the guise of seeing how she was; perhaps this could be a bonding experience for them – maybe some good could come of it all. They would drink wine and confide in each other, sharing secrets and how they were worried about what this awful man might say next. Perhaps Karla and Felicity would invite them over to their next get-together, and they could all remember poor Erica and how much she loved a party, how she was the one who kept them all coming together, but it was okay because they had each other now.

And then you'd say something matter-of-fact that would upset one or all of them, without even realising and you'd have to move house. Remember that time you asked Felicity who did her Botox? There's a reason you have no friends, Miranda.

There it was, that little voice again that made an appearance every time she even considered going to that get-together, or crossing the road to have a chat with someone she knew. It had got worse since she'd given up her job – at one time she was sure she could hold a conversation without the little bastard in her brain assuring her afterwards that she'd spoken too loud again, been too opinionated – and couldn't she stop speaking long enough to listen for a change? What made her think that people wanted to hear what she thought about everything? Never mind that she barely ever got more intelligent conversation than which 'LOL Surprise' doll was the best, which is what made her want to discuss anything and everything with anyone who stood still long enough to listen.

She straightened up from rummaging in her bag just as the car pulled in through the gates, and her jaw slackened. So, this was it, then? The news had said that the police had decided not to pursue a new investigation of Erica's death, but they had apparently changed their mind. One by one, they would all be questioned, and the cracks would show. And judging by the fact that it was Mary-Beth's house they were pulling up to, they had decided to start with her.

Maybe Miranda would look for a new candidate for a best friend.

'So I'm thinking that this guy just named us because we were all there that night. If you think about it, it's the only possible way he could have gone with it. It's a classic murder mystery set-up. A Halloween party – I mean, you couldn't get more perfect really, that bit sort of just fell in his lap – the suspects are obviously going to be the people at the party. I mean, if he'd called out six random people who hadn't been anywhere near Severn Oaks that night, it would have presented him with a load more difficulties. Like how they got in, for example. Plus it's much more exciting this way. The killer is inside the walls and all that crap. He'll come out at the end and say it was all fiction and we'll sue for emotional distress.'

'I thought your lawyer said—'

'Yeah,' Karla interrupted, and Felicity let her go with it. She seemed on a roll now, almost as if she wasn't discussing their lives but an episode of some soap or crime drama. If this was how she wanted to deal with things, fine. Felicity kicked off her pumps and bent down to rub her foot. 'He said we couldn't sue until the guy gave something away to indicate he was talking about us. Me and Marcus, I mean. Well, he's going to have to, isn't he? The party was at our house. He's not going to be able to talk about us as suspects without mentioning it was our house the party was in, and Bingo! He's implicated us.'

Karla pulled open her sizeable American-style fridge freezer and pulled out a tray of hors d'oeuvres wrapped in cling film and labelled 'Karla for book six'.

'Try these,' she urged. 'I need to know if they taste like crap before I add the recipe to my latest book.'

'Looks yum,' Felicity said, picking up a slice of cucumber covered in cream cheese with a roll of salmon on top and shoving it in whole. She chewed, nodded enthusiastically and swallowed. 'Those are lush. But what if he doesn't come out at the end and say it's fiction? People will always wonder. Look at all those Netflix documentaries about true crimes, just mentioning people's names in the same sentence as the word murder is enough to make people wonder. Our lives will be ruined.'

'You're being dramatic. No publicity is bad publicity, remember? Look at Queen Martha. She went to jail, and it didn't stop her. There might be a film. I'd be played by Charlize Theron. You'd probably be played by someone ten years younger. George Clooney would be Peter, Marcus would be the sexy one from *Breaking Bad*. Worst-case scenario we could start a tour. "And this is where she hit her head . . ."' Karla grinned at her friend's gaping mouth.

Felicity threw a grape at her. 'I'm glad you can joke about it. What if the police reopen Erica's case?'

Karla's grin froze. 'Why would you think that?'

'Well, because he's saying there is evidence. What if there is? What if one of us killed Erica?'

'Don't be ridiculous, Felicity.' Karla wasn't used to seeing her best friend like this, and it was unnerving. Felicity was usually so together – the calm, collected one who had a list of goals for every day and an hourly plan on how to achieve them. She was the kind of person Karla thought she herself should be – maybe if her agent was a bit more like Felicity she would be on *Real Housewives* by now. 'This guy can't possibly have evidence that the police don't know about. If he has then he's been obstructing the course of justice, and revealing it puts him in the frame as much as any of us.'

'Except no one knows who he is.'

'You heard the news. The police aren't looking into the case.'

'They're not?' Felicity asked, gazing out of the double patio doors. 'Then why have they just pulled up at Mary-Beth's house?'

14

DS Harvey looked steadfastly ahead at the path leading up to Peter and Mary-Beth King's home, trying to force himself not to look left at where the Kaplans' house stood, imposing and equally as determined not to be ignored. The memory of that night ten months ago sat on his shoulders as if he had just woken from the night shift, an eager trainee ready to present his findings to his DCI, desperate to impress. He shuddered to shake away the memory of that meeting now. The words imprinted on his mind. *We don't need a scandal involving the Kaplans.*

'You were here that night, weren't you, sir?'

The voice of Detective Constable Allan at his side reminded him that he was Detective Sergeant, someone's 'sir' now – no longer the lowest in the CID food chain. Ordinarily he wouldn't even be here at this early stage but the minute his boss had got wind of a disappearance from Severn Oaks, Barrow had summoned him into his office to insist he accompany DC Allan. Which is why what would usually be a job for a police constable had become a two-CID-ring circus.

'Yes.'

Not put off by his superior's curt response, Allan pushed on. 'What were they like? The people here?'

Harvey restrained himself from groaning. This one was keen.

Untouchable had been the first word to come to his lips as he remembered them all, standing in the Kaplans' garden, tears running down the women's cheeks, and yet when they looked at him it was with defiance. *You won't find the truth here.* Had it really been less than a year? It felt like a decade ago. A lot of good things had happened to his career since then, thanks to DCI Barrow. None of them had sweetened that sour taste he got when he thought of Severn Oaks.

'Distressed,' he replied, realising Allan was still waiting for an answer.

'Understandable, I suppose. What do you reckon to this podcast then? The one that's saying it wasn't an accident?'

Harvey pushed open the gate, aiming a glower at DC Allan, hoping it would shut him up – suspecting it wouldn't. He couldn't blame the young trainee for being inquisitive, really. But that didn't mean he had to indulge him. The truth was that the minute he'd listened to that podcast last night he'd got in the car, gone to the gym and worked out until he'd thrown up.

'You should take the lead on this,' Harvey replied after a silence. 'Are you okay with that?'

'Yes, sir, I appreciate the opportunity, thank you.'

'Remember that seventy per cent of runaways turn up absolutely fine in a few days. She's more than likely to have taken off with the plumber, but he's not going to want to believe that.'

DC Allan's hand froze halfway to the doorbell. 'Do *you* believe that? Even given the timing?'

Another glower. 'Yes, I do. I'm sure you've been waiting for some big exciting case to come along, and I understand that, but this isn't it. Don't try and make this into something it isn't.'

He heard himself speak the words and at the same time heard them coming from someone else, in another place and time. Harvey screwed up his nose. It was the truth, this time. He wasn't turning into Barrow. He wasn't.

15

Peter took a deep breath in and wiped his hands on his grey suit trousers before opening the door. From the moment he'd seen the police pull through the gates he knew that this could be it. It could all be over. People would be gossiping already, but let them. This wasn't some sordid tale you could tell over appetisers, this was his life. Today he looked every one of his forty-eight years, stubble shading his usually smooth face, angry purple triangles under his bright blue eyes. Peter knew he was attractive and usually he took the utmost pride in his appearance, regular facials, a personal trainer three times a week. Right now he looked like shit and for once in his life he didn't care.

'You've found her,' he announced, not waiting for either of the officers to speak.

They shared a 'look' that Peter would analyse for at least an hour after they left.

The younger of the two men cleared his throat. He looked nearly as nervous as Peter felt. 'No, Mr King, I'm afraid we haven't, and I'm really sorry to worry you. Can we come in?'

He was perhaps late twenties, which immediately put Peter

at ease. Surely if they thought he was some kind of wife killer they would have sent someone whose mum didn't still iron his trousers? He looked like a nice enough lad, though, with his ginger hair cut short and spiked, a smattering of freckles dusted across his nose and a redness in his cheeks that made him look more like a boy scout collecting donations than a police officer. His colleague, older, harder faced, stood with his hands in his pockets, his face clearly stating that he couldn't care less if they were invited in or not.

'Yes, sorry, of course.' Peter moved into the house, gesturing them to follow him. 'We can talk in here. The children are upstairs, probably both with headphones on. I haven't told them anything – I don't know what to tell them.'

He led them through to the room that his wife reserved for fancy guests, glancing around to check there was nothing the police officers shouldn't see. He wiped his palms against his suit trousers and gestured at the sofa. 'Take a seat. Would you like a drink?'

'No, we're fine, thank you.'

The younger officer sat, his partner remained on his feet.

'I'm Detective Constable Allan. This is Detective Sergeant Harvey – he's here to supervise.'

The first thing Peter noticed about DS Harvey was his height. Or rather lack of it. He was perhaps around five foot five, and had clearly spent a lot of time in the gym trying to make up for it. His shirt was straining slightly across his shoulders and yet baggy in the waist – perhaps the job didn't pay well enough for tailoring. He had closely shaven blond hair, and as he stepped forward to shake Peter's hand, he got a whiff of menthol chewing gum and expensive aftershave. Apparently, the pay wasn't too shabby. Maybe he just wanted people to notice his muscles as they looked down on him from above. Yet there was something about his face . . .

'Have we met?' Peter stared at him.

The older officer looked familiar somehow, but seeing the police wasn't second nature in Severn Oaks. The last time had been . . .

'Did you come when Erica fell? Harvey, yes, I remember you.'

The officer inclined his head. 'You have a good memory.'

'Not really,' he said. 'We just don't get many occasions to see the police here. It's usually very quiet. People here look out for one another generally. You were only a trainee then? You've done well for yourself in less than a year.'

The sergeant reddened. A sore spot? Although Peter couldn't see how a promotion could be cause for discomfort; he was a man who believed that the top was the only place to head. No use competing for last place and all that. DS Harvey didn't seem to agree, judging by the way he changed the subject so swiftly.

'No CCTV any more, I see?'

Peter shook his head, tried to look regretful that their every move wasn't on cameras for the world to see. 'There used to be CCTV, the developers paid the contract for the first five years as part of the deal – although of course they put the cost onto the house price. After that, Erica took care of it and we all just paid her. Then after she died, no one else bothered and it lapsed. My wife kept meaning to . . .'

'That's Erica Spencer?'

The younger officer looked at his partner, who nodded back slowly but didn't elaborate.

'Why don't we kick things off?' prompted the sergeant.

The younger officer reddened and pulled out his notepad. 'Okay, Mr King—'

'Peter, please.'

'Okay, Peter. We're following up on the missing person report you filed on your wife. Firstly, has anything changed since you made your report? Has Mrs King made contact at all?'

'No.' Peter shook his head. That much, at least, was true. 'I haven't heard from her.'

'Okay.' DC Allan made a note. 'It's going to seem like I'm asking questions you've already answered in the report but I just want to make sure we get a full picture of what might have happened.'

To see if my story changes, more like, Peter thought, but he wasn't worried. He'd gone over the story a million times, he'd thought of little else.

'Of course,' he said. 'I'll tell you everything I know.' He didn't know what to do or say, what the correct procedure was, the way one should act when one's wife has been missing for days. Would he be a suspect? Wasn't that what happened on TV? The police look like they are trying to help, but they are trying to get you to incriminate yourself? Could you try and look too innocent?

'So, we need to establish if Mary-Beth is what we call "high risk".'

'High risk?' Peter repeated. 'Isn't everyone who goes missing high risk?'

'Not necessarily, no,' Harvey replied, speaking for the younger man. 'There are a lot of reasons why someone – especially an adult – might go away without telling anyone, and they don't always equate to that person being in danger. What we need you to do is give us every bit of information you can so that we can make an informed decision about how to proceed with the investigation.'

'But there will be an investigation?' Peter rubbed sweat from his palms onto his trousers and hoped the officers didn't notice.

Allan nodded. 'There will always be an initial investigation, we just need to know what we're dealing with.'

Peter pushed the heels of his hands into his eyes. When he released the pressure the room swam for a second before coming into focus. DC Allan was talking again.

'When was the last time you saw your wife?'

'Monday morning, about eight a.m.'

DC Allan made a note in his book. 'But you didn't report her missing until nine p.m. last night?'

'No, well, I only realised she was missing then. The kids stay over at Mary's mum's on a Monday anyway. It wasn't until Mary's mum phoned yesterday to say she hadn't been to get the kids – had we forgotten them? – that I even realised there was anything wrong.' Peter stood up, then sat down abruptly. He didn't know what to do with himself, his limbs seemed to demand to move around irritably. He laced his fingers together to stop them flexing.

'You didn't speak to her at all after you left Monday morning? Was that normal?' DS Harvey didn't even try to hide the incredulous tone in his voice.

'No, it wasn't, but it wasn't abnormal either, if you know what I mean. Well, probably you don't. I tried calling her when I arrived on Monday, but the phone went straight to answerphone. The signal around here is really bad, so that didn't surprise me, but usually, she'd call back. I had a few drinks in the hotel bar after the training and went to bed – it only occurred to me in the morning that she hadn't called back, but by then I was in another training session. I tried her from the car on the way home but it just rang out. I wasn't worried or anything – I mean, why would I be? Your wife doesn't answer a couple of your calls, you don't automatically think that—' He stopped short, unable to say the words.

'Of course you don't,' DC Allan said, sounding as though he was aiming for a soothing tone. 'So when you realised she hadn't picked the children up, what did you do then?'

'I called her again.' Peter recalled the sound of a phone ringing and ringing with no one to answer it. 'And of course, she didn't answer. I went over to Mary's mum's to pick the kids up and I tried her all the way home, over and over, trying not to panic the children, making jokes about silly Mummy leaving her phone on silent. She did that all the time anyway. When I got home I sent the children to play while I searched the house. Everything was tidy and in place. None of her clothes seemed to be missing, the suitcase was where it always is.'

'And that was when you called the police?'

'Not straight away. I went out into the street, caught one of our neighbours, Larry Gorman from next door but one – he hadn't seen her since Monday, but he works funny shifts. I banged on Jack – Spencer, that is – from next door but there was no answer. I popped next door to Felicity, but I think she was on the phone, then I saw Marcus in the drive. He looked a bit shell-shocked, not his usual self, so I asked him if he'd seen Mary-Beth and he said not since the picnic.'

'The picnic?'

'I'd forgotten all about it. The community picnic, the one at the school every year. Erica usually organises it, but with her gone . . .'

'That's Erica Spencer again?'

'Yes, she and Mary-Beth were very close. She took on a lot of the work for the picnic – that's what she's like, she can't say no to anything. She was at the picnic and dropped the kids off afterwards. No one has seen her since.'

'Right, sorry, Mr King, I just want to make sure we have all the details. So you checked with your neighbours, and then you reported your wife missing?'

'Yes. I mean no, not that very instant, but almost. I went back inside, and I was wondering what I should do next, whether I should bother the police when she could walk back in any second and apologise for forgetting to pick the children up. I think I called her phone again, sent a text for her to call me. I called a couple of her friends from the school – we have this pyramid letter with all the phone numbers on, so I just tried names I recognised. Then I called the police, and they asked me to come to the station to file a report.'

'Okay, thank you, Mr King. I know that you must be anxious about your wife, but these next questions – we're only asking them to get a full picture of what's happened here. They might seem a little personal.'

Peter sighed. 'Go on. Ask anything you want. I just want her found.'

'Right. Would you say your wife was acting normally on Monday morning before you left?'

Peter nodded. 'Nothing about her behaviour stood out as unusual. She was making the kids' breakfast, flicking through Facebook or Twitter or something. I showered, dressed, came down and kissed her goodbye. Said I'd see her tomorrow and she said to drive safe. She always said that, like if she forgot and something happened it would be her fault.'

'And the days before? Anything unusual?'

'Not that stands out, no. I suppose everyone says that.'

Allan ignored the remark. 'Okay,' he said, jotting something down. 'I'm sorry, sir, I have to ask you this but . . . were there any problems in the marriage? Any reason she might have left? Any reason to believe she was having an affair?'

Peter felt sick at the word. 'No, no, and no. I know everyone probably says that but even if there was anything wrong, or she wanted to leave me, she would never leave the children.'

'Have you got access to your bank account online? Perhaps you could check the recent transactions? Sometimes, when women do leave, we find small withdrawals over several months, kind of like a pot so—'

'She didn't have a pot,' Peter spat. 'And there won't be any transactions.' He groaned, like an animal in pain. 'Sorry. I'm sorry. It's just, God, of all the things I can think of, the best-case scenario is that my wife has left me for another man. How fucked up is that? Because if she hasn't run away . . .'

DS Harvey made a small gesture and DC Allan stood up.

'It's an incredibly stressful situation, sir, and I'm not going to patronise you with statistics, but I do want to say that most of the cases we see have a perfectly good explanation and the people turn up fine. We'll have a wander around, talk to your neighbours and get back to you as soon as we have anything to go on. Will you be okay?'

'I'll be okay when you find out what happened to my wife.'

16

The door clicked closed behind them and DC Allan turned to look at Harvey. His supervisor had both hands shoved into his pockets and Allan had a sudden urge to stick out his foot and let him fall on his infuriatingly vacant face. He didn't understand why Harvey was so cagey about this case – about Severn Oaks in general, actually. Was there more to the Erica Spencer case than he'd let on? He seemed reluctant to discuss it – even more reluctant to admit that this new disappearance could have anything to do with what happened last Halloween.

'You still think she ran away?'

'Yes.'

Allan resisted the urge to sigh. Surely he wasn't stupid? Allan had heard all about DS Harvey, about how he completed his training and made DS faster than anyone in the department, not long after the incident with Erica Spencer last year. He wasn't exactly showing any of the intuition that had got him promoted right now.

'He said there was CCTV.'

'He said the CCTV hadn't been working since Erica Spencer died.'

'Exactly. Which means it was working the night she fell out of the tree house.'

Harvey looked at him sharply. 'What's that got to do with this investigation?'

'You can't just dismiss the idea that the two are linked. Was the CCTV checked in the initial investigation? Perhaps I should check out the files.'

'Perhaps you should write up the missing person report and let the DCI decide what happens next. That's how this works, we don't get to just go running around looking for mysteries. We have a budget to think about. And before you go dragging up what happened here last year – the CCTV was checked. I did it personally. Only one person who didn't live in Severn Oaks entered those gates. A woman drove up towards the Kaplans' drive. The CCTV was trained on the street, not the private houses, so you can't see the house anyway. After less than thirty minutes the woman returned, drove straight out and didn't come back. It was two hours before Erica went missing. There was no way that woman had anything to do with Erica's fall.'

'Did you ask Karla who she was?'

Harvey scowled. 'Of course I did. She said the woman was a friend, she'd been dropping something off. There didn't seem any point in wasting any more resources on it.'

He shrugged as though it was no big deal, but Allan sensed there was something his sergeant wasn't telling him.

'Shame they didn't keep that CCTV running. I'd like to know if Peter King was telling us the truth about when he last saw his wife.'

'You think he was lying?'

'Didn't you hear what he said? When he was talking about Mary-Beth telling him to drive safe?'

'Yeah, so she was superstitious. What's wrong with that? Apart from being a pile of crap.'

'He said, "She always said that, like if she forgot and something happened it would be her fault."'

'Yeah, so?' Harvey's voice was bordering on the aggressive.

'He used the past tense. About his wife who's been missing barely forty-eight hours.'

Harvey snorted. 'You're reading too much into it. People make those kinds of mistakes all the time. This isn't some TV drama where one throwaway comment unlocks the mystery. I understand you're eager to solve this but—'

'Whatever.' Allan looked up at the houses encircling them, all with their expensive cars in the driveways and their empty windows, and felt that each one was watching them. 'I still think there's more to this one. I think Mary-Beth King is in danger, and I intend to find out why.'

17

'They're coming out,' Felicity hissed, jumping back from the patio doors. 'What do you think is going on? Mary-Beth isn't with them.'

'Maybe the podcast guy gave them his evidence, after all,' Karla speculated. She scrolled through her phone and clicked Marcus's number. 'Babe, it's me. The police are at the Kings'.'

'Oh, shit, I wonder if it's to do with Mary-Beth?'

'That's what we said. Do you think they're fingering her for Erica's murder?'

'Erica's murder? Fingering her? Shit, Kay, you need to watch a lot less TV. Anyway, I don't mean that. I saw Pete last night and—'

'They're coming here,' Felicity announced, hopping from one foot to the other. 'They are coming. Up. The. Driveway. Right. Now.'

'Shit. Marcus, get back here now. And call your lawyer,' Karla hissed into the phone, and hit the 'end call' button.

'Lawyer?' Felicity's eyes widened. 'Bloody hell, Karla, I don't have a lawyer. I mean, I know lawyers, for the business and all, but I've never actually needed to use one. I never thought I'd need one. What do you think they're going to say?'

'We're about to find out,' Karla grimaced as the doorbell rang.

She flung open the door and announced, 'You will have to speak to my lawyer.'

The two police officers on the front step looked alarmed.

'Your lawyer?' the younger one repeated stupidly.

The older one grinned. 'Celebrities,' he said by way of explanation. 'Mrs Kaplan, isn't it? If you wish to have a lawyer present while I ask you when was the last time you saw your neighbour then, by all means, go ahead and call them. We'll pop back to you once we've asked the rest of the street. The ones who aren't acting like they are on the set of *Law and Order*.'

Karla felt her face redden. 'My neighbour? Do you mean Mary-Beth?'

'Yes, her husband reported her missing yesterday evening, and we're trying to get a picture of when she was last seen. Would you mind if we came in, or do you still want your lawyer?'

'Sorry,' Karla mumbled, stepping aside to let them in. 'Got a bit carried away. We don't have police here often.'

'You'd be surprised at how many people go *Miami Vice* on us, start referring to people as "perps" and asking us if we've "fingered" the criminals. This is DC Allan, and I'm DS Harvey.'

Karla gave a tinkling laugh and scowled at Felicity, who had stuffed her fist into her mouth to stop herself from laughing. 'Ha! Idiots. Wait . . . Harvey? You were here last year. You've lost weight.'

Harvey's face coloured. 'A bit,' he admitted, before the other woman spoke up.

'I'm Felicity Goldman.' She held out her hand, and both officers shook it. 'I'd say good to see you again, DS Harvey, but I'd be lying. I don't know if you remember but I live across there,' she pointed at her house, 'next door to Mary-Beth and Peter. I can't believe she's missing, though. Are you sure she hasn't gone to her mum's?'

'Does she do that often? Stay at her mum's? Were there problems in the marriage?'

Felicity clapped a hand to her mouth. Dropping it, she pointed at the police officer. 'Ooooh, I forgot that you're good.'

'Do you want a drink?' Karla asked, appearing from the kitchen with a tray. 'Hors d'oeuvres?'

'We're fine, thank you. So, Miss Goldman . . .'

Karla noted the annoyance on Felicity's face. She bloody hated being called 'Miss'. Said it made her sound about twelve years old.

'. . . Mrs Kaplan, when was the last time you both saw Mary-Beth?'

'Well, she was at the picnic,' Karla replied. 'On the gate, doing the tickets. She said she was going to meet us on the grass afterwards but she never came to find us.'

'Wouldn't it have been quite busy? Perhaps she couldn't find you.'

'Possibly,' Karla admitted. 'Although she's got all of our numbers. I went to look for her when that post went up and I couldn't find her anywhere.'

'Post?'

Karla groaned. 'Good job I'm not a criminal, I suck at it. I may as well tell you, I'm surprised Peter didn't. There was a post, on the school Facebook page, that said our friend Erica's death . . . that she was murdered. And that one of us did it. I know,' Karla gave that tinkling laugh again, 'it's ridiculous, right? You were here, you know it was an accident. And then there was a podcast last night which threatened to dredge the whole thing up again and unmask a murderer. Completely vulgar. No respect at all. So I knew Mary-Beth would be upset – she was Erica's best friend.'

'And what time did this post go up?'

'I'm not sure . . .' Karla looked at Felicity.

'The picnic started at twelve, so probably about twelve forty-five, maybe one?'

'And you didn't see Mary-Beth after that?'

Both women shook their heads. 'No,' Karla said. 'We thought she'd taken off early.'

'But you weren't concerned?'

Felicity frowned. 'Why would we be concerned? When you have children, a thousand and one things can stop you from doing whatever it is you have planned. When the twins were two years old, I clean forgot my own birthday. Just woke up, got on with the day and didn't realise until I checked my emails at the end of the day and saw the date. We assumed she hadn't even seen the post and had just gone to take the kids to her mum's – they stay over on a Monday.'

The police officer smiled. 'Okay, well, if you think of anything that might help – if Mary-Beth confided in you about her marriage or wanting to leave or anything at all that might shed some light on where she's gone, be sure to let us know. In the meantime, we'll look up this podcast, the timing does seem suspicious. Perhaps it upset her, and she went away to clear her head.'

'Yes, to clear her head,' Karla mused as she closed the door behind them. *Or her conscience.*

Taking a last look at both screens and seeing two small blonde heads, both face down, and pyjama-clad bottoms shoved into the air, Felicity set the monitors down on the patio table and crept around the edge of the garden until she reached the far end. She'd done this so many times that she had the perfect formula now; she knew the right shoes to wear (either her UGG boots or her fluffy booted slippers), knew where to stand to avoid the security lights flooding the entire back garden with stark white light, knew which boards behind the bushes on the left-hand side were loose enough to sneak through, which she did now, her blouse snagging on the branches of the conifers as she crawled in. She slid aside the loose feather-edge boards and squeezed her athletic frame through and into an identical set of conifers on the other side. Out of the darkness, a hand appeared to guide her through, which she grasped, pushing aside the branches and throwing herself into the arms of the man waiting beyond.

Peter pulled her into his chest and wrapped his arms around her whole body, and in an instant, Felicity felt calmer, safer. He pressed his lips against the top of her head, and she breathed in his scent.

'You've been smoking,' she said, trying to keep her tone from sounding accusatory. 'Mary-Beth will hate that.'

'I know. I've just been listening to that fucking podcast again.'

Felicity grimaced. 'Where are the kids?' She looked up at the house beyond, which was clothed in darkness.

'Mary's mum took them to hers. In case . . . in case I had to go anywhere.' Peter's words came out strangled, and Felicity laid a hand on his arm.

'You really have no idea where she's gone?' she whispered, studying his face.

He shook his head but didn't meet her eyes. 'I assumed she'd found out about you and taken off to teach me a lesson.'

'God, when the police came round—'

'You didn't tell them about us, did you? That young one – he's . . . I don't think he believes that Mary-Beth ran away.'

Felicity shook her head. 'Of course not. It's not my place. So you're saying Mary-Beth didn't find out about us? Then why would she run away? Are you sure she did?'

Peter shrugged. 'Maybe not. Maybe she had an accident?'

Felicity wondered why he couldn't look her in the eye. 'But—'

'I don't know, Fliss,' he snapped. 'There's just literally no sign of where she went after she dropped the kids at her mum's. Nothing is missing. There's no suspicious activity in the accounts.'

'You've checked *all* her accounts?'

'What do you mean all her accounts? Look, do you want to come in? There's no one here and . . .'

'How's that going to look if the police turn up? No, the twins are asleep but I can't hear the monitor from inside yours. Listen, I know you must be going crazy over this but there's bound to be an explanation. Do you think it might be anything to do with the podcast?'

'I don't know. I suppose it depends what time she left. That post didn't go up until after midday, and even then Mary-Beth apparently wasn't mentioned until the podcast came out on Tuesday night. No one remembers seeing her car after the picnic, but no one remembers not seeing it either. This is all so fucked up.' He ran his hands over his face and groaned. 'Why wouldn't she speak to me? If she was in any kind of trouble, if she had anything to do with what happened to Erica – why just run away?'

'She couldn't have had anything to do with what happened to Erica. Erica fell, it was an accident, the coroner said so, remember? And this guy – this Andy Noon, whoever he is – well, he knows nothing.'

'And who is he? He's got to be someone from in here, right? From inside Severn Oaks? Which means he's been watching us – he could be watching us now.'

They both glanced around, as if they might see a periscope sticking up from over the fence.

'And what's all that about a diary? If that's true, he'll know exactly what Erica knew, which was pretty much everything about everyone. She never could keep her fucking nose out of anything.'

'Did she know about me?' Felicity already knew the answer. As Peter said, Erica knew everything.

Peter nodded, and Felicity's heart sank at the confirmation.

'She knew. About me and you, about the twins – who their father was . . .'

Felicity squeaked. 'How the . . . ?'

'Don't ask me.' Peter shrugged, and Felicity knew in an instant he was lying. 'She cornered me at the party and asked if we'd enjoyed the zoo – do you remember, we'd gone the weekend before, while Mary-Beth was away at that spa? A stupid risk, but I'd been so desperate to spend the day with you and the girls. And we were so pleased with ourselves that we'd got away with it. She said she was going to give me a chance to tell Mary-Beth myself – that she had a right to know – and if I didn't tell her, she would. Then she fell out of that tree house, and Mary-Beth was so upset and—'

'So what you're saying is that Erica Spencer threatened to expose you as Dad of the Year on the night she died? That's just brilliant, Peter. I'm not sure what that's called in your world, but here in the real world, that's called a motive. And it lands both of us in it. And now Mary-Beth is gone and . . . oh!' Felicity clasped a hand to her mouth, felt her chest constrict, and her breathing quickened. 'Oh God, oh God.'

'What, what is it?' Peter grasped her arm. 'Are you okay? What's wrong?'

'They're going to think you killed her. They're going to

think you killed Erica, and Mary-Beth found out, so you killed her too. And they're going to think I was in on it. They're going to think we killed them both, and we're going to go to prison.'

18

Marcus stepped down from the back of the stage, sweat sticking his too-long fringe to his forehead and trickling down the back of his neck. His stage highs were the greatest feeling on earth, the kind of euphoria you get when your kids were born, or you drive your first supercar. Back in the auditorium people were still chanting his name – *his name* – and he knew he would have to take the entire day off tomorrow to reply to middle-of-the-night emails from fans telling him they were so excited to turn their lives around that they couldn't sleep, thanking him for changing their entire outlook, their whole lives.

He changed lives. It may sound braggish and exaggerated but Marcus Kaplan had lost count of the amount of people who had contacted him over the last two years to say that they had been in the darkest depths of despair and depression, not knowing how they were going to get out of bed and make it through the next day, when they had heard him talking on the TV or the radio and been inspired to start living again. Then there were the lives he saved through his Bringing You Home initiative, funding the search for teenage runaways living on the streets who felt, for one reason or another, they couldn't go home. Marcus had made it his mission to help as many people in his life as possible. He had been given this gift, this amazing opportunity, and it would be ungrateful of him not to help others. He wasn't doing it for the recognition, either. Bringing You Home wasn't an organisation that was often on the news, and he didn't throw swanky charity balls or show his face in the newspapers constantly.

'Mr Kaplan, that was amazing.' The organiser of the event crossed over to Marcus, took him firmly by the hand and shook it. 'You had the whole room in the palm of your hand. How do you do it? How do you talk with such passion and enthusiasm?'

'Because I'm genuinely passionate about what I'm talking about,' Marcus replied with a shrug. 'You just need to find a subject you love.'

'Well, the audience sure does love you.' The organiser beamed. 'I hope you'll consider extending your time here? Tonight's gig was a sell-out, and there were thousands of people on the waiting list, we would love to be able to provide some extra dates.'

'I'd be happy to talk about that tomorrow,' Marcus replied with a smile. 'I'm a bit—' The words died on his lips as he saw the woman walking towards him. 'I thought no one was allowed backstage.'

The organiser followed his gaze and his face fell. 'No one is supposed to be. We have a meet and greet planned on the last night, but they have to pay extra for that, and there are only a hundred spots. No one should be back here. I'm so sorry, Mr Kaplan, I'll get rid of her immediately.'

Marcus held up his hand. 'No,' he said quickly. 'There's no need for that. I'll deal with this one myself, just make sure no one else gets back here, okay? I've just done a three-hour spot, I don't need to be mobbed right now, I'm bloody exhausted.'

The organiser nodded his head enthusiastically. There was no way he wanted Marcus unhappy. 'Of course, of course. I'll make sure you're not disturbed again, Mr Kaplan, I'm very sorry.'

He glowered at the woman as he passed her and went to speak to the security guard.

'Marcus . . .' The woman smiled as she approached him. 'It's been a while. I heard your gig tonight, you sounded amazing.'

'What are you doing here?' Marcus hissed, his voice low and dangerous. 'I thought we had an agreement. You're not supposed to be here.'

His heart thumped in his chest. Why was she breaking their agreement now? God knew, she was the one with all the power in this relationship, just one interview with her could blow everything apart. The boys, Karla, they would never forgive him. His entire reputation, everything he had worked for over the last few years would be shattered with one word from this woman.

The woman held up a hand. 'You don't need to worry, I'm not here to cause trouble. I don't want trouble for you, you must know that. It's just, I still love you, Marcus. And nothing will ever change that, I don't think.'

Marcus sighed. 'We've been through all this,' he said, rubbing a hand over his face. 'You said you only wanted the best for me. You agreed.'

'I know.' The woman shook her head. 'I know what we agreed, I do just want what's best for you. I'm not here to cause trouble. It's just, I miss you.'

Marcus refused to look into the woman's eyes, those bright blue eyes that he knew so well. He couldn't look at her, he couldn't see what his decision had done to her. How he had chosen his career, his family, his money over her.

'I love you too,' he said, his voice catching in his throat. 'I just . . . I just don't know . . .'

'I shouldn't have come here.' The woman began to back away quickly. 'I'm sorry, I shouldn't have, I know what we agreed. We can't be seen together.'

'No, no, I'm glad you did.' Marcus caught hold of her hand as she turned to leave. 'Really, I'm glad you did, it's good to see you. I just can't . . .'

The woman looked up past him sadly. 'I know,' she said quietly. 'You just can't tell the truth now.'

19

'I'm so glad you could all make it.' Miranda stood in front of the group and smoothed down her shoulder-length auburn hair. *It would have been so much easier to do this at Karla's*, she thought, looking at the large group of people assembled in her living room on an assortment of dining-room chairs, sofas and the floor, but then that would have put Karla Kaplan front and centre, and that would defeat the object. This was her job, as Erica's successor to the head of the Neighbourhood Watch, and as much as Alex had grumbled about having to go out late last night for an array of nibbles and refreshments, she did love to play hostess. She scanned the faces of the residents of Severn Oaks. Jack Spencer was noticeably missing, along with Mary-Beth of course – but they wouldn't be here if she hadn't disappeared. And her husband, working late. Felicity would bloody love that.

'As you all know, one of our number is currently missing. The police are involved, but it doesn't seem as though they are treating her disappearance as "high risk" – is that how they put it, Peter?'

Peter King, his face grey and his clothes crumpled, nodded. He looked as though he'd slept in the shirt he was wearing, although it might be more accurate to assume he hadn't slept at all. It was shocking to see him like this – he was usually so handsomely turned out, his dark hair silvering at the temples but always well styled, his clothes smart, and he *always* smelled amazing. Miranda wondered how the poor children were coping. She hadn't seen Hannah and Teddy since the police showed up yesterday.

'Yeah,' he said, his voice cracking. 'There were no signs of, um, foul play,' he took a deep breath, 'at the house. Her purse, phone and car are gone, although her passport is still here. They are assuming she went of her own accord until there's evidence to suggest otherwise—'

'Which we feel there is,' Miranda interjected, taking charge of the conversation once more. 'Her bank account hasn't been accessed since Tuesday, there's no evidence that clothes or a suitcase are missing, and her toiletries are still at the house. The major issue, however, is that she hasn't contacted her children, which – as those of us who know Mary-Beth would agree – is very unusual. So I called this meeting to take on some of the things we feel the police should be doing.'

'But what can we do?' Simon Barker from number eight asked, quite unnecessarily putting up his hand to speak. Simon was a nice-enough man, always smartly dressed, with a good car and clean, polished shoes, which – in Miranda's eyes – put him in the 'right kind of person for Severn Oaks' bracket. His wife, Gilly, was a thin, mousy woman who kept herself to herself but always chipped in with a helping hand when it came to community matters. They were childless by choice which, of course, meant that they were on the fringe of the community – having children in Severn Oaks gave you the golden ticket into the Parent Brigade – but one could hardly hold that against them at times like these. 'I mean, what can we do that the police can't?'

All heads turned at the sound of the front door opening. Alex appeared in the doorway, a bashful, apologetic grin on his face. 'Sorry I'm late, babe,' and before Miranda could reply, 'I bought some of these.' Alex produced a huge box emblazoned with the words Planet Donut on the front.

Miranda's anger fizzled down to a tiny spark. Alex had, once again, charmed his way out of trouble. As everyone helped themselves to donuts amid a chorus of 'I really shouldn't', Miranda cleared her throat.

'Good question, Simon. What can we do that the police aren't?' A question Miranda was ready for, of course. She walked brusquely into the dining room and returned with a stack of A4 sheets of paper. 'I had these printed this morning.' She began handing them out, Mary-Beth's face staring up at everyone from each sheet, with the words 'Have you seen this woman?' emblazoned across the top. 'As well as this map of every business in Cheshire. Every coffee shop, hotel, bar and retail outlet. I've divided up the areas by colour, and I thought that in pairs we could distribute these leaflets to our designated areas, speak to the business owners and see if anyone has seen anything. We could also—'

'I thought we were assuming she hadn't run away?' Karla interjected. 'If she's come to harm she's hardly going to be shopping in River Island, is she?'

Miranda forced a smile onto her face. 'Of course not, but by targeting businesses and asking them to display the posters, we are ensuring the maximum number of people see Mary-Beth's face. That way, if anyone has any information about who might have taken her—'

Peter King made a low, guttural sound in his throat. 'Sorry,' he whispered. 'I just can't . . .'

Felicity jumped to her feet and rubbed his arm. 'It's okay,' she soothed, in the way you might speak to a young child who has lost their teddy. 'She didn't mean it like that.'

Miranda was sure she did mean it like that – what else were they all doing here if they thought Mary-Beth hadn't come to harm at the hands of someone else? If she had just taken off with some secret boyfriend then what was the point of all of this? Still, her cheeks coloured at Peter's obvious distress, and she cleared her throat, hoping to salvage something of the meeting.

'Gosh, yes, sorry, Peter. I'm sure nothing like that has happened and that she'll be found ali— perfectly well, soon. Sorry, this must be so upsetting for you and the children.'

And where are your children, Peter? Why have you shipped them off as soon as Mary-Beth is out of the picture? And why is Felicity's hand still on your arm?

'Of course, I'm sorry, Miranda. You're just trying to help, and I'm so grateful. It's just—'

But none of them would find out what it was 'just' . . . because at that moment Peter's phone began to ring in his pocket.

'I'd better get that, it might be news or the kids.' He manoeuvred his way through the people on the floor and disappeared into the dining room.

Miranda heard the back door slam.

It was as if a spell had been lifted. Without Peter's presence, the residents of Severn Oaks all had their questions ready.

'Did anyone see her on the day she left?' Kelsey from number four asked, looking around at the shaking heads. 'Do we know she's only been missing since Monday evening?'

'Peter did,' Felicity answered, an impatient tone clear in her voice. 'And I don't really think that kind of—'

'Is it true that Erica Spencer was murdered, do you think? The timing is very suspicious, what with that podcast saying Mary-Beth and Peter were involved.' Larry Gorman from the far corner – three-bed, barely any driveway – asked. His

85

trainers were filthy, Miranda had noted, as she'd requested they de-shoe at the door.

'It also said that Marcus and I were involved,' Karla spoke up sternly. 'So I'd be really careful about what you say about that bloody podcast.'

'Yes, but you're still here, aren't you?' Larry wasn't backing down. 'You stayed to face the music. The only one who has run scared is—'

His words died on his lips as Peter appeared back at the door, his mobile phone hanging limply by his side. 'That was the police. They've found Mary-Beth's car. By the River Dee.'

20

High risk. Suspected suicide. Prepare for the worst.

The words swirled around in Peter King's head, smashing into other thoughts, thoughts he'd been trying to shove aside. That was until the call from the police to say Mary-Beth's car had been found next to the river. This was good news, wasn't it? He knew the car would be found. This was what he wanted. So why did he feel so sick?

Peter knew what everyone else thought of his wife. She was the quiet one, wouldn't say boo to a goose, never stood up for herself. That's why they all took advantage of her. Oh, Mary-Beth, you couldn't be a sweetheart and take Emily to the ballet tonight, could you? How do you make that soda bread taste so beautiful? You'll have to give me the recipe. I put your name down for costumes for the school play – that's okay, isn't it?

And she would smile, and say, of course, it was fine, she'd love to. She didn't complain when the play turned out to be *The Little Mermaid*, and she had to sew individually hand-crafted scales onto a tail for Miranda's little darling Charity, or when her Great Aunty Helen's soda bread recipe turned up on Karla Kaplan's website described as a 'family tradition'.

'Well, technically it is,' she'd said when Peter had expressed his frustration.

'Yes, but your family, not hers.'

Mary-Beth had shrugged. 'What does it matter? One recipe isn't going to turn me into Karla Kaplan. It's more use to her anyway.'

Peter pressed balled fists into his eyes to stop himself from crying at the memory of her. Her soft voice, her small mischievous smile. What would happen to them now? What would happen to the children?

As soon as he'd received the call he'd left Miranda's fake concern meeting and headed straight to the station. The kids were staying with Mary's mum until he could figure out what was going on. Of course they couldn't stay away indefinitely. But hopefully, she wouldn't be away indefinitely.

'Mr King, through here, please.'

He'd run into DC Allan as soon as he'd arrived. The constable had looked temporarily blind-sided, and Peter wondered if they hadn't told him the whole story over the phone.

'They said on the phone they'd found Mary's car?'

'Yes, that's right.' DC Allan nodded. 'Look, I should probably get the family liaison officer, I've already alerted DS Harvey, he's on his way down and—'

'Family liaison officer? Why do I need one of those? Have they found something?'

DC Allan shook his head furiously and looked like he was royally screwing things up. 'No, no, Mr King, they haven't found Mrs King. We still don't know where she is. It's just . . .'

The door opened, and Peter had never seen anyone look so relieved in his life.

DC Allan jumped up. 'DS Harvey, I was just asking Mr King if he wanted a drink.'

'And I was just saying I'm fine, thank you.'

'Mr King, thanks for coming in. How are you doing?'

'What kind of a question is that? My wife is missing and you won't tell me what's going on. How do you think I'm doing?'

DS Harvey sat down at the table and gestured for Peter to do the same. He placed a brown cardboard file on the table between them, and all of a sudden everything seemed to be getting more serious.

'As my colleague told you on the phone, Mary-Beth's car was found next to the River Dee earlier this evening.'

'Whereabouts?' Peter asked, picturing the scene in his head, the engine running, the door flung open and abandoned in a fit of spontaneity.

'Pretty close to the weir there, Mary-Beth's car was parked up on the left.'

'But that's miles away. Why would she drive all that way just to abandon the car?'

'The car was found close to the bridge.'

DS Harvey looked down, waiting for Peter to understand.

'So you definitely think she jumped?' Even saying the words hurt his chest. Had they given up on her just like that? And if so, why allocate a detective to the case if they already thought she was dead?

'Other than the car at the bridge there's nothing to suggest Mary-Beth is in the water. It's a pretty busy bridge, and no one has reported seeing your wife climb the rails or jump in. In fact, she hasn't been sighted at all. After finding the car where we have, we've escalated Mary's disappearance to high risk.'

'What, so she wasn't high risk before? What does that even mean?'

DS Harvey sighed, and Peter could tell he was grappling to find a way of saying what he wanted to say without sending him into a fury or spiralling down into depression. Why couldn't he just be open with him?

Because you're a suspect now. It's always the husband. Unless it's the lover.

'Mr King, I'm going to be candid.' Harvey laid both hands on the table, as if he'd read Peter's mind. 'When your wife first went missing there was nothing to suggest she hadn't left of her own accord. Wait—' He held up a hand. 'I know you're about to say she wouldn't do that, she has children, you're happy together, but you wouldn't believe how many times we hear that, only to find out later that the wife – or husband – has been holed up in a hotel trying to make a point, or has left with someone else. The truth is that your wife made sure your children were safe and well looked after before she disappeared. People who have been kidnapped usually don't do that. And as much as we are all influenced by the media, the majority of missing person cases aren't kidnappings or stranger murders. Most people don't have a dark past that comes back to haunt them. And if they do, it doesn't happen out of the blue. The general public doesn't know this, but the police usually have a good idea of who has committed murder within a few hours – a dispute or a domestic, witnesses, some form of evidence. So until we found Mary-Beth's car, we had no reason to treat her as high risk.'

Peter sighed. 'Okay, so now she's high risk. What does that mean? Where do we go from here?'

DS Harvey nodded, glad of the response, and opened the folder in front of him. 'Now we have a team allocated to finding your wife. There are officers out now walking the edges of the River Dee—'

'But you said—'

'I know I said that there was no evidence Mary-Beth has committed suicide, but we still have to look. Quite frankly,

90

the location of the car is the only lead we have. So I'm here to ask you to go over every inch of your life, give me every conceivable person Mary-Beth could be staying with, and every single person who might have wanted to hurt your wife. None of this means we think she has committed suicide, run away or been hurt. What it means is that we are keeping an open mind and looking at every single angle. And we can only do that with your co-operation. Is that okay?'

'Of course.' Peter looked down at his hands and discovered he was twisting his wedding ring, over and over. Felicity's words from the other night came back to him, ringing in his ears as if she was standing in the room next to him.

They're going to think you killed her. They're going to think you killed Erica, and Mary-Beth found out, so you killed her too. And they're going to think I was in on it. They're going to think we killed them both and we're going to go to prison.

'She wouldn't kill herself,' he said, trying to sound confident. *And I didn't kill her either*, he wanted to add, but he didn't want those words out there, he didn't want them free to embed themselves in the detective's mind, a seed to take root. 'But there are some things you should know.'

21

'You told them.' Felicity knew she was breaking one of their rules by calling Peter on his mobile, but it wasn't like Mary-Beth was about to overhear them, was it? She was hardly screening his calls these days.

Callous, Fliss, she reprimanded herself. *What if something really awful has happened to her? Like Erica?*

She couldn't help it. Peter made her feel like a petulant schoolgirl, stamping her feet and having a tantrum. She knew all the reasons they had to be so secretive but it was beginning to grate. She had been about to give him an ultimatum when Mary-Beth disappeared – in fact, her disappearance seemed to have been timed to perfection. No one could question her about the night of the party, about what she'd done to her best friend. And once again she was back in first place with Peter, number one, with Felicity relegated to second best.

She'd heard every excuse in the book. *Think of the children, how awkward is it going to be with you living next door . . .?* Okay, so it wasn't ideal – the kids would be furious about their father's affair, but in time they would forgive him and accept Felicity. Maybe even be a family. She'd been waiting for the secret to come out in a way she couldn't be held responsible for, for so long, and now it had happened and she was stunned.

'I had to. If they're going to find Mary-Beth they need to know the truth, however difficult.'

'Do they know who I am?'

'If they do, it's not from me. I just told them I'd fathered children by someone else and it was possible Mary had found out. They aren't exactly about to go spreading the gossip all over the street, are they? DS Harvey said they would be discreet.'

Felicity sighed. How had this all gone so terribly wrong? She'd settled down here, found Peter . . . was an easy life too much to ask? She had a sudden urge to speak to someone outside these godawful gates – gates that had made her feel so safe and secure, but now made her feel like a prisoner.

'Have they asked you about the podcast? About Halloween?'

'He asked if there was any way Mary-Beth was involved in what happened to Erica, if that's why she might have disappeared on the very day the Facebook post about the podcast appeared.'

'And you said . . . ?'

'I said that Erica fell out of the bloody tree house.' Peter sounded irritated now.

Felicity flinched. She knew she had to tread carefully – if this became too difficult for him, he could just cut her out of his life completely. 'So of course she didn't have anything to do with it.'

'And you didn't mention anything that happened before she fell?'

'What is this, the Spanish Inquisition?'

Felicity sighed. 'I just need to know what to say if they ask me, Peter. The worst thing in the world is that we mix up our stories now and get caught lying. How will that make us look?'

'Guilty,' Peter muttered. 'But then neither of us are exactly innocent, are we?'

22

This is The Truth About Erica *and you're listening to me, Andy Noon.*

As promised, tonight I'm going to read an extract from Erica's diary – or her 'burn book' as it's been referred to within the walls this last week. This diary came into my possession – no, I can't tell you how – just a few weeks after Erica's murder, and although some of it was written in short-hand, and some using initials and references known only to Erica, I've managed to make sense of almost all of it. If you want to see the whole thing I'll be releasing extracts every week on my new blog, www.thetruthabouterica.com.

Here's what Erica wrote on the first of March 2018. Let's see if you can guess who she's talking about.

'It's ironic, really, that she has made a fortune from being the perfect specimen of womanhood when I've never seen her so much as make a lasagne. Had an interesting conversation with Jess a few months ago who questioned if K had even read her own books. Marcus is always stressed – back on the cigs, and Sterling Dual stubs follow his path like breadcrumbs.

As for improving relationships with family – after what he did, I'm surprised half her family isn't in prison.'

I think we can safely assume that the K referred to in Erica's diary is Karla Kaplan and that Jess refers to a person Karla would deny even exists. As investigators, we can dismiss the somewhat disingenuous and slightly spiteful claim that Karla hasn't so much as made a lasagne – as much as Erica knew about her neighbours, she couldn't be there for every family meal. So what was it that Erica knew about the person she only refers to as 'he'? And was it enough to get her killed?

'Karla and Marcus are gaining momentum in the celebrity world faster than Posh and Becks did.'

What you're hearing now is an interview with one of Karla Kaplan's fans, a young woman in her late twenties who I approached when I saw her buying a copy of Entertain and Be Entertaining *by Mrs Kaplan herself.*

'She's just got her shit together, you know? She isn't just Marcus Kaplan's wife – even though she doesn't need to work – she's got her own brand. She's an inspiration.'

Ah yes, Karla Kaplan's brand. Karla has a range of books and products dedicated to helping others live their Level Ten Life. Managed by her good friend Felicity Goldman, over the course of four books Karla helps us poor mortals improve relationships with our family, friends and children, helps us reorganise our lives, achieve financial success and, of course, 'Entertain and Be Entertaining'.

So did a death at one of Karla's parties affect her brand?

'Of course not,' *the fan tells me conclusively.* 'It was an accident. Even the most professional party planner can't stop someone falling out of a tree house.'

So, if the Kaplans have made their fame and fortune on the back of Karla being the perfect mother and hostess, how far would she go to protect that image?

SOMEONE IS LYING

Karla Kaplan mentioned in her statement to the police that she had seen Mrs Spencer on the landing of the house at 'somewhere around midnight' when she said she was just going to pop out for a cigarette. Yet did anyone else see Erica smoking that night? No, they didn't. Because Erica Spencer had quit smoking four weeks previously. Of course everyone has the odd relapse – especially when they are drinking. Possibly. Although Erica wasn't drinking that night either, despite what our six 'witnesses' will tell you. And yet she was found with cigarettes in her pocket – Sterling Dual, as a matter of fact – and alcohol in her blood stream.

So I must be mistaken, I can hear you say. Erica must have fallen off the wagon – one mistake wouldn't matter, right? One evening of abandon just to climb back on the horse the next morning. Except the stakes were higher than cutting back for her own health. Because she wasn't just looking after herself on the night she died. Erica Spencer had stopped smoking and drinking because she was pregnant. Whoever killed Erica killed her baby that night too.

Goodnight, listeners . . . and until next week, stay honest.

23

'I don't give a shit how busy he is, I want him round here within the next hour, or I'll find a lawyer who is available when I call.'

Marcus slammed the receiver back into the cradle, and Karla winced. Her husband didn't get this angry unless he was really rattled.

They had barely said a word to one another since the podcast had played into the kitchen half an hour ago. Zachary had been banned from listening in the first place and, as the final bars of the end tune played, Brandon had silently picked up his phone and gone up to his room. Karla didn't have the energy to follow him.

A mixture of relief and dread peaked in her chest as the doorbell rang. The police already?

'It's Felicity.' Marcus came back into the kitchen. 'I'm not letting her in. I've closed up the front of the house and locked everywhere. Let everyone get their gossip somewhere else.'

'Doesn't that make us look guilty?' Karla picked up her mobile and put it back down again without reading any of the six messages. 'Add that to our lawyer turning up, and we may as well get "I killed Erica Spencer" T-shirts printed.'

'See, that's what I love about you.' Despite how irritated he'd seemed on the phone, Marcus grinned. 'You see a difficult situation and immediately think, "How can I monetise this?"'

Karla glanced through the hallway blinds and watched Felicity's front door close behind her. Guilt prickled at her – Felicity would only have been coming over to show support – now was not the time to be sending friends away. But Marcus was right, they just needed to close ranks until they had figured out a plan of action. This latest podcast didn't mean anything. Okay, it wasn't the best reflection of their lives, but it was hardly the damning evidence of murder that Andy Noon – whoever the fuck he was – had claimed to have on them. But what if this was only the beginning?

'Did you hear how he talked about everyone? *To everyone*? As if he knew us. It's got to be someone who lives here. He said "our community", for God's sake. Why can't we find out who he is?'

'What do you want me to do, start hammering on all the neighbours' doors, asking them if they've been accusing us of murder? We can't start turning on each other, Karla. For all we know, it's someone outside trying to make us believe they live here. Maybe they think we'll all start burning each other's houses down, smoking the bastard out.'

Karla sighed. 'I know, it just seems so stupid that there are only thirteen houses here and we have no idea who this guy is.'

'It might not even be a guy,' Marcus reminded her. 'You

remember what Brandon said about voice distortion. It's more likely to be a woman – wouldn't a guy have used a woman's voice as a disguise?'

Karla thought of the woman she'd confronted the night of the Halloween party nearly a year ago. Could Andy Noon be . . . ? But why? She was angry, yes, but angry enough to set them up for murder? Or was this just her way of exposing their lies so she could sweep in and pick up the pieces – have Marcus back, the way she wanted? Karla wanted desperately to ask Marcus if she'd been in touch, if he'd seen her again. But that would mean talking about it, and once they pulled it out into the fresh air instead of burying it deep, an unspoken knowledge between the two of them, who knew where it would end?

'I'm going out.' Brandon's voice broke into her thoughts.

Marcus was at the bottom of the stairs before their son could get halfway down.

'Not now, mate. We're all staying in tonight, keeping a low profile and all that.'

Brandon raised his eyebrows. 'What, so because Mum lied to the police I can't—'

'Your mother did not lie to the police, and you need to watch what you're saying. The papers get hold of you saying something like that, and you'll end my career, probably your mum's too.'

'Oh, and that would be devastating,' Brandon replied, his voice laden with sarcasm.

'In there.' Marcus directed his eldest son into the small living room the family kept for themselves, the room they had always referred to as 'the snug'. It was there that Karla had breastfed her children, where she and Marcus had sat up all night watching horror movies under piles of fleecy blankets, and where the boys had retreated to when they felt ill, feet up on the squidgy sofa, watching back-to-back episodes of whatever TV show had been popular when Brandon was younger. Karla could hardly remember him being young, these days – it felt as though he'd always been a surly sixteen-year-old.

'Zach?' Marcus shouted up the stairs to their youngest.

Karla followed Brandon into the snug, immediately feeling calmer. The wall to the left of the door was lined with bookshelves, crammed with everything from Jenny Colgan to Shaun Hutson, books from every decade of their family life. There were box sets of Secret Seven novels and true-crime compendiums. The carpet was a muted scarlet, mostly covered by a woven multicoloured rug Karla had found on a market in Benidorm. A DVD cabinet housed box sets like *Lost* and films like *Taxi*. The desk in the corner was covered in Zachary's homework, and pictures of the family adorned the wall above – not huge canvases taken by professional photographers but actual photographs – family camping holidays, Bran on his first bike, Zach on the potty. An electric guitar lay propped up in the corner; it had been there for four years, and Brandon had barely touched it in three. This was the only room in the house that showed who the Kaplans were when they weren't being famous.

Karla took up residence in the armchair, pulling her feet underneath her, while Brandon slumped into the corner of the sofa. Marcus sat on the floor and Zachary appeared in the doorway, the only one who had no idea of what was going on.

'What? What is it? Is someone ill?'

At Zach's words, Karla realised just how long it had been since they had gathered together as a family. How was this so unusual that it had to mean bad news to their ten-year-old son? How had they built a brand out of showing others ways to craft the perfect family when their own children couldn't remember the last time they had all spent together?

'Listen, we need to talk about what this guy is saying, this anonymous podcaster. It's imperative that if the press ask you anything, you don't make a comment. In fact, it's best if you don't comment on it to anyone, not kids at school, not—'

'What's he saying?' Zach looked confused.

Karla beckoned for him to come to her and when he did, she pulled him onto her knee.

'He's saying Mum lied to the police,' Brandon said, a hard edge to his voice that Karla didn't like. 'He's saying that Dad planted cigarettes on Erica Spencer's dead bod—'

'Brandon!' Karla's hand flew to her mouth, but Marcus shook his head.

'Don't, Kay, he's right. We heard what he said: that Erica had written in that bloody journal of hers that I was smoking again, and that my brand of cigarettes were found in her pocket when she had quit smoking months ago. So for once in a long time, let's treat our kids like the adults they are growing into. If they can't talk about it here, they will only talk at school.'

'Spoken like a true self-help guru,' Brandon muttered, rolling his eyes.

'What is your problem?' Karla snapped. 'Just what is it that we've done to you that is so bad? We've given you everything – probably too much, by the looks of it – but we always thought we had taught you to be respectful of how much you have, to appreciate our good luck. We volunteer at shelters, we donate to food banks – Dad has his own charity, for fucksake – and still, you're turning into a spoiled brat. What is it, Bran?'

'Why don't we see Nana Randley?' Brandon asked, looking his mother level in the eye.

Karla flinched.

'You know why,' Marcus interjected. 'I haven't spoken to my mother in years. You don't need to know the details, but we had a falling out, and we thought it best she wasn't part of your lives.'

'Because she abused you.'

Karla gasped. 'Who told you that?'

When Brandon didn't speak, Marcus answered for him. 'You've read my book.'

'What, did you really expect me not to? When all anyone at school can talk about is my junkie dad whose mum beat the shit out of him. Do you know how many times I've been asked if Mum's books have any recipes with dog food in? Or if the pair of you have plans to work together on a hash brownie book?'

'Oh, Bran,' Karla breathed.

Marcus just looked white. Zach still looked confused by the whole outburst.

'You mean hash brown,' he corrected his brother.

Brandon scowled.

'Mate, I'm sorry—' Marcus started, but Brandon jumped to his feet.

'And I'm not your mate, why do you have to call me that? You think you're so cool and hip because you've been on drugs, but everyone I know thinks drugs are for losers. So what does that make you, *mate*?'

Without waiting for a reply, Brandon stormed from the room. Marcus looked at Karla, and she felt as though her heart was breaking. While they had been busy building an empire, she hadn't ever realised how opening their family life to the public would affect the two most important people in it.

Karla heard Brandon's door slam.

'I'll talk to him tomorrow,' Marcus said. 'I need to go out.'

'Wait, where are you going?' A vision of long blonde hair, watery blue eyes, flashed into her mind.

Marcus hesitated. He could still decide to stay. It wasn't too late yet. He shook his head. 'Just out.'

24

Karla leaned over to the laptop that was balancing precariously on the arm of the chair and pressed 'refresh'. It was getting late, dammit, and Marcus still wasn't home. She wasn't expecting anything other than the 'coming soon' notice that had been taunting them since the first podcast, so when the website began to load she almost fell off the chair.

The landing page of *The Truth About Erica* was a montage of black-and-white photographs that looked as though they had been taken by a deranged stalker. Which they probably had. Karla could make out herself, out walking Gigi, at the beginning of summer by the looks of it. She was wearing a dark-coloured vest top and tiny cut-off shorts, with Grecian sandals. From the angle it had been taken at, her legs looked dumpy – how dare they! Her legs were her best feature.

There were others: Marcus outside his accountants, Felicity and Peter talking in Felicity's front garden, Miranda in her car, Mary-Beth looking over her shoulder. The photographs were arranged at angles, laid over each other as though spread over a table. Above the middle of the montage was a menu bar with options:

Halloween 2017
Erica's Diary
The Severn Oaks Six
What is the truth?

Karla clicked on the tabs one by one and scanned each page. Information about the night Erica fell. Pictures and biographies of each of them: Felicity, Peter, Mary-Beth, Miranda, Marcus and herself. Her cursor hovered over the tab 'Erica's Diary', not wanting to look but knowing she was going to anyway. The page loaded and Karla gave it a quick scan – there it was, in black and white, Erica's alleged scribblings about how Karla had never even made a lasagne. But nothing new. She let out a sigh of relief. What had that horrid man said? That he would be releasing extracts every week? Perhaps he was waiting for his big reveals to be on the podcast. She clicked on 'What is the truth?', her heart rate lowering. There wasn't anything new here – Marcus's lawyers could probably get it taken down, perhaps they could even find out who the owner—

She gasped as the last page loaded. The only thing on the page was a full-sized picture of Erica, the word 'MURDERED' scrawled across the middle in blood-red letters.

'Brandon!' Karla shouted up the stairs. She didn't want her son to see this but with a physical link to the podcaster now, surely that made him more traceable? 'BRANDON!'

He appeared at the doorway of the snug, headphones slung around his neck and his trainers on.

'I was just going out,' he said, his face still sullen from their earlier argument.

'At this hour? I need your help with something,' Karla said, spinning the laptop to face him. 'This website – do you know how to find out who owns it?'

Brandon took a few steps into the room and leaned down to scan the screen. 'Shiiiit.'

'Yes, exactly,' Karla said. 'Shit. Can you trace the owner or something?'

Brandon shrugged. 'Depends. I doubt they would have left their personal details visible but I can try.'

He took the laptop over to the sofa and Karla crouched down next to him, watching as he pulled up a site called Whois.com.

'Usually this will just show you the host details, unless the owner has made their details public. It's unlikely this guy would do that – unless he's stupid – so it will probably just show LCN or HostGator or some . . . oh fuck.'

'What? Show me,' Karla demanded, shifting for a better look. 'I don't understand . . .'

'Me neither,' Brandon said, his eyebrows raised. 'It says here that the domain name owner is Dad.'

25

'Of course, I didn't know she was pregnant,' Felicity said, nudging her way up the queue. 'Did you?'

'She never said a word to me. I wonder whether Jack knew?'

Miranda looked awful. Felicity had called her as soon as she'd left Karla's last night – her best friend hadn't answered her repeated door ringing or text messages, and Felicity had needed to speak to someone, at that point – even Miranda would have done.

'Surely he must have,' Felicity mused. 'More to the point – where the hell is Jack? Have you seen him since any of this crap started?'

'No.' Miranda shook her head. 'I thought maybe he'd taken the kids away, but the curtains have been opening and closing as usual. The car hasn't been on the drive, but it might just be in the garage.'

'Could be the cleaner opening the curtains.'

'What about Peter?'

'I'll get these,' Felicity said, ignoring the question. 'You sit down. What do you want?'

'Oh . . .' Miranda looked as though no one had ever

bought her a drink before. 'Can I get a hot chocolate, please? No cream but I'll have the sprinkles.'

Felicity watched Miranda make her way to a free table, taking in just how different she looked today. Her usually sleek auburn hair was pulled back into a messy bun at the nape of her neck and she'd obviously been forgetting to tan because she looked a shade paler than white. One of her gel nails had come off. This would usually warrant an emergency trip to the house for her regular nail woman – Miranda didn't go to nail bars like the rest of the mums, she had a 'woman' – but today she'd obviously had other things on her mind.

'What can I get you?' The guy behind the counter was someone Felicity had never seen before. Where was her friend when she needed him? A complimentary muffin would go down like a dream today.

'Flat white and a hot chocolate, no cream, sprinkles. To drink in, please.' She wanted to ask where the other guy was, even if just to make the point that she came here all the time, but what difference did it really make? Was it really so important to her to be more special than the other customers. *Eurgh, I'm no better than Miranda.*

'Hot chocolate, flat white. That's four eighty.'

Felicity paid, finding that she was paying particular attention to his voice. She'd been doing it with every man she'd spoken to since the podcast. Could he be the mystery podcaster? No, his voice was too young, and he spoke too fast. Andy Noon spoke slowly, with a deeper husk. But wouldn't he be disguising his voice? *Face it,* Felicity thought, *he could be anyone, and we'd have no clue.*

Carrying the drinks over to where Miranda was sitting with her back to the rest of the coffee shop, Felicity was glad – she couldn't bear thinking that everyone she met was whispering about her, nudging one another. No wonder Karla had gone to ground, it must be a hundred times worse for her and Marcus – two of the most recognisable faces in Cheshire.

'Did you go to the website?' Felicity asked, placing Miranda's drink down in front of her.

'Thanks. I tried, but it just said "coming soon". Did you?'

'Same. I haven't checked today.'

'He didn't mention Mary-Beth,' Felicity said, voicing something that had been on her mind since she'd heard the second podcast. 'He didn't say anything about her disappearing.'

'What does that mean?'

Felicity shrugged. 'Maybe nothing. Maybe he'd recorded it in advance and couldn't be bothered to edit it after she went missing.'

'I don't have a clue how that works. Logan would know more than me.'

'Do you recognise the voice?'

Miranda shook her head. 'I've listened to it twice – as much as I hated it. It just doesn't sound like anyone inside the gates to me – does it to you? I mean, there's Marcus – and I definitely don't think it's him, for obvious reasons. Then there's Peter, and God knows he's got enough on without all this.'

'Karla says that Brandon said that it doesn't even have to be a man. The voice sounds like it's been altered, with distortion software. It could be anyone. It could be you.'

Miranda let out a tinkling laugh but her face didn't reflect amusement. 'Well, I think we both know it isn't me.'

Felicity was inclined to believe her. For a start there was the blog. *The Truth About Erica*. Felicity could hardly see Miranda sitting in front of her computer setting up websites and recording podcasts. She would have had to ask Felicity what an FTP was, why LCN were hosting and where the party was. The idea that she would be behind all this was laughable really.

'Have you spoken to him, by the way?'

Felicity started, realising that Miranda had been speaking to her. 'Sorry, who?'

'Peter.' Her voice sounded innocent enough, but that was the problem with Miranda. When she was making an effort to sound innocent, you should beware.

Felicity felt colour flood her face. 'No, why would I have?'

Miranda pulled a face. 'Well, he left in such a hurry the other night, after saying that the police had found Mary-Beth's car. I expected him to come back and tell us what was going on but when he came home, early hours that morning, all I saw was the garden security light go on. I haven't seen him since.'

The garden security light. Was that Miranda's way of telling her that she knew about Peter and Felicity's garden meetings? Or was she just being paranoid – everything felt like a personal dig these days.

'I suppose one of us should go and see him.' Felicity shrugged, trying to look nonchalant. 'After all, where they found Mary's car, I mean, you know how that looks, right?'

Of course Miranda knew, Felicity thought. How could she not? Mysterious disappearance after being named as a suspect in her best friend's murder, then her car shows up at the side of the river? Things did not look good for Mary-Beth.

'I'd have no idea what to say to him.' Miranda looked down into her hot chocolate. 'Or poor Jack. Sometimes I . . .' she hestitated then shook her head. 'Have you spoken to Karla?'

'No. Everything's closed up, and she's not answering her phone.'

'No police have turned up, though?'

'Police?'

'Well,' Miranda took a sip of her drink and looked away, 'you know, what with her having lied to them about why

111

Erica was going outside and with Marcus planting those cigarettes on her . . .'

'Miranda!' Felicity gasped. 'You have no right saying things like that! All the podcast said was that she had cigarettes on her—'

'Those weird clicky dual ones Marcus smokes,' Miranda pointed out. She gave a little shrug. 'I'm just saying.'

'Well, you'd better not let Karla hear you "just say". Otherwise you'd better hope Karla does get arrested – otherwise she'll kill you.'

'And make it look like an accident, I'm sure,' Miranda muttered.

Felicity glared.

'Stop it. You know Karla would never hurt Erica, and neither would Marcus. And what is this guy saying, that they killed her because she's never seen Karla make a lasagne? Ridiculous.'

'Yes, of course,' Miranda murmured. 'Let's hope the news vans I saw driving towards us this morning think the same.'

26

Miranda surveyed the mess around her and closed her eyes. She counted to three but when she opened them again the saucepan and plates were still piled up next to the sink, crusty with the remnants of uneaten mash and gravy. Stray peas littered the countertop and a cup of what could only be described as 'juice-mush' sat on the table, where Charity had tried to sink her leftovers into her drink so that she would be allowed to leave the family dinner Miranda had slaved over.

She couldn't blame lack of time for the carnage that was strewn through the living room, kitchen diner and into the bedrooms. Logan was staying overnight at Jesson's, Charity was at her mother's all day, then she had ballet at 4 p.m., which her grandmother would gladly sit through, so she wouldn't be home until after five. Miranda probably wouldn't have to cook later, as Grandma would likely have prepared a tasty stew or nutritious steamed chicken for after class, delivered to Miranda's in a still-warm casserole dish so it was clear that it was home-made. No, Miranda's house was in a total state of disrepair because she just couldn't be fucked to clean it. What she wanted to do was to get back into her pyjamas and lie in bed all day, tucked up under the plush duvet, and binge-watch trash TV – *Real Housewives of Cheshire*, or something equally as brain-numbing.

It hadn't always been this way. Before the kids came along, she had a job, she was something other than an unpaid cleaner. It was a bloody good job too – she had been a Business Continuity Planner, and multinational companies all over the country had called on her to help them safeguard their futures. Nowadays the only people who called her were the school, wanting to know why Charity only had one welly in her forest school bag, or demanding last week's dinner money payment. All those countless 'What Career Should You Have?' questionnaires in school and she couldn't remember ever once answering that she wanted to follow a small child and a grown man around the house flushing toilets after them.

She took a deep breath and counted backwards from five – something she'd mocked Felicity for – to clear her mind and refocus on the task ahead. Then, as she hit one, she began to move automatically towards the kitchen.

Speaking of Felicity – she'd been particularly on edge when they had met for coffee today. Then again, there didn't seem to be a member of the Severn Oaks Six – bloody hell, now even she was thinking of them with that awful moniker – who looked themselves lately. Well, Miranda supposed no one knew what Mary-Beth looked like, given that she hadn't been seen since the first podcast had aired. And how did that make her look? Guilty, that's how. That's why Miranda had stuck around so long; running made you look like you have something to hide. And with all the focus suddenly on Marcus Kaplan and the brand of cigarettes he smoked, no one was looking at her.

At least, not yet.

The sound of a car engine entering her driveway and being

switched off pulled Miranda to the window. Bugger! What was Alex doing home? Quickly she opened the dishwasher and began shoving plates in, scooping up the peas from the counter and tipping them into the bin. As he walked into the kitchen she closed the china cupboard on the cup of soggy leftovers and prayed he wouldn't try and make himself a drink.

'What are you doing back?' Miranda smiled and tried to look as though she'd been cleaning for hours. 'Home for lunch?'

One glance at Alex told her that he wasn't just home for lunch. His perpetually tanned face was grey and his eyes looked bloodshot. Had he been crying?

'Jesus, you look like shit! What's wrong? Are you coming down with something?'

Alex shrugged, throwing his coat onto the back of the sofa – Christ, she hated it when he did that. It was two extra steps to hang it up, for goodness' sake. 'I feel like shit. I'm going to go and lie down.'

He barely looked at her. Miranda wanted to tell him about the podcast she'd listened to alone last night – he'd told her he wasn't interested in that crap after she'd made him listen to the first one with her. She wanted to talk to her husband about the coffee shop this morning, where she was certain people were watching her and Felicity, talking about them in hushed tones. Two of the Severn Oaks Six, out in public! It seemed like the whole population of Cheshire was holding their breath, waiting to see what was revealed next. But Alex clearly wasn't in the mood to be bothered, and he would only tell her she was being paranoid – besides, hadn't he told her to stop listening to the podcasts in the first place?

'Shall I bring you some lunch? Soup?'

'I don't really feel like anything. Thanks,' he added as an afterthought.

As he left her standing in the kitchen, staring after his back, she realised he hadn't even got close enough to give her a kiss.

Breathing in deeply through her nose, Miranda busied herself, the tidying and cleaning seeming more appealing now that she needed a distraction. She picked up Alex's coat and was hit by the stench of alcohol – had he been drinking?

No, that was ridiculous. Alex had his shortcomings but being a drunk wasn't one of them. Especially as his car was on the driveway – he'd driven home from work, and he would *never* drive after drinking. No. No, definitely not.

Miranda hung the coat in the cloakroom, pausing at the bottom of the stairs. There was a voice coming from her bedroom – probably Alex on the phone. She took a couple of stairs. It wasn't eavesdropping if the person was your husband – right? And the way he'd looked when he'd come in, she was worried about him. If it was the flu it had come on awfully quickly.

It was a man's voice, but it didn't sound like her husband. Perhaps his boss on speakerphone, she thought, but dread rose in her chest with every step she mounted. Because that voice was familiar, and it wasn't Ged – Alex's boss. It was a voice she'd heard more recently than that – last night, in fact, with her earphones on as the bath water cooled around her, too horrified to move. Despite everything he'd said about not listening to that crap, and it being some kind of wind-up, her husband was playing last night's podcast. Obviously he did think it was a big deal, after all. Had someone at work told him she was on it? Maybe he suspected what she'd done at the party. Maybe he thought she killed Erica.

Miranda stood frozen on the stairs, until the slamming of their en-suite door jolted her back into life. She padded down the stairs as quietly as possible and out into the back garden, behind the shed, where she crouched down and pulled a packet of cigarettes from inside a fake plant pot. Hands trembling, she lit one up and inhaled deeply. Just hearing that voice put her on edge – enough even to risk being caught smoking by her husband.

Leaning back against the shed, she exhaled and pulled her phone from her back pocket. Checking social media was like picking a scab. Even as she told herself she shouldn't be doing it, that it would be painful and leave her feeling worse than before, she couldn't help but click on the Facebook app and scroll through her newsfeed.

'Any chance I could steal one of those?'

Miranda jumped at the voice. She'd been so deep in thought and automatic screen-scrolling that she hadn't even heard the back gate open or seen Jack Spencer walk in.

27

'I don't know what's more insulting – that you think I would be such an asshole to you and Mum, or that you think I would be stupid enough to use your details to register it.' Brandon opened the door of the American-style fridge and pulled out a tub of butter.

'Nobody said you were an asshole, Bran. I had to ask.' Marcus ran a hand over his face. He was exhausted; he and Karla had stayed up half the night in the snug, her head in his lap, covered in blankets, while they debated what exactly was going on, and how they were going to deal with it. The police were yet to speak to them about the allegations being made by Andy Noon, but with Mary-Beth's disappearance being upgraded to 'high risk', whatever that meant, and thinly veiled accusations that Karla had lied to them in her statement, it wouldn't be long. Plus the press were beginning to realise how big this story was getting, and articles were already showing up in local newspapers loaded with snark about Karla and her fitness to tell others how to raise their families. If this guy turned out to be one of their kids, it would end her career – and possibly his.

'Can't you just get it taken down? If you own it?'

Not for the first time, Marcus was surprised at how quick-thinking his ten-year-old son was. It had taken an hour of hand-wringing before either he or his wife had had the same thought.

'Close, Zach, but no cigar, I'm afraid. I don't have the email address or password for the account. It's in my name, and our home address is listed, but the email isn't actually mine – it just looks like it is. I've emailed LCN, the people who host the site, but Dean doesn't think there's much we can do about it other than get them to contact the owner to change the address.'

'Can't they get the IP address of the customer?'

Marcus raised his eyebrows. 'What do you know about IP addresses?'

Zach shrugged and spooned Rice Krispies into his mouth. 'They ping a signal to tell you where a computer was used,' he said through a mouthful of cereal and milk.

'You are too clever.' Marcus ruffled his son's hair. Karla had thought they should keep the kids out of all of this, but he knew now that he was right to involve them. Despite what Erica obviously wrote in that fucking journal of hers, they were a close family and thought of themselves as good parents. They treated the boys as the young adults they were, and they never kept secrets. Well, almost never, but what kind of parents told their kids everything? Some things needed to be private. He cringed as he thought of the Halloween party the night Erica fell from their tree house. Yes, some things were best kept between the adults. 'But unfortunately they can't give us the IP address. Confidentiality. The police could get it, if they thought a crime was being committed, but free speech means this guy can say what he likes.'

'Unless it's libel,' Brandon pointed out. His toast popped out of the toaster and he proceeded to butter it directly on the work surface, leaving beads of toast sweat and crumbs in his wake. 'Then you can sue him.'

'We're looking into it.' Karla walked into the kitchen, looking like death warmed up. She was still wearing her dressing gown, her blonde hair wild around her head like a frizzy halo, and dark rings of yesterday's eyeliner under her eyes. 'We could sue for loss of earnings if *Real Housewives* use this as a reason to refuse me a slot. And use a plate, for God's sake.'

Brandon rolled his eyes. 'Being accused of murder hasn't affected your ability to bust my ass, I see.'

'Bust your ass? God, these YouTubers have a lot to answer for. Besides, I haven't— Oh, never mind. Stop winding me up and put the kettle on. What time is Dean coming?'

She crossed the kitchen to Marcus, who stooped to give her a kiss.

'Morning, baby.' He glanced over at the Alexa on the counter. 'Half an hour, maybe. Did you get any sleep?'

It had been 2:30 a.m. before they had finally gone upstairs, Karla already half asleep when they got into bed.

She nodded. 'Didn't wake up once, actually. Although I must have dreamed a ton because I don't feel rested. I'd better get ready before Dean shows up.'

'I'll bring you up a cup of tea.' Marcus smoothed down her unruly hair, then reached down to squeeze her ass. Karla grinned and pretended to swat his hand away. He watched his wife leave the kitchen and sighed. He had no idea where this was all going, but he hoped they would still be a family by the end of it.

28

They sat on the swinging chair at the end of the garden, Erica's husband and Miranda Davenport. Jack sucked on his cigarette wordlessly, Miranda fidgeting with her hands and wondering what on earth to say. None of the neighbours had seen anything of Jack or Erica's children – Max and Emily – since the first podcast had been announced, and now Miranda realised that maybe she should have tried to contact him sooner.

'We thought it best to give you some space.' She settled on the easy lie.

The truth was that she'd been scared to go and knock on the door of the house Jack and Erica had shared for six years, scared that he might yell at her, or question her too closely about just where she'd been at the moment Erica 'fell'. The truth was, Jack had no fight left in him. He'd been using all the energy he had to keep his family afloat since his wife's death. He had always been the breadwinner, working all the hours God sent in project management, while Erica did the hands-on parenting. The last year had been like climbing a mountain of compromise and discovering that it was near impossible to do anything well when you were trying to do *everything*.

'The kids don't understand,' he replied, letting her off the hook. 'They haven't heard the podcast and I intend to keep it that way. I snuck them out in the middle of the night after the first one, told them it was a surprise holiday. We went to Erica's cabin.'

'They'll be back at school soon, Jack. You'll have to tell them something before the other kids do.'

Jack nodded. 'I know. I just don't know what to say to them. It's hard enough for them to accept their mum's death as an accident – but to have to tell them someone might have hurt her, that someone took their mum away from them on purpose . . .'

His words trailed off, and Miranda looked at him sharply.

'You believe what this guy is saying, then? That one of *us* hurt Erica?'

Jack sat in silence, the way he had when his father died, the way he had when Erica died. That was his way, he'd never been any good at opening up about what was on his mind. Then he began to talk.

'This is going to sound weird,' he said. 'But part of me wants to believe it. Part of me – the part that has been furious at Erica for being so stupid, for leaving me and the kids. If it had been done to her, I could focus my anger on someone else, I could blame someone other than Erica – and myself.'

'Why would you blame yourself?'

Jack hesitated. How much was he going to tell her? After all, it was easy to get carried away when you were talking one-on-one to someone, in such an intimate setting, light-headed from your first cigarette in nearly a year.

He recovered himself in time and shook his head. 'Doesn't everyone, when the person they love dies? If I'd been with her on the balcony, if I'd gone looking for her sooner – those questions haunt me every day.'

'Have the police spoken to you?'

Jack scoffed. 'Who, Harvey and his new sidekick? He's different now, don't you think? Harvey? Not so keen for the truth this time. He barely speaks, just lets his new lapdog ask all the questions.'

'I don't really remember much from when . . . from the first time he was here,' Miranda confessed. 'I think I was a bit of a mess. I remember him asking a lot of questions, though, and he didn't seem to believe anything we said. I remember Felicity saying she thought he didn't believe us. She was all panicked – I remember, because she's usually so calm, so in control.'

'They suspected me,' Jack said, surprising Miranda.

She'd never considered Jack would be a suspect – he loved Erica, for all her faults.

'Did you know about this diary?'

'No,' Jack said, a little too sharply. 'Not until this fucking podcast. Who is it, Miranda? Who's dragging this all up again?'

Miranda couldn't answer. She had one more question, one she didn't feel like she should ask, but she was going to anyway.

'Did you know she was pregnant?'

Jack winced. 'Not until afterwards. The coroner ordered a post-mortem because the death wasn't a result of natural causes. Her pregnancy wasn't mentioned at the inquest because they didn't have any evidence it was related to cause of death – but the senior coroner told me. I didn't even tell the kids. I didn't want them to know they'd lost a mum and a brother or sister in the same night.'

'I'm so sorry,' Miranda breathed, and to her credit she looked it. 'Did they say how far along she was?'

'Thirteen weeks . . .' Jack sniffed. 'I spoke to her doctor. She'd already been to see him about the baby. The thing is—' He stopped, put his face in his hands.

'What? What is it?'

'I had the snip, Miranda.' Jack couldn't meet her eyes. 'I'm too old for more children. The baby wasn't mine. Erica was sleeping with someone else. Maybe that's why she was murdered. So no one would find out who the father really was.'

29

'I told you. Didn't I tell you?'

Felicity held in her sigh. She'd known as soon as she'd made the decision to call her sister that she was going to have to listen to the whole 'I told you so' thing before Melissa would switch on the sympathy. Plenty of other people would have held back, let the words go unspoken, but not Liss. The good thing about her sister, though, was that once it was out of the way, she wouldn't dwell on it, or harp on about how she'd told her that Peter King was bad news. It was as though she had to get that superior 'I was right all along' spiel in so that it didn't sit between them for the entire conversation. Felicity switched the phone to her other hand and flicked on the kettle.

'It's worth the grief, Liss, I promise. You should come and meet him. He's . . . I just think you'd like him, that's all.'

'Yeah, maybe,' Melissa replied, but Felicity knew from the tone of her sister's voice that she didn't mean it. She'd already decided she didn't want anything to do with Peter, and she could hardly blame her. It wasn't exactly a conventional relationship.

'So go on, tell me what's going on.'

Felicity glanced at Mollie and Amelie, who were playing on the sofa at the 'family' end of the kitchen diner. They looked preoccupied enough and the front door was locked, as was the side gate. Despite how safe Severn Oaks was, she could never shake the feeling that she needed to know where the twins were at all times. They were only five at the moment, and so her overprotectiveness was fully justified – the only problem was that she didn't think the urge to keep them close would miraculously subside when they were eight or nine, or even fifteen. If anything, this feeling of panic whenever they were out of sight would get worse as they got older. She knew what could happen to fifteen-year-old girls if they were allowed too much freedom – she'd been one herself once.

Pouring her cup of tea, she carried it over to where the twins were playing with the modern equivalent of Barbies, wide-eyed female dolls with faces full of make-up.

'You remember I told you about that woman who died at that party I was at last year?'

'Erica Spencer.'

Felicity rolled her eyes. She should have known that Melissa would remember Erica's full name – her sister never forgot anything, and never missed a trick. There was no point in trying to keep secrets from her, she had a way of getting to the truth – and had since they were kids. Felicity had accepted it by now, and told her sister almost everything. Almost.

'That's the one. Well, someone has started a podcast claiming that Erica's death wasn't an accident.'

'What's a podcast?'

Felicity almost choked on her cup of tea. 'What's a podcast? Liss, are you serious? Have you never heard of *Serial*?'

'I'm going to assume you don't mean the stuff I had for breakfast,' Melissa replied dryly. 'So no, I've never heard of *Serial*. Is it a game?'

'A podcast is like a prerecorded radio show.' Felicity realised she had adopted the tone she used when explaining things to the twins. Only usually it was words like 'obnoxious', not 'podcast'. 'You listen to it on an app. You know what an app is, right?'

'There's no need for sarcasm. I don't have kids like you to keep me up to speed with these new trends.'

Melissa wasn't old at all, she was Felicity's twin. The difference was that she was 'old school'. Unlike everyone they knew, Melissa had refused to start any social media accounts, she had never used Twitter or Snapchat or Instagram. She ran her own business making jewellery and didn't even have a website – much to Felicity's chagrin. As a brand awareness manager Felicity had asked – no, begged – Melissa to go digital but her sister claimed to have more customers than she could handle through word of mouth, and what would the point be of trying to garner more if she didn't have time for more orders?

'Don't you want to expand?' Felicity had asked. 'You could take on some staff, have a team. You could get some machinery . . .'

Liss had sighed heavily, as though the very thought of it all was exhausting her. 'I just want to make jewellery, Flick. Not conquer the world.'

'Okay,' Felicity conceded now. 'Although my five-year-old daughters didn't tell me what a podcast is, by the way. You learn these things when you connect with the real world, not sit in a mud hut in the back garden all day like a hippy.'

'It's not a mud hut and I'm not a hippy.' Melissa's studio was a dilapidated old shed that she insisted she would have renovated when it gave up – probably one more year. That had been four years ago and the hut showed little sign of falling down, almost as though it had heard the conversation

127

and was determined not to be euthanised. 'Tell me about the podcast on the app.'

Felicity grinned. Satisfied that the girls would be fine on their own for ten minutes, Felicity carried her cup of tea into the front room, settled herself down on her oversized navy-blue sofa and pulled the mustard teddy bear throw from over the back and tucked it around herself. From this point she could see the entrance to Karla's driveway, a portion of her best friend's front door as well as – if she turned her head sideways – the entrance to the street, and Miranda and Alex's house. The huge bay windows in the front room had been an absolute nightmare to buy blinds for but had served her well in the long run – she had one of the best views in the street, second only to Erica and Jack's. Well, just Jack now. Speaking of Jack – had he just come out of Miranda's side gate?

'Flick? Am I going to hear the story, or do I have to wait until one of the twins tells me?'

'Sorry . . .' Felicity remembered her sister on the other end of the phone. 'It started a couple of weeks ago. There was this post on Facebook – you do know what Facebook is, right?'

The person who looked suspiciously like Jack Spencer made his way down Miranda's driveway and down the street to Jack Spencer's house. So he was back. No one had seen him since this whole mess had started. Where had he been? And what was he doing in Miranda's back garden? Miranda and Alex were both home – Felicity had seen Alex's car pull up much earlier than usual today. Was something going on?

'I've heard rumours,' Melissa retorted, dryly. 'Go on, what did it say? This post.'

'It was by a fake account and it said that there would be a podcast starting that would tell us the truth about what happened to Erica. That she was murdered and there were six suspects.'

'Who were . . . ?'

'They didn't give names but it was clear who they were talking about. For a start, there were only about eight of us there when Erica died – although I'm not sure why that doesn't make it eight suspects.'

'Well, because one of them is this podcaster, so that would be seven anyway,' Melissa said.

'Huh?' Felicity was gazing out of the window so intently, waiting for something to happen on the street, that she almost missed what her sister had said. 'What?'

'Keep up, Felicity, you're supposed to be the smart one. This person wouldn't say eight suspects because they obviously don't suspect themselves. The pod person has got to be someone who was there – otherwise, how would they know what really happened?'

'Well, that's not technically true, is it? I mean, there were eight of us there but Zachary's tree house could be seen from any of the windows on that side of the street. No, not from number eight probably – that's Simon and Gilly's. Possibly the Pattersons'. But definitely from Jack and Erica's—'

'Who were at the party, so that's useless information. Jeesh, Detective Goldman, thank God you're not in charge of the investigation. Who else lives on that side?'

'Mary-Beth and Peter, who were also at the party and have both been named as suspects. And number ten, which I think is still empty. It used to be that couple with the white dog – Julie and whatever her husband was called – but they split up. They were going to rent it out, but I haven't seen any cars going up there.'

'So the only people who could have seen what happened from their houses weren't actually in their houses. Who does that leave?' Melissa sounded triumphant. 'The three people not named as suspects. Erica herself, and who else?'

Felicity thought back to the people left at the end of the

party, eight shocked faces drained of blood, blue and red lights lighting them up to the beat of her thumping heart. Red, *Miranda*. Blue, *Marcus*. Red, *Peter*. Blue, *Mary-Beth*. Red, *Karla*. Blue . . .

'Alex,' she whispered.

Red . . .

'And Jack.'

30

It had been one week since the last podcast and everyone in Severn Oaks knew what that meant. Tuesday nights were no longer ordinary nights, and with tomorrow being the first day back at school for the children of Severndale Primary, tensions were particularly high in the houses behind the gates. What would they find out about the night Erica died tonight? What would be the topic of conversation tomorrow at the school gates?

Over the last couple of weeks of the school holidays Felicity, Miranda and Karla had been able to pretend it wasn't all happening to them – that the anonymous voice behind the screens of their smartphones and laptops could be referring to anyone – like any true-crime podcast that had gripped the nation, it belonged to someone else, other people's lives that were good for a bit of salacious catching up around the water cooler or leaning up against the door of their cars after the kids had been safely deposited in school. Only this time the tragedy that was being played out in delicious detail every week was *their* lives, and there would be no escaping it tomorrow morning when they had to venture out into the wider world. Felicity assumed they had all been clicking 'refresh' on the blog as often as she had, cringing every time the photographs of them all loaded. Who had taken them? None of them felt safe any more, the one thing they had always taken for granted in Severn Oaks.

The journalists weren't letting up. It would have been bad enough if none of them had been under suspicion, with cars parked outside the gates all day, beady eyes glinting through the windscreens and dictaphones glued to the hands of those whose job it was to turn real life into entertainment. Karla and Marcus's celebrity had notched the story up a level – who would dare accuse Cheshire's power couple of murder?

'I wonder what *she'd* have done,' Felicity mused, accepting the glass of wine that Karla handed to her in her own kitchen. 'Thanks.'

'Who, Erica?'

Erica's name hit the air like a noxious fart. It was funny how they'd all avoided talking about her in the weeks since the revelations had been rolled out by the stilted, slightly robotic voice they had all grown to hate. The conversation Miranda had had with Jack in her back garden – so out of left field and surreal that she wasn't even sure it had really happened now – was the first time Erica had actually been front and centre of anyone's mind. They were all so busy worrying about what it meant for them.

'She'd have been the one holding the cards.' Miranda spoke for the first time since they had all arrived at Felicity's house, twenty minutes ago. It struck Felicity that this was the first time they would all be in the same room since the first podcast aired. No, not all, of course – Mary-Beth still hadn't come home.

'True . . .' Karla sat down next to Miranda at the breakfast bar. 'How was it that she always knew so much about everyone?'

'Knowledge is power,' Felicity offered. 'She made it her

business to squirrel away every nugget of information she could about us, about everyone she knew, so that she had a level of control over everyone. There aren't six suspects, there are bloody dozens. Do you remember when Marianne Gilespie's daughter wanted to play the violin in the talent contest?' She took a slug of her wine, finding it easier with every mouthful to speak ill of the dead. 'And we all knew that Emily was going to play the violin. What did I say to you, Karla?'

'That Mary-Beth would be on stage doing a striptease before Erica would let her daughter be upstaged by Tiffany Gilespie.'

'And what happened?'

'If the answer is that Mary-Beth did a striptease then I'm going to start attending the school talent shows.'

The three women looked up to see Miranda's husband, Alex, in the doorway. 'Sorry, the front door was open.'

Miranda scowled. 'Do you always have to be so inappropriate? Mary-Beth is missing,' she practically hissed.

'And Erica is dead, but that hasn't stopped you three sitting here like the Witches of Eastwick stirring your cauldrons.'

'Oh, do fuck off, Alex.' Karla grinned and stood up. 'Do you want a drink? I don't suppose you saw my husband on your way over, did you?'

'He was on the phone in the garden. Something about getting a refund on a hit he'd organised.'

Miranda looked as though she was about to be sick. Alex grinned and Karla shook her head. Karla had often wondered how it was that someone so laid-back and mischievous (not to mention attractive) as Alex Davenport ever ended up married to the hot mess that was Miranda Clarke (as she was back then). Oh yes, to the outside world Miranda might appear to be completely in control of her life, but these days Karla was beginning to suspect the truth. Miranda had always been desperate to be top of the heap, valued, *important*. It was so crucial to the core of her being, her self-worth, that she be seen as super-organised, always the one that people turned to in a crisis. She'd have been hosting the crisis meeting they were at now, if Felicity hadn't flat-out refused to leave the twins in bed alone while she went across the road. It had annoyed Miranda – what did she think would happen, for goodness' sake, they lived in the safest neighbourhood in England – but she'd acquiesced, of course. As she frequently reminded herself, arguing with people only got you a name for yourself. There was more than one way to skin a cat. Instead, she'd ordered a selection of biscuits from Selfridges Foodhall, arranged them on expensive porcelain, and popped a tub of Whittard's Rocky Road Hot Chocolate in her handbag for the opportune moment.

Now – for the sake of appearances – she forced a smile. Alex smiled back over his beer glass, knowing he would pay for his flippancy later, no doubt.

'It's all right for you, joker,' Felicity said. 'You're the only one who hasn't been called out as a suspect by this guy.'

'It's my innocent face.'

'Oh, yeah?' Marcus Kaplan appeared in the doorway. 'Picture of innocence, you. Sorry I'm late.'

'It hasn't started yet,' Felicity said, checking the huge black-framed clock on the wall. 'Five minutes. I thought Peter was coming?'

'He's having a cigarette,' Marcus replied. 'I didn't know he smoked?'

'He's not supposed to,' Felicity said, without thinking. Quickly she added, 'Mary-Beth wouldn't like it.'

'Have we heard anything about Mary-Beth yet?' Miranda spoke in hushed tones, as though Peter might hear his wife's name through the two walls that separated them.

'There wasn't anything in the car that proved where she might be. But it was right next to the river, so . . .'

'So what's our best guess? Mary-Beth kills Erica, then does a runner when this Andy guy threatens to out her on his podcast? Jumps in the river? Or fakes her death to live in Mexico?' Alex offered.

The doorbell rang before anyone could answer.

'Saved by the bell,' Marcus quipped. 'That must be Peter. I'll let him in.'

'At least someone has some manners,' Felicity frowned, 'although I hope he hasn't woken the girls.'

Peter and Marcus burst into the kitchen and slammed the door shut. Marcus flicked off the light, and everyone in the room began to shout at once.

'Hey, mate, what's the problem?'

'Marcus? What's going on? Is it the police?'

'Sssshhhh! *Sssssshhhh!*'

Felicity made her way over to the light switch and flicked it back on. She looked seriously at the two men. 'We're at the back of the house. The gate is locked. And the blinds are closed. Is there any need for the panic? Who's out there?'

'Jack!' Peter put a finger to his lips. 'He looked like he was coming here, so we hid behind the fence and legged it inside when he went back to check his front door was locked. Are you sure the side gate is locked?'

'I always keep it locked, except on bin day. The girls disappeared over to play with Emily once without me knowing, and I was frantic. Anyway, what's so wrong with Jack coming over? He might not want to be alone, knowing another one of those hideous episodes is coming up.'

'And you want him in here listening to it, do you?' Marcus raised his eyebrows. 'While one of us is dissected, while all the reasons we had to kill his wife are laid out in stereo?'

Felicity's face coloured. 'I suppose not. I guess I just don't like to think about him sitting there, night after night, all alone. And now, with all this going on, I just feel . . .'

'Guilty?' Alex offered, with a grin. 'Maybe it's your episode tonight, Flick.'

Felicity saw Miranda's face slacken. She'd obviously never heard her husband call Felicity by her childhood nickname before, and Felicity wanted to thump him. He only did these things to wind Miranda up, and she'd walked right into it at one of their community barbecues at the beginning of the summer. They'd all carried their meat over to Miranda's front garden, where Alex had held court at the barbecue while Miranda pulled out a steady supply of couscous and potato salad. Felicity had made the mistake of telling Alex that her sister didn't call her Fliss, like her new Severn Oaks friends – mostly because her name was Melissa and they hadn't wanted to be Liss and Fliss. Instead, they'd ended up as Swish and Flick, which neither of them had liked any better.

Felicity glowered at him now.

'We're about to find out . . .' Karla held up her phone. 'It's gone up.'

31

Good evening, listeners, you're listening to The Truth About Erica, *and I'm your host, Andy Noon. Regular listeners will know that each week we delve a little further into the unexplained and so-called 'accidental' death of Severn Oaks resident Erica Spencer. Tonight, on week three of* The Truth About Erica, *we hear about the exact order of the events of that night.*

The date is October the 28th, 2017. Erica Spencer and her husband, Jack, have waved goodbye to their two children, Max and Emily, and Jack pours them a glass of wine each as they take their time showering and dressing for their favourite night of the year – the Kaplans' annual Halloween party. As Erica slips on black ballet pumps, adjusts her long black wig and rings her eyes with thick black eyeliner, a stark contrast to the deathly pale of her face, Jack pulls the white stocking over his head.

'I don't know how I'll drink anything in this,' he complains.

His wife smiles and smooths down the front of her short white nightdress. 'You usually manage.'

He doesn't notice that she hasn't touched her wine.

The Spencers arrived at the party at around seven thirty

p.m. Karla remembers in her statement to police that they were one of the first couples to arrive.

'They were always on time,' she told police. 'And Erica would always show up with a hostess gift. This year she brought a dozen red roses, mixed with a dozen satin black ones – for Halloween. She was so thoughtful like that.'

The party was open house – you see the Spencers and the Kaplans live within the walls of Severn Oaks, one of the most exclusive gated communities in Cheshire. They had no concern that anyone unsavoury might wander in – in fact, it was the Kaplans' own son Brandon who – at sixteen – posed the biggest threat to the party. The last thing Marcus Kaplan, author of the YOU self-help empire and his wife Karla, Cheshire's answer to Martha Stewart, wanted was for their teenage son's friends to crash their party and cause a scene.

They had no need to worry. Brandon Kaplan told police that during the party he was 'as far away as possible', which transpired was a friend's house in Warrington.

By eight thirty the Kaplan residence was full of party guests in their Halloween finery. Karla Kaplan wore a skin-tight black leotard over black fishnet tights, with long black gloves and a circus master's top hat and long-tailed jacket. Her husband wore a similar circus master outfit: a black tuxedo jacket with a red satin trim, and top hat. His face was painted white, with black make-up around his eyes and stitches drawn from his mouth. There was a mummy, the Bride of Frankenstein and a female Freddy Krueger. Miranda Davenport from number five arrived alone, wearing a witch's costume and promising that her husband, Alex, would be there soon. Peter King and his wife came as Beetlejuice and the Grim Reaper. Everyone had made a real effort for one of the nights of the year they enjoyed the most. Felicity Goldman walked in with Alex Davenport, the last couple to arrive, at eight thirty-five. Even after twin daughters she **claims** are the result of a one-night stand, Felicity has an enviable figure and was showing it off dressed as Harley Quinn. Alex appeared to have come without a costume – the only person other than Severn Oaks resident Larry Gorman not to have come in fancy dress.

The night proceeded smoothly, the guests taking full advantage of the free alcohol – over five hundred pounds' worth that the Kaplans had provided. After the fact, no one would recall what Erica Spencer was drinking, although she had brought two bottles of wine along with her and it was assumed she was drinking as readily as everyone else. Her husband would later find a receipt for those two bottles, along with the Jack Daniel's she had purchased for him – although he never appeared to realise from the receipt that the wine Erica had taken to the party was non-alcoholic. The post-mortem revealed her blood alcohol level to be 0.24, three times over the driving limit in the UK.

The only potential bump in the road for the Kaplans' perfect party came at just after nine p.m., when Miranda Davenport demanded to know why her husband had turned up late, sans Friday The 13th costume and at the exact same time as Severn Oaks' most eligible bachelorette. As he tried to calm down his furious wife, Alex made the mistake of opening his jacket to show her that he was wearing a costume and, with a look that has been described as 'ridiculously pleased with himself', revealed a suicide bomb vest. Witnesses say that Miranda hit the roof and insisted that Alex throw the tasteless costume choice away, go home and retrieve the outfit she spent a bloody fortune on and stay the fuck away from Felicity Goldman.

As far as parties went, this one was fairly tame. Severn Oaks, you see, is a community comprised of the most prestigious 'regular folk' Cheshire has to offer. These aren't footballers or Real Housewives (although Karla Kaplan tells everyone she has *turned down the show twice). These people are lawyers, business moguls, interior designers to the stars. They occupy the rungs of the corporate ladder people aspired to before reality TV and Instagram Influencing existed. And Severn Oaks was a safe space, concealed behind its wrought-iron gates. Any danger was firmly on the other side. At least, that's what Erica thought.*

The usual suspects tailed off early. Simon and Gilly made their excuses around 10:30, according to Simon.

'Three hours drinking is more than enough for Gilly. Any more than that and she's apt to throw up on the AGA and fall asleep the moment her head hits the pillow. And no bloke wants that when they spent all night trying to get their wife drunk enough to forget it's not a birthday or Christmas, do they?'

Larry Gorman – minus costume – left at eleven, and distinctly remembers a highly inebriated Ben carrying his wife, Martha, down the road towards the house, on his back.

'He was stumbling around and shouting, "It's Michelle. Get it? MY SHELL." I think Martha is literally the only person in the world who thinks Ben is hilarious. Just as well they married each other.'

When questioned about whether he saw Erica before leaving the party, Larry is suddenly quite cagey.

'It's like I told the police, we'd all been drinking quite a bit and time gets away from you. I'd go to say goodbye to someone and get caught up in conversation for another ten minutes. So yes, I saw her at one point, before I left, but I can't be sure what time. She was talking to someone who I thought was Karla – she had the top hat and jacket on, and blonde hair – but I could only see Erica's face. She had this strange look, a bit mean, I thought. Like a spiteful smile a child would give you before they crashed your favourite monster truck into a wall. And Karla was waving her arm – her right arm, I think – but neither of them was raising her voice. Then, as I left, I ran into Karla in the kitchen and went to thank her for having me. She was wearing a big jumper – I suppose it had dropped too cold for that skimpy leotard – and her hat was gone. So it couldn't have been her talking to Erica, could it?'

This theme of 'costume swapping' will come back to us in our quest to find out what really happened to Erica at this elite gathering, but for now, let's not forget that we are at a Halloween party. All Hallows Eve, a night when evil spirits come out to play. And it was after the peripheral guests had left the group that the real party began. Unsurprisingly, the Severn Oaks Six are cagey about what happened after the others left them. The following is taken from Peter King's statement to the police.

'We just stood around, chatting. Once people started to leave and there were fewer of us, we moved into the formal living room, but people were still in and out. I didn't even notice Erica leave.'

And from Alex Davenport.

'I don't remember much after eleven-ish. Someone suggested drinking games in the living room, and Karla lost her shit because Marcus knocked over a green shot and the carpet is cream, or beige, or whatever. That's it, I think. Nothing else really happened.'

So we've already moved from 'standing around chatting' to drinking games. Is this how Erica ended up with a blood alcohol level three times the legal driving limit? But why would she partake in shot games when she had specifically taken non-alcoholic wine to the party? And how did she end up climbing into the tree house that would later be the death of her?

The real question for this week then, listeners, is what

happened at that party after the other guests left? And why are the Severn Oaks Six so reluctant to talk about those lost hours? Stay tuned – you might find out.

Next week, part two of The Party – Motive.

32

No one had spoken throughout the entire episode. As the final bars of the theme music played, Felicity opened her eyes and looked around the kitchen. Everyone looked frozen in place, like one of those films where the superhero can stop time. Miranda over on the sofa had her head in her hands. Karla, opposite Felicity at the breakfast bar, held her glass of wine suspended in mid-air, almost as if she'd forgotten some time ago that she had wanted to take a sip. Marcus stood behind her, a hand on her side, underneath her arm – a more intimate gesture than on her shoulder, which made it look as though he was holding her up. Peter had spent the entire episode at the kitchen end of the kitchen diner. Leaning against the worktop, staring at the cream-tiled back-splash. Predictably, Alex was the first to speak.

'Well, I didn't think that was too bad. Although poor Ben will be pissed off at Larry for saying that Martha is the only person who finds him funny. It's true, though. What did you think?'

Miranda let out a long-drawn-out groan, almost as if she was waking up from a particularly awful nightmare. 'Were you even listening to the same thing as the rest of us? All that stuff about "after the other guests left" and us being "cagey about what happened". It sounds like we all conspired to kill bloody Erica! And what was all that about her blood alcohol level? And how the fuck did they get hold of *your police statement*?'

It was as though Miranda saying the word 'fuck' had jolted the rest of the room back to life, like a cuss word from Severn Oaks' most restrained resident could break any spell. Everyone began to talk at once.

'Who was talking to Erica in the garden when Larry left?'

'Did you see her drinking? I could have sworn she was drinking.'

'I didn't notice her not drinking, if you know what I mean. I'd have noticed if she was on soft drinks.'

'Why is he doing this? Who is the little fucker?'

Felicity spoke, quietly at first, and then when she realised no one could hear her over the sound of their own, more important ramblings she raised her voice. 'Jack,' she said, as loudly and forcefully as her voice could manage after what felt like a punch-to-the-stomach realisation. 'It has to be Jack.'

'What makes you say that?'

Everyone had stopped talking now, and they were all staring at her. Felicity looked up at each and every one of them and realised they were all hiding something. It wasn't just her. They were all petrified that something about that night, or something Erica knew about them, would be the next words out of Andy Noon's mouth. *How could we all be so stupid as to think we'd be able to live in this privileged existence for ever?*

'At the start. He started by talking about Erica getting ready – and something she'd said to Jack. That wouldn't have been in police statements, would it? He wouldn't have given a statement about what they said and did before the party even started. And Jack and Erica are the only ones who know what they said to each other before the party, and Erica is very definitely dead. We all saw her, we buried her, for God's sake. The only one left then is Jack.'

'She's right.' Peter's voice sounded hard to Felicity's ears. She hadn't heard him sound that way before. 'And he's the only one not to be called a suspect. Isn't the husband always a suspect? Why not this time? Because it's him.'

'The bastard!' Marcus's face was an angry, blotchy red. 'I'll kill him.'

33

Marcus thumped on the door of the house Jack Spencer had once shared with his wife. The group had spilled out onto the street after Marcus had made his threat, half wanting to stop the scene that was about to unfold and half wanting to know what Jack was going to say for himself when confronted with the realisation Felicity had come to moments earlier. Felicity herself stood on her driveway, torn between wanting to witness the confrontation and not wanting to leave the twins in the house on their own. Karla had stormed after her husband, trying unsuccessfully to reason with him, begging him not to do anything stupid. Miranda just looked lost, whereas her husband was enjoying the show immensely. Peter stayed by Felicity's side, his face ashen.

'Marcus, stop it, please! What are you hoping to—'

The door flew open and Jack appeared from behind it. He looked broken. Felicity, abandoning the idea of staying close to her girls, stalked towards where Miranda and Alex were watching at the end of Jack's driveway, with Peter following close behind. He laid a hand on her arm protectively.

'What do you want, Marcus?' Jack kept his voice quiet. 'My children are asleep upstairs.'

'Don't you dare hide behind those poor kids.' Marcus sounded as though he was straining not to shout. 'Come out here and face us, you fucking coward.'

Jack stared at Marcus and in that moment Karla thought he might be the first one to throw a punch. *Look at him*, she silently pleaded to her husband. *Does he look like he's behind all this?*

He shook his head and muttered something, then stepped forward and closed the door behind him. He followed Marcus to the end of the driveway, Karla trailing behind them helplessly.

'What is all this then?' he asked, looking at the group. None of them but Marcus could meet his eye. 'What are you all doing here?'

'We listened to your podcast,' Marcus hissed, poking a finger at Jack. 'And we want to know what the fuck you're playing at, making out that one of us killed Erica.'

At the sound of his wife's name Jack flinched, and Karla felt yet another stab of sympathy for the man in front of them. He'd lost his wife and his baby, maybe even his mind. Who were they to judge him, even if he was behind the accusations? Especially herself and Marcus. Perhaps that's why her husband was having such an extreme reaction to the whole thing – he knew that he had something to feel guilty about.

'Did you, Marcus? Did you kill my wife? Her unborn baby?'

Marcus stepped back as though he had been punched. 'How fucking dare you!' He lunged forward, fists clenched, and Karla grabbed his arm.

'Marcus, no!'

'Go on!' Jack shouted. 'Hit me, if that's what you want to do! It won't change a thing. And for your information it's not my fucking podcast.'

147

Felicity stepped forward. 'We heard it, Jack. Only you could know what Erica said to you while you were getting ready – what you said to her about not being able to drink through the costume you were wearing.'

As she said the words out loud Jack's voice sounded in Karla's head – not from right there and then, but from another night, one much like this. They were all together but it was a happy occasion. A party. A Halloween party.

'I told Erica earlier that I wouldn't be able to drink through this stupid thing,' followed by a laugh, deep and throaty, one that she hadn't heard in nearly a year. 'Cheeky cow said I'd find a way – that I usually manage.'

'It could have been any of us,' she whispered, but no one was listening.

'And that means I'm the one, am I? Andy Noon? I've been here all night, listening to the fucking thing, on my own – not like you lot, I see. Nice to be invited to the party – although I think I'll be steering clear of parties with you lot in future. How could it be me, if I'm here?'

He doesn't even know how they work, Karla thought. She went to speak again but Felicity beat her to it.

'It's not live.' Felicity's voice was small, as though she too was doubting that Jack could be behind this. 'It's prerecorded and uploaded. You could have . . . I mean, *someone*, could have done it at any time.'

'Someone?' Karla flinched as her husband rounded on her best friend. 'Oh, so now it's someone? It was you who said he must have done it.'

'I said . . . I mean, Jack, you are the only one who knows what you said to Erica before the party, in private.' But now she didn't look as sure of herself. Her blue eyes were shining and Karla noticed that Peter's hand was gripping her arm.

A thought shot through her mind. *Are they . . . ?* No, Felicity would have told her, and now wasn't the time for jumping to any more conclusions. Marcus was doing so much of that, he could have been on a trampoline.

'He wasn't.' Karla found her voice at last, aware of her husband's gaze turning towards her. 'The only one, I mean. He said it – at the party. He said that he'd told Erica he wouldn't be able to drink through the mask and she'd said he'd manage. It was early on, before we'd all drunk much. Anyone could have known that.'

Marcus's eyes widened and she felt a sinking awfulness in her chest. She'd let her husband make an absolute fool of himself.

'And you're only just mentioning this now?' His words weren't the angry tirade he'd unleashed on Jack. He never spoke to her like that. He never really got angry at her at all. It was like she was such a part of him that to yell at her would have been akin to yelling at himself, they just didn't operate that way.

'I'm sorry, Marcus.' Tears filled her eyes. 'I literally just remembered. And you took off so fast . . .'

Marcus shook his head and sighed. Raising his eyes, he met Jack's.

'I'm sorry, mate. I should never have . . . we're all just— But then you're going through worse, much worse. I just can't imagine . . .' He trailed off and hung his head.

Jack sniffed. He still looked furious but also as if he just didn't have it in him to argue any more. Marcus and Jack, and all the men on the street really, had always been such good friends – better than the women, in a way. The women enjoyed closer proximity, they saw each other every day at the school gates and stopped in the street for a chat. Mary-Beth and Erica had been as close as Felicity and Karla. But apart from that, the women all secretly barely tolerated each other. The men, however, didn't see one another nearly as much, but when they did, they seemed to genuinely like one another; there was none of this underhanded competition and sniping with them. Would any of their relationships survive this?

'Forget it. It's a crazy situation. I shouldn't have asked you that, about . . .' His voice cracked. 'About Erica. It's just – who the hell is this guy? How does he know so much? And what does he want? I'd never thought for a second that Erica's death was anything more than a stupid accident. Now I'm asking my neighbours if they fucking killed my wife like some paranoid conspiracy theorist. It's just fucked up, is all.'

Marcus did something then that Karla had never seen him do to another man, apart from his son. He stepped forward and pulled Jack into a hug. A manly one, but still a hug.

'We're really sorry, Jack,' Felicity spoke up, 'that we accused you, and that we didn't invite you. We were just . . .'

We were just worried about what you might hear, Karla thought as her friend's sentence broke off. *We were worried you'd find out what really happened to Erica.*

34

'Come on, Charity, I've asked you to get in the car, so will you just put that down and . . . no, for goodness' sake, I don't know where the bloody unicorn is!'

Six-year-old Charity's face crumpled and Miranda sucked in a breath. Holy shit, the last thing she needed this morning was an epic breakdown over a horse with a stick on its forehead. 'I tell you what,' she spoke quickly and quietly, as though there was bound to be someone listening to this display of awful parenting, 'if you get in the car and strap in without a fuss I will buy you two unicorns as soon as you get home from school.'

Charity raised a blonde eyebrow and Miranda was struck by the sudden realisation that she was raising the spawn of Satan. She was just like her fucking father.

'Three unicorns,' she stated. 'And a Slush Puppie.'

Miranda let out a breath. 'Okay, fine.' At this point her daughter could have asked for a pony and a holiday home in the Bahamas and she'd probably have acquiesced. Anything to get her in the car.

It was the first day back at school, the night after the third awful podcast and that horrific showdown with Jack Spencer that her bloody husband had loved every second of. He'd been practically gleeful when they'd finally got back into the house, grinning as though he'd just come out of a Bruce Willis movie – Alex loved Bruce Willis.

'Best entertainment I've had in a while, and I didn't have to remortgage the house to get it. No hotdogs, though.' He frowned, looking genuinely disappointed that there hadn't been hotdogs at the highly embarrassing street brawl Marcus Kaplan had almost had with a grieving widower. God only knew what the rest of the street thought of them. Perhaps they'd be kicked out of Severn Oaks, the Severn Oaks Six shunned by the community and sent to live Beyond The Gates. It would serve her right, after what she'd done.

It had taken every ounce of strength she'd had to sit there and listen to that podcast with the others, as that frightful man talked about what had happened after the other guests left, as if perhaps they were a bunch of cultists just waiting for the 'normal' couples to leave before they sacrificed one of their members. It was an accident, everyone knew Erica had been drunk – they all saw her, taunting poor Felicity and Peter, sniping at Karla. And she was all over Marcus, not that Jack had seemed bothered. Not that Miranda herself could remember too much at all after that point – she'd drunk a little more than intended, especially after Marcus brought out those disgusting purple shot things.

She swung into her usual space outside the school and killed the engine. Twisting herself around to help Charity unclip, there was a bang on her side window. The round, pink face of Jean Whittleby, Severndale Primary's parking enforcer, gate unlocker and fount of all knowledge, was pressed up against Miranda's driver's side window. Miranda forced herself into school mode, something she'd been prac- tising for years. She plastered on a huge smile and flicked the engine back on to open the window. 'Jean! Morning!

We've missed your smiling face every morning, haven't we, Charity?' Without waiting for her daughter to say that actually she'd never seen Jean smile, she launched into a second charm offensive. 'Did you have a nice summer? At least we had some decent weather this year, although it always goes too fast, doesn't it? Charity dear, are you ready?'

Switching to an apologetic smile, Miranda motioned towards the back seat. 'Better get her in then – don't want to be late on her first day in a new class, do we, sweetheart?'

'You can't park there.'

The words were so unexpected that for a second Miranda didn't even register what the other woman meant. Was she wonky? Did she need to straighten up?

'Excuse me?' Never let the smile falter. You can say what you like to people if you smile, she'd found over the years. Even if you felt like you would rather poke someone in the eye with a Pritt Stick, you could win them over with a smile and some eye contact.

'It's for taxis and the school bus . . .' Jean faltered. 'You need to park somewhere else, Mrs Davenport.'

So it was Mrs Davenport now? Jean had always called her Miranda before, and although she knew she technically shouldn't park in this spot, the school bus had already dropped off and she had always parked there.

'It's never been a problem before. Everywhere else is full now, we'll be late.'

Jean's expression faltered for a split second, then her face hardened again. 'I'm sorry, but it was brought up at a meeting. The head's orders. You'll have to move.'

A meeting? But Miranda was a parent governor – they didn't have meetings without her! She took one last look at Jean's determined expression and sighed. The last thing she needed today was an argument outside the school gates. 'Fine,' she said, her face burning as she pressed the button to close the window. With a satisfying whirr it zoomed up, closing Jean out before she could launch into any kind of Jobsworth speech. Miranda's face burned as she pulled out of the space, noticing the passing mums watching with interest as she drove away.

'Where are we going, Mummy?' Charity asked. 'Don't we have to go to school today?'

It crossed Miranda's mind to say no, there was no school today, to drive straight back to the safety of Severn Oaks and slam a few doors. Fury built up inside her. It was what the old Miranda would do. That or drive straight onto the school playground and fuck the lot of them. But she didn't have the energy to fight today – not after last night – and besides, she couldn't let Charity blot her attendance record on the first day because of her mother's stubbornness. Pick your battles was another rule she'd learnt about keeping up appearances. She wouldn't let that bitch Jean know that she had ruffled her. She'd just report her for smoking in the toilets – poor Jean thought she was the only one who knew things.

'We just have to park down the road today, darling, they need that spot today. It's just a little walk.'

But as predicted, the rest of the road had filled up almost completely and Miranda found herself having to park almost two streets away. By the time she'd got Charity, complaining about having to actually walk to school, out of the car, along with her bags, PE kit and Forest School attire, it was three minutes to nine.

'Come on, Charity, hurry up, darling! I know, but it's not that far and we don't want to be late on the first day!' Miranda was *never* late. She would usually pull up right outside the school and stride Charity through the door in under two minutes flat. When she got back to the school Jean didn't even look in her direction. *Enjoy your job while it lasts, Smokey Joe.*

She heard the bell ring from the entrance to the school gates. Shit! Now she would have to go through reception, the walk of shame she'd seen so many other parents do as she looked on, judging them for not being more prepared, or not having the presence of mind to park closer to the school.

'Morning, Mrs Davenport.' Gina on reception had obviously been informed of the change in title. She couldn't remember the last time she'd been addressed at the school by her full name. She had become as much a part of the school in the last year as Gina, or bloody Jean. 'Running a little late today?'

Miranda bit back the angry tirade threatening to spew from her lips and forced a smile. Gina had better be careful, or she'd find her violation of the 'no phones in school' rule making its way to the head. 'Just a few teething issues, getting used to the new regime,' she said, hoping that was enough to make the point that her daughter's tardiness was through no fault of her own. Charity seemed oblivious at least, and ran off happily towards her new classroom. Her teacher held up a hand and gave a weak smile as the little girl went to join her classmates.

There was one positive about Charity being late, Miranda supposed. There would be no bumping into the other mums at the back gat—

Miranda's heart sank as she left via the reception only to see three of the mums from Charity's class huddled together chatting.

Just breeze past, Miranda told herself. *Just keep walking, head up, smile and . . .*

'Morning!' she beamed, certain that she was going to make it right past without bursting into tears. See? She had it all under control.

'Miranda!' In unison the three women split apart and

spread themselves across the path, almost blocking her route entirely. If she hadn't felt such a sinking feeling of despair, she would have laughed at how perfectly choreographed it all looked. Perhaps they should try out for the school talent show – or the school 'no talent' show, as she privately referred to it.

'How are you doing?' Cynthia Elcock's voice was dripping with concern, her head tilted to one side the way people do when you have some sort of incurable disease.

'I'm fine, thank you.' Miranda took a step forward but couldn't get any further without shoving linebackers Pria Hamilton or Stephanie Green off the pavement. 'In a bit of a rush, actually.'

'Yes, I was just saying it's a surprise to see you run in so late. Where's your car?'

'It's down the road – Charity wanted to walk today, bless her. She's spent all summer going on about fitness – must be their age.' Miranda was almost certain Pria had been going through the gates when Jean had banished her from her usual spot, but if she'd seen the encounter she was saving the story for when Miranda was safely back in the car.

'Oh, well done, Charity.' Yep, they definitely already knew. 'Listen, we were wondering if there was any news on Mary-Beth? We saw their nan dropping the kids off earlier and didn't want to ask . . .'

'I don't know anything,' Miranda said flatly.

'Oh.' Cynthia looked distinctly put out but recovered quickly. 'And how are you coping with all these silly rumours about Erica's death? We wanted you to know that, of course, none of *us* believe you had anything to do with it.'

The implication clearly being that some people did. Miranda swallowed down her fury. *They are just looking for a reaction. The next bit of gossip. It's nothing personal.*

'I should think so, you all being *far too intelligent* to listen to someone's idea of an extremely sick joke.' Miranda watched Stephanie's face falter. Had Cynthia not been there, she'd have won the room with that remark and been able to walk off safe in the knowledge that they felt appropriately chastened. But Cynthia was like a pit bull – simple psychological warfare would get her nowhere with this one. Her face had taken on this smug glow, as if she was thoroughly enjoying Miranda's discomfort.

'Joke, yes. It's just that it's not very funny, is it? And what this person knows . . . well, it seems like they've certainly done their research.'

'Yes, well, you did your research on Brexit when you shared all those pictures on Facebook of Boris's bus – and look where that got you. A bus full of horse shit.'

Stephanie and Pria recoiled, looking both horrified at the turn the conversation was taking and fascinated all at once. Cynthia gave a smile and her eyes flashed, the way a python's might before it struck you dead.

'I just can't imagine being accused of *murder*.' She elongated the word as far as it could be stretched, complete with breathy Hollywood-style voice.

Miranda resisted the urge to insult the limits of Cynthia's imagination.

'It's really not as awful as you think,' Miranda replied with a smile. 'It makes it much easier to get a seat in the coffee shop.'

'But not a parking space.'

Miranda gave a tinkly laugh. 'This was so much fun, Cynthia, but I really have to get going. I left the arsenic brewing on the stove.' She moved past Pria, who sidestepped quickly, clearly realising she was out of her depth here.

'Just one more thing?'

Miranda turned to see Cynthia practically glowing.

'Is it true what people are saying about the baby? That it

wasn't Jack's? That the father was someone *very close* to Erica?' She didn't wait for an answer. 'Wouldn't it be just horrific to find out your husband had fathered a baby by one of your friends? I'd just want to die. Or kill them, maybe.' And with a smirk she pushed past Miranda, leaving her feeling like she'd been punched in the stomach.

35

'Okay, thanks for being here,' Detective Sergeant Harvey's voice brought everyone to attention and dimmed the hum of noise in the room. Three faces looked up at him – not a large number for a search team but as many as the budget for Mary-Beth King's disappearance could afford. On the board to his left the information was sparse; there had been no leads since Mary-Beth's car had been found at the side of the River Dee nearly two weeks earlier. Until today.

'I've called you here today because, as you've probably heard, there has been a tip come in via the hotline regarding Mrs King's movements on the 20th of August – the day she disappeared. The call came from a taxi driver who saw Mrs King's picture on the TV and says he believes he had her in his taxi at approximately seven p.m. on the evening of her disappearance.'

'Why's it taken him so long to come forward?' DC Allan asked.

'He was a bit cagey about that, but the extremely astute hotline operative managed to ascertain that his licence had expired and he waited until he had renewed it to call us – a fact that we are going to overlook if he remains helpful. Anyone free to go and speak to him today?'

'I'll go.' DC Allan held up a hand again. *Quelle surprise.* Had he really been that keen once? He remembered his hand shooting up whenever DCI Barrow asked if someone would be willing. That was what had led him to Severn Oaks the first time. The first time he suspected there was a murderer within the gates.

'Good, thanks. Before we wrap up, I assume everyone has been listening to our very own murder mystery podcast?'

Three heads nodded. Of course they had – it seemed like everyone in Cheshire, and probably beyond, was talking about *The Truth About Erica*. Even his mum had called him last night when it had finished to ask which of the Severn Oaks Six killed that poor woman. The Severn Oaks Six, for God's sake.

'Right, well, so have the country's finest parasites, it seems.' His blood pressure rose just thinking about the journalists sitting next to their smartphones, salivating over every salacious detail. It helped – or didn't, as the case was – that the drama was taking place in Severn Oaks. It added to the mystery – murder behind locked gates, and all that – and it was always more tantalising when the people involved were well off. And for Marcus and Karla Kaplan to be involved as well – it was a tabloid jackpot. *Just like Barrow suspected a year ago.* 'So I think it's a good time to reiterate that no one speaks to the journalists – you can refer them straight to me so I can ignore their calls personally.'

'Are we reopening the case, sir? Erica Spencer?'

He'd been waiting for the question and he might have known it would come from Allan. This man just— Did. Not. Give. Up. Ever since the podcast started, Harvey had been thinking of nothing but the night he had first visited Severn Oaks. They might not have recognised him straight away but he could remember each one of their faces: Karla Kaplan and Felicity Goldman looking tear-stained, with expensive mascara smudged across their faces; Miranda Davenport staring straight ahead the whole time as if she was in severe shock. The men's voices overly confident to mask how nervous they were. DCI Barrow's voice as he made it clear that no one wanted a scandal involving the Kaplans.

Harvey tried not to sigh loudly. 'No, we are not. Mrs Spencer's death was ruled an accident and so far we've not heard one shred of real evidence that suggests otherwise. To reopen the case based on some true-crime junkie trying to be the next Sarah Koenig – don't look so surprised, Allan, I am well up with the popular culture, innit? – would cast doubt on our original investigation, which was handled impeccably by yours truly. So while I'm not saying that Mrs King's disappearance doesn't have anything to do with the podcast, I am saying that Erica Spencer's death was an accident and I don't want anyone on this team so much as thinking out loud that we might have made a mistake. Those bastard journalists can smell police incompetence all the way from Fleet Street. Go on, meeting's over.'

36

'Wouldn't it be just horrific to find out your husband had fathered a baby by one of your friends? I'd just want to die. Or kill them, maybe.'

The words had swirled around in her mind, smashing into one another until they failed to make sense any more. I'd want to die. Kill them. Fathered a baby. Kill the baby. Kill your friends. Horrific. Horrific. Horrific. *I'd want to kill them.*

Had she wanted to kill Erica? She didn't think so, it had never crossed her mind to ever hurt anyone. Okay, so she'd done some things in her life that other people would consider bad, but only things that those same 'other people' would do in a heartbeat if they knew there was no chance they would ever get caught. Like that time she'd clutched her car keys between her fingers and dragged them down the side of that dreadful man's car – the one who had called her a stupid bitch when she'd pointed out that he was parked in a parent and child space without a child in sight. The sound of metal against metal as the key gouged a deep silver crevice into the black paintwork had been more satisfying than any orgasm she'd ever had. And there was the phone call she'd made to the DVLA when a van driver had slammed his fist on the horn because she'd taken three seconds too long to turn into her street. She'd written his number plate down from her dash cam and checked his details online. Tut, tut, his MOT was overdue by six days.

But none of those things had physically hurt anyone. They were small, petty acts of revenge – no one had died.

Except, this time, someone had.

She twisted the hem of her shirt around and around in her fingers, wrapping the thin material about her index finger until the tip went pink. Every time the door swung open, clanging against the wall and making such a noise she thought it was coming off its hinges, Miranda's head snapped up. The final time she looked up, the pretty PC with the blonde hair was walking through.

'Mrs Davenport, I'm told you have some information regarding the death of Erica Spencer.'

'Yes, I, erm . . .' Suddenly this didn't feel like such a good idea. In fact, it felt like a terrible one.

The woman looked at her and narrowed her eyes. 'Don't say anything here,' she instructed. 'Come with me.'

She turned so sharply that Miranda had to leap to her feet to follow her. Where were they going?

You're going to be interviewed, arrested probably. Take a good look around, Miranda. This might be the last thing you see as a free woman. She wished with a sudden ferocity that she had said a proper goodbye to her children. That she had kissed them for so long that they would remember the touch of her lips for ten to fifteen years. She'd barely spoken to Alex on the way out of the door, afraid that she would blurt out that she wasn't going to the shop, that she was turning herself in. Would he have tried to stop her? Would he have cried, knowing what she was doing for him? How different would all this have been if she had just been honest?

The PC had picked up speed now, apparently oblivious to the fact that Miranda had no clue where they were going. She hurried after her, down a long thin corridor, like the one in that film the kids used to love, *Willy Wonka & the Chocolate Factory*, a corridor that got thinner and thinner until it pressed in on you from all sides and you couldn't breathe.

Miranda couldn't breathe.

37

The September sunshine shone brightly through the trees, making Felicity squint every time Amalie came back down to earth. Felicity gave her daughter a hard push, and she sailed up into the sky again. 'Higher, Mummy!' Amalie squealed with delight. 'Higher!'

'How has this week been?' she asked Karla as she gave Amalie another shove towards the sky.

Karla sighed. 'Zach's been really quiet this week.' She watched Mollie digging with her hands in the dirt underneath the tree at the bottom of the garden. 'I've asked him if there is anything wrong, but he won't talk to me. I get the feeling it must be something to do with the podcast. I bet all the kids in his class are talking about it and his murderous parents.'

Felicity sighed. 'I feel so lucky that the girls are too young to know anything is going on,' she said. 'Although, unfortunately, that isn't the same for the mothers. Did you hear about what happened to Miranda? I heard one of the other mothers say that she'd been forced to park on the street with the rest of the commoners. She was practically gleeful about it.'

Karla nodded. 'I heard too. It's like everyone's just been waiting for something like this to happen. I also thought we were part of the community there, even though we lived in here. That's what I liked about this place. We just always felt like part of the family. Now it seems like everyone I thought was my friend was just waiting for us to be torn down in one way or another.'

'It's human nature, I'm afraid. I've been lucky to miss most of it because the girls go to breakfast club so early, but at pickup I still get the sense that every time I walk over to a group of people, they've been talking about it.'

'They need to find something else to talk about,' Karla snarled. 'But to tell you the truth, if it weren't happening to us, we'd be talking about it too.'

Felicity shrugged in agreement. 'You're right, I know you're right. It just seems so unfair. No one is willing to ask us outright what they want to know. It's like we have no right of reply. We just have to be accused of these awful things, and we can't put our side across, for fear of looking even guiltier.'

'Actually,' Karla started, concentrating all of her attention on the nail she was chewing off, 'in the spirit of just asking, there was something I wanted to ask you. Something about the last podcast . . .'

'It's about the girls' father, isn't it?' Felicity looked as though she'd been waiting to have this conversation, ready for the moment someone asked. 'I wondered if anyone had noticed that, should have known it would be you. You want to know if I know who he is.'

'You always just said that he was a one-night stand,' Karla said, looking uncomfortable. 'But the podcast made it sound like you know. I know that he's just clutching at straws. If you tell me you don't know who their father is, I'll believe you.'

Felicity sighed. 'I wasn't exactly truthful about not knowing who he is.' She sniffed and pulled her cardigan closer around her chest. The sun was shining but the day was still cold, or maybe she was just cold. Maybe this whole subject gave her chills. 'I know his name. In fact, I know everything about him. It wasn't a one-night stand, Karla, it was an affair. He's married.'

Karla nodded as if she'd been expecting as much. 'Why didn't you just tell me?'

'It was a mistake, a huge mistake. The worst kind. The kind that could ruin everything for a person. I just wanted the girls to grow up without the stigma of their father being some kind of liar, and cheat, and awful person.'

'Do you want to tell me about it?'

Felicity said nothing.

'You don't have to,' Karla said quickly. 'You don't have to tell me anything if you don't want to, I mean, I just thought you might want to talk about it.'

'I don't understand how this person could know.' Felicity looked at her girls; Amalie was still laughing in delight and demanding to be pushed higher and higher, and Mollie seemed to be looking for Australia. They weren't listening, and even if they were listening they probably wouldn't understand, adult relationships were beyond their comprehension at their age. They were too young, too innocent to know that grown-ups could make mistakes.

'I can't,' She said, her voice full of regret. She wanted nothing more than to tell someone everything about it, about that whole awful period of her life where she had made so many mistakes. But it wouldn't just be her life she was ruining. It wasn't just her secret to keep. 'He was married, and it was a mistake, that's all I can say. I came here to start again, to give him another chance.'

'Another chance at what?' Karla asked.

'Another chance at the life he should have had. Another chance at being a father without the stigma of what we'd done.'

'And how is that working out for you?' Karla asked, raising an eyebrow.

'It's not, is it?' Felicity replied. 'It just feels like sometimes you can't escape your past mistakes, no matter how hard you try. You're just doomed to repeat them, over and over again, until someone finds out. Until someone puts you on trial.'

'You're not on trial, Felicity,' Karla said. 'You made a mistake, you haven't done anything a million other people haven't done before you.'

'If only that were true,' Felicity replied. 'If only—'

A shout from the front driveway cut her off mid-sentence.

'Who's that?' Karla crossed the garden to the back gate. 'Alex?'

'Hi, sorry to interrupt.' Alex appeared in the opening, looking dishevelled and slightly frantic. 'Have you seen Miranda? She went out this morning, and she's not answering her phone.'

'No, sorry.' Karla glanced at Felicity, who had stopped pushing Amalie and shook her head in agreement. 'Where was she going?'

'To the shops, she said. But that was six hours ago. I've called her at least ten times. Do you think I should call the police?'

Karla and Felicity exchanged worried looks, both clearly thinking of Mary-Beth.

And then there were four, Felicity thought grimly. 'Yes,' she said out loud. 'I think you should.'

38

'So if you could just tell us what time it was that you picked up the woman you now believe to be Mrs King?'

The man nodded with more enthusiasm than was strictly necessary – it wasn't as if he'd actually found the woman. 'Yes, yes, I've got it all written down here . . .' He fumbled in the back pocket of the too-tight jeans that sat uncomfortably underneath a beer belly massively out of proportion to his short, stocky frame. Pulling out a piece of paper folded so many times it should resemble a swan, he smoothed it out on the table in front of him, obscuring the flecks of rolling tobacco clinging to whatever sticky substance coated the surface.

'Here, I wrote it down off the system. It was seven p.m. on Monday the 20th.'

'And where did you pick her up from?' DC Allan leaned forward and squinted at the paper, but it might as well have been written in Orcish with the state of the handwriting.

'Cherry Grove Primary School,' he announced proudly, as though this was some great achievement.

'On Chapel Lane?' Allan wondered if DS Harvey would

try to deny the significance of Cherry Grove Primary School's location to their case. Would he use this as proof Mary-Beth had run away? From what the taxi driver was saying, Mrs King wasn't coerced into getting in or out of the taxi in any way.

'That's right. She was waiting outside the school. I remember because usually I hate going anywhere near them – schools, that is – on account of the roads always being crammed with arsehole parking. Sorry . . .' He flushed, as if DC Allan hadn't heard the word 'arsehole' before. The detective was just thankful it wasn't being directed at him, for once.

'No problem. You were saying?'

Jeff looked confused for a second, then nodded. 'Oh, yeah. Well, it was okay at that time, wasn't it? So the road was empty, except for her waiting.'

'And you're sure it was this woman?' DC Allan pushed the picture towards Jeff again. He'd had the taxi driver make an identification the minute they had walked into the shoebox taxi-rank office, but he got the impression Jeff had barely looked at it. He'd already convinced himself he had picked up 'that woman they were all looking for'.

'Yeah, that's definitely her,' he said, glancing at the photo briefly.

'Right, thanks. And where did you drop this woman off?'

'Like I said when I called, that's how I was so certain it was her. She wanted dropping at Dalton campsite. That's where she's from, isn't it? That fancy estate isn't far from there, right? Severn Oaks?'

'You've been really helpful.' DC Allan stood up. 'One more question, did the office take a name with the booking?'

Jeff nodded so vigorously that Allan worried his head would pop off. 'She said her name was,' he peered at his origami notes, 'Spencer. Erica Spencer. That's not what they called her on the news, though, is it?'

'Let me get this straight – the woman this guy picked up from Chapel Lane said her name was Erica Spencer?' Harvey ran a hand over his face. 'Fucksake. The press are going to love this. It doesn't go any further for now – understood?'

'But—'

'Oh, for God's sake, Allan, I'm still your superior. Now am I understood?'

'Understood, sir.' DC Allan nodded, biting his lip.

Harvey sighed. He felt about ten years older than he had two weeks ago. 'And he positively ID'd Mary-Beth King?'

'Well, he did the first time, sir. The second time he positively ID'd Jennifer Lopez.'

Harvey scowled. 'So we don't even know that it was her.'

'Except the places he picked her up and dropped her off, they fit, don't they? Chapel Lane is just a thirty-minute walk from where Mrs King's car was found at the weir. And Dalton campsite is less than a half-hour walk from Severn Oaks, ten minutes' drive. Although I don't understand why she would dump her car and then get a taxi back to where she started.'

'Unless she wanted it to look like she'd jumped in the bloody river. Is this woman having us on? Or is someone else taking the piss out of us?' He felt like kicking something. Or *someone*. Allan was the closest. *Unfair*, he thought. He let out a sigh. 'All right, good job, Allan. Do you think you could get onto this campsite, see if they have anyone renting a caravan there under the name Spencer, or King – and if there is, tell the receptionist *not* to alert her. She might have been under our noses the whole frigging time.'

The door opened and the front desk PC appeared, her cheeks pinkish as if she'd run all the way from the front desk. 'Sir,' her breath caught in her throat, 'there's someone downstairs confessing to the murder of Erica Spencer.'

DS Harvey's heart plummeted into his stomach.

So here it was, the end of his short career.

39

The room was small, with filthy grey walls that looked as though they hadn't been painted since the days when suspects were allowed to smoke in interview rooms. Miranda wished she could smoke now.

She sat at the fake pine table, picking at the loose skin around her thumbnail. She was alone in the room, DS Harvey having gone to call the lawyer whose number she had given him when he'd first shown her into the room. She hadn't even considered that she would need a lawyer, although it seemed apparent the moment he'd asked her if there was anyone she wanted him to inform of her presence. It was as if, with the utterance of the word 'representation', the magnitude of her situation had hit her. She was going to be charged with murder.

Was it murder, though? She'd watched enough TV shows to suspect that her lawyer might argue manslaughter – after all, she'd had no intention of killing Erica Spencer. In fact, she'd had no intention that any harm should come to the other woman at all – but then she hadn't known a year ago what she strongly suspected today. That her husband was the father of Erica's unborn baby. In fact, she hadn't even known there was a baby, and when the news had come via that horrific podcast, she hadn't for a second suspected that her husband might have had anything to do with Erica or the child. It wasn't until Cynthia had made her scathing comment that she had realised she must be the last person to know – her husband and Erica were having an affair. And that was when another shocking thought had come to her. What if Erica had told Alex she was pregnant at the party? Would the dawning realisation that his lies were about to be revealed have forced him to do something stupid?

It was the thought of her husband following Erica into that tree house. Perhaps she had told him that there was something to discuss, or maybe – and this thought made her feel sick – they had arranged to meet for sex, when she uttered the words, 'I'm pregnant. And it's yours.' Miranda could even see the look on Alex's face, that stupid but beautiful expression he got when he was struggling to compute something she'd said – as if he was trying to work out $3,520,042 \div 75$ in his head.

She could picture the scene now.

They begin to row, Alex yelling at Erica that she'll have to tell Jack the baby is his. Erica refuses – she's going to tell everyone what they have been up to. There is a fight and Alex, her husband, the love of her life, shoves Erica. She stumbles backwards, arms flailing, trying to grab hold of something before losing her footing, the alcohol in her system making it impossible for her to regain her balance.

That was the vision that had propelled her to the police station this morning.

'Miranda?'

Miranda jumped to her feet, her hip smashing against the table. 'Oh!' Her face crumpled and her eyes filled with tears. It didn't even hurt that much, but the combination of the sudden pain to her hip and the arrival of their family solicitor, a friendly face in a hostile environment, was too much.

'Rob, thank God you're here.'

Robert Lavistock sat down next to her and laid his briefcase on the table. He pulled out a yellow pad and looked Miranda square in the eye.

'You're better off getting the duty solicitor,' were the first words out of his mouth. Miranda went to object, but he held up a finger. 'I'm not a criminal lawyer. They told me on the phone you're here to confess to a murder? Does Alex know about this?'

Miranda shook her head. 'No. I don't want you to leave me. Will you stay with me for the interview?'

'I don't know,' Rob admitted. 'I've sat in on a few interviews before, but it's crucial I advise you to get proper representation. Tell me everything, and I'll decide if I can get you out of this mess.'

40

'Peter, it's DC Allan.'

The words made him feel sick. Despite the fact that DC Allan had been updating him regularly on the progress of the investigation into Mary-Beth's disappearance, this time his voice sounded different.

'Have you?'

'No, no, it's not that. But we've had a lead that I want your help to look into. Do you know any reason why Mary-Beth might have gone to the Dalton campsite?'

'The one just down the road?' Peter shook his head, then remembered that the officer couldn't see him. 'No, why would we go there? If we were going to have a holiday, we would hardly drive ten minutes down the road for one.'

'And she doesn't know anyone there?' DC Allan asked. 'She doesn't have friends who run it, or family members?'

'No,' Peter said firmly. 'Why are you asking me this? Is she there? Do you know where she might be?'

DC Allan sighed as if he might have made a mistake calling. 'I'm not sure I'm supposed to be telling you this,' he said. 'We're still looking into it. It seems that a taxi driver thinks that he picked Mary-Beth up from Chapel Lane on the day she disappeared, and dropped her at Dalton campsite. I've called the campsite, and there's no one booked in any of their caravans under that name or the name she gave the taxi driver.'

'What name did she give the taxi driver?' Peter asked.

There was silence on the other end. Peter thought that DC Allan might be regretting this entire phone call.

Eventually, he spoke. 'She said her name was Erica Spencer.'

Peter cursed. 'I'm going there.'

DC Allan spoke quickly. 'You can't do that, Peter. We are looking into it ourselves. If Mary-Beth is on the campsite, we will find out. We are going to interview everyone staying there, in case she booked in under a different name. We're taking her picture there right now, in fact. I just thought I might give you the heads-up, and find out if there are any family connections, any reason the owner might be lying to us or protecting her.'

Peter sighed. 'Nothing I can think of,' he said. 'But Mary-Beth has lots of friends, contacts that I might know nothing about. For all I know, one of the mums at the school owns the campsite. I mean, it's likely to be run by local people, isn't it? And Mary knows everyone around here.'

'Okay,' DC Allan said. 'We'll bear that in mind. When we show them the picture, we will be able to tell if the owners are lying about knowing her anyway. Most regular people don't know how to lie to the police. They might be able to do it on the phone, but in person, it's a different kettle of fish. I'll call you as soon as we've been there and let you know, okay? In the meantime, have a think about whether your wife has ever mentioned the campsite or the school in Chapel Lane. It was closed on the day she got picked up, so it's unlikely she has any connection to the school, and her car was found by the weir, which is half an hour's walk away. It seems quite far to walk to get a taxi for no reason – unless she was trying to throw us off the scent. But then why she would use Erica's name to get the taxi is beyond me. If she wanted to be completely anonymous, surely she would have used a completely made-up name?'

'Maggie May,' Peter breathed.

'Excuse me?'

'Maggie May,' Peter repeated. 'It's the name she would have given herself, had she had the choice. She hated the name Mary, she said if her parents were going to give her an old-fashioned name it was just her luck that it wasn't one that has come back around, you know? Like all the old names are doing now? Florence, Martha, Maggie, they're all cool again now, but she said Mary would never be cool. She said if she could rename herself, she'd like to be called Maggie May, like the song.'

Peter could almost hear DC Allan processing this information. 'Thanks,' he said. 'That's really useful. We'll keep an eye out on the caravan register for any Maggies.'

'So you think . . .' Peter started, but he didn't know how to finish the sentence. 'So, do you think she's still alive then? You think she's run away, rather than anyone hurting her?'

'We're keeping our options open, Mr King. All of them.'

41

Felicity and Karla stood in the Kaplans' kitchen – the centre of operations for any crisis. They could hear the delighted shrieks of the twins upstairs as Zachary thundered after them, pretending to be some kind of monster, moaning and groaning.

'He's so good with them.' Felicity smiled.

'It's nice to actually hear his voice,' Karla admitted. 'He's barely spoken to us since he went back to school – except, of course, to announce over dinner that he knew all about his father being abused when he was younger. Some little shit called Jeremy has apparently read Marcus's book.'

'Oh shit.' Felicity made a sympathetic face. 'What did Marcus say?'

'What could he say? It was hardly the time to talk about it. Especially with Brandon so furious, for some reason, that he can't see his grandmother. I mean, for God's sake – why would he want to meet a woman who had done those kinds of things to his father? What does he expect? That we're just going to invite her round for dinner? Marcus acts strong, but he's not that strong. No way.'

'I bet Brandon understands that really,' Felicity said. 'He's a sixteen-year-old boy, which is a hard enough age as it is, without all this stuff going on about Erica. Has he had any stick about that at his school?'

'How would I know? I'm only his mother. Why would he tell me anything? I don't know, Fliss, sometimes it feels like I'm in danger of losing him, and anything I do could make the situation worse.'

'Losing who?' Marcus came into the kitchen, yawning and stretching. He was wearing a pair of grey tracksuit bottoms and nothing else. Felicity's face burned at the sight of his muscular physique. Marcus wasn't ripped – when he was wearing clothes, there was no way you could tell that he was in such good shape.

'Jesus, Marcus, put some clothes on! Poor Felicity hasn't had sex in months.'

Felicity grinned and swatted Karla's arm. 'Now, now, it's his house. Honestly, Marcus, you wear as little as you want.'

'Thanks, Felicity. My wife is just selfish. What are you two witches brewing up now, anyway?'

'I was just telling her about Bran and his attitude problem.'

Marcus snorted. 'Gets it from his mum.'

'Asshole. Listen – are we all getting together Tuesday to listen? I know it didn't exactly go swimmingly last time . . .'

She side-eyed Marcus, who held up his hands.

'I know, I know. I'll be good this time, I promise. Are we going to ask Jack? I know he was pissed off last time about not being invited, but I still think it's a bit weird to sit there listening to ourselves being accused of murder with the husband of the woman we're supposed to have murdered.'

'Think how he must feel,' Karla murmured.

The doorbell rang.

'I'll get it!' Karla jumped up. 'You put some clothes on,' she slapped his bare stomach, 'it might be my agent.'

But it wasn't her agent, it was Peter King.

'Hiya, I, erm . . . just needed to talk to someone . . .' He looked over Karla's shoulder as he spoke.

'Felicity's inside.' Karla stepped aside, and Peter didn't even try to hide his relief.

'Thanks, Karla.'

'What is it?' Felicity asked, jumping to her feet as soon as Peter entered the kitchen.

Karla frowned, but her friend didn't seem to notice.

'I've just had a call from the police about Mary-Beth. A taxi driver is claiming he picked her up on the day she disappeared.'

'Where from?'

'Chapel Lane. I've googled it, it's near the town centre – about half an hour's walk from where her car was dumped.'

'Is he sure it was her?' Felicity demanded. 'Where did he take her?'

Peter shook his head. 'It doesn't make any sense, but he says he dropped her off at Dalton campsite.'

Karla snorted. 'Well, she's hardly likely to be there. Can you see Mary-Beth camping?'

Peter shrugged. 'None of it makes sense.'

'Maybe it wasn't her,' Felicity said. 'He could be wrong.'

'She used the name Erica Spencer.'

There was silence.

Eventually, Karla sighed. 'When will this all end?'

'Maybe it just has,' Marcus replied, appearing in the doorway, Alex Davenport at his side. 'Tell them what you just told me.'

Alex shook his head, like he couldn't quite believe it himself. 'I wondered if I could bring the kids over? I'm on my way to the police station now.'

'Oh God, Alex, of course. Have you reported her missing?'

'I tried,' Alex replied. 'But they know exactly where she is. She's already there – she's been there all day. Apparently, she's confessed to Erica's murder.'

42

'So what you're saying, what you're telling me, is that you have walked into a police station and confessed to murder when what you really mean is that you got Erica Spencer drunk?' DS Harvey could barely contain his disgust. He'd waited almost an hour for her lawyer to turn up, the whole time reviewing Erica Spencer's case notes, wondering how the hell he could have missed the fact that she was murdered by Miranda Davenport. And now this?

'Well, yes, but that makes it sound so innocent! I don't mean "got her drunk" like you get your best friend drunk on their twenty-first birthday! I'm telling you I switched her drinks entirely. I suppose you could say I drugged her, although the only drug was alcohol, and I'm not sure whether that's even classed as a drug . . .'

DS Harvey was grateful for Miranda's solicitor clearing his throat to make her stop talking. Even he looked as though he didn't have a clue what he was doing here. When he'd arrived at the station, he'd informed Harvey that he wasn't a criminal lawyer and likely wouldn't be taking the case. Obviously, after speaking to Mrs Davenport, he felt equipped enough to witness her ludicrous 'confession'.

'So let me make sure we have this correct. On the night of the 28th of October, while at a Halloween party at the Kaplan residence, Erica Spencer asked you to pour her a drink. You knew the wine she had brought to the party was non-alcoholic, but instead, you poured her an alcoholic version.'

'And added a shot of vodka.' Miranda nodded.

'Right. And you didn't mention to Mrs Spencer that you'd done this?'

'No.'

'Can I ask why you felt the need to get Mrs Spencer drunk?'

Miranda hung her head, her cheeks flushed pink. 'It was just a bit of, well, I suppose you'd call it revenge. There was this one time, this Bingo night at the school, when I'd had one too many glasses of wine. Erica was serving me, and I'm sure she was pouring more into those white plastic cups than she was giving the other mums. I . . .' Miranda faltered, as if the memory was painful. 'I made a bit of a fool of myself. I'd had a row with Alex, my husband, about some comment he'd made about Felicity Goldman, and so I was feeling a bit rubbish anyway, and by the end of the night I, erm, I got into a bit of a situation with Mr Jenkins, the kids' PE teacher. I suppose – oh God, this is embarrassing – but I suppose I tried to seduce him. Pathetic, I know. He was very good about it, very, um, very gentlemanly, you know, told me that I was a very good-looking lady, but there were rules about him getting involved with the mums and all that . . .

'Well, I was mortified, of course. And who, somehow, knew about the whole thing? Erica, obviously. She never told anyone else – not that I know of – but she was always mentioning it in this snide way she had. She looked down on all of us, you know? Even when she was drinking, she never got drunk, never made a fool of herself. She was head of the PTA, and on about four charities, she was . . . well, she was bloody perfect, and I was fed up of it.

'So when I saw she'd brought non-alcoholic wine with her, I decided that it was about time she lost control of herself a bit. I was just hoping that she'd do something a bit embarrassing that I could poke her with for the next twelve bloody months. I never thought—'

'So it was just one drink?' DS Harvey interrupted. He thought his head might just explode with all the bloody suburbanness of it all. Drunken fumbles at Bingo nights! He had been employed to deal with criminals, for God's sake, not PTA mums.

'Not exactly,' Miranda mumbled. 'More like six. Or seven.'

'And you think Erica didn't notice she was drinking alcohol? You don't think she would have been able to tell that she was getting drunk?'

'Erica hardly drank at all,' Miranda replied. 'She'd never have more than one cocktail at any of our gatherings. I think that perhaps, after that first wine and double vodka—'

'Double?' DS Harvey raised his eyebrows.

'Well, I wasn't exactly using a measuring glass. I think perhaps she was a bit tipsy after that first one and stopped caring enough to question it.'

'So after you got her drunk, what then? Did you ask her to meet you in the tree house? Was there a fight? She fell, perhaps?'

Miranda looked horrified. 'God, no, I was nowhere near the tree house when she fell. But it was still my fault, don't you see? If she hadn't been drunk, she never would have fallen. I killed her, even though I didn't mean to. So you can stop investigating now, can't you? You know who that horrible podcast person is referring to – me. So you can just arrest me and leave the others alone.'

43

Anticipation of the fourth podcast sat between them like a nasty smell no one wanted to admit to causing. Their numbers had dwindled to four. Miranda and Alex had, unsurprisingly, not turned up, and although Felicity had seen Alex's car pull into the drive she hadn't been able to see who got out. Alex had texted Karla and asked her to send the kids over but hadn't elaborated.

'What, you didn't ask?' Marcus had demanded.

'What was I supposed to do, text back and ask if Miranda was in prison for murder?' she'd hissed back.

Marcus had shrugged. 'I would have.'

Now they were all assembled – Peter, Felicity, Karla and Marcus – gathered around the breakfast bar, laptop open in front of them, refreshing iTunes and waiting for the next episode of *The Truth About Erica* to load.

'It's eight p.m.,' Karla said, unnecessarily. None of them had taken their eyes off the time in the corner of the screen.

Marcus clicked 'refresh' again.

'Click there, on "feed",' Felicity said, pointing at the screen.

Marcus clicked, as instructed, but that only brought up the three podcasts they had already heard.

'Okay, give it here.' She started tapping away at the keyboard, switching windows and running searches.

'It's not there. Maybe he's running late,' Karla suggested. 'Check the website.'

'Maybe he's given up now the murderer has confessed,' Peter countered.

'Oh, come on,' Karla replied. 'Do you really think Miranda killed Erica? And then just came back to the party with the rest of us?'

'Well, whoever killed her did just that,' Felicity replied.

'No one killed Erica,' Karla stated flatly. 'She climbed up into that stupid tree house, which, to be honest, was a crazy thing to do in the first place, and she fell. End of.'

'What was she even doing up there?'

'Maybe she was meeting someone?' Karla raised her eyebrows. 'Maybe she was having an affair?'

'Maybe she was meeting Alex,' Marcus replied. 'Perhaps that's why Miranda shoved her out of the tree house. I don't know.'

What they did know was that, an hour later, there was still no podcast that night accusing anyone of my murder. Or any other night that week.

It was, it seemed, as Peter had predicted.

It was over.

44

Peter's foot slipped through the slick mud and he grabbed the edge of a caravan to steady himself, nearly dropping the mobile phone he was using as his only source of light. Where was he now? The darkness was disorientating and he wasn't sure where the hell he was. Faint lights glowed through the curtains of a few of the caravans; it was almost the end of the holiday season and the park was only half full. A door slammed somewhere, making him start.

Out of nowhere, a voice.

'Stop right there, this is the police.'

A flashlight shone in Peter's face, then the beam dropped. Peter could just about make out the fresh face of DC Allan in the dim light.

'Peter King?' DC Allan sighed. He turned and shouted into the darkness. 'I've got him. It's fine, I'll meet you at the car.' DC Allan moved towards him and took him by the arm. 'Come on, over here.' He shone the light on the ground until they came across a small children's playground with a bench. 'Sit down.'

Peter sat without protest.

'What are you doing here? Didn't I tell you that we

knocked on the door of every caravan here and no one has seen Mary-Beth? We spoke to the owner, who said that they've never seen her before either. Even the taxi driver admitted he didn't actually see her go into the campsite, he just dropped her outside.'

'It's been three weeks, and this is the only lead you have to go on,' Peter snapped. 'No one else has seen her, it's like she's just disappeared off the face of the earth. Do you know what it's like sitting here not knowing if she's alive or dead? Not having any idea why she's walked away from me and our children, or if she's ever coming back? What do I tell the children?'

DC Allan sighed. 'I do understand, Peter. It's why I'm doing everything I can to try and find her, but unfortunately this isn't my case, and we haven't got the budget to do any more than we are currently doing. Despite what you think, I've been following up leads in my spare time.'

'What leads?' Peter asked quickly. 'You never told me about any other leads.'

DC Allan shook his head. 'No, because they came to nothing. In a case like this you can get a hundred calls a day with sightings – it would only get your hopes up if I called you every time someone saw a slim, dark-haired woman in a beige mac. But I've followed up every single one, I promise. Most of them turned out to be a different woman altogether, the others led us nowhere. Nothing was as concrete as the taxi driver, especially with the name he gave, but we're starting to think now that he'd heard Erica's name associated with Mary-Beth's case and his mind filled in the blanks.'

'And her car?'

'It's still in with forensics. These things aren't nearly as quick as you see on TV, I'm afraid. But as soon as we find anything, you will know. You just have to trust us.'

'I'm finding it hard to trust anyone at the moment.' Peter thought of Felicity's relief when the podcast hadn't aired the night before. Was she hiding more than even he was aware of? Just because of their relationship, that was no reason to think she would be one hundred per cent honest with him. After all, he hadn't been with her.

'Understandable . . .' Allan nodded.

The radio on the detective's jacket crackled and Peter heard the words 'Severn Oaks'.

'What was that? What did he say?'

'It was a missing person shout.' DC Allan pushed himself to his feet. 'Missing person in Severn Oaks. Come on, you'll have to follow me back. I'll say I chased off the intruder. Less paperwork.'

45

No one was surprised when they saw the blue and yellow car pull in and turn the corner. They had spent the previous twenty-four hours alternating between relief that no podcast had been forthcoming this week, and fear of what would happen next. Because it wasn't really over, was it? Mary-Beth was still missing, and Miranda – of all people! – had admitted to killing Erica.

Felicity had thought a lot about the night of the Halloween party – not just since the podcasts had started, but before as well. She'd be at Karla's, gazing out of the window at the spot where the tree house used to be, and she'd picture what Erica might have seen in the moments before she died. The dead tell no tales, they say, and yet it seemed that, even a year after her death, Erica was still telling tales on all of them.

It had started with that bloody shot game. The drinks had been flowing all night and everyone was plenty drunk enough, but still Marcus had decided that the party hadn't been eventful enough, and now that the 'others' had gone – that was how he referred to the guests who weren't part of the inner circle – they could let their hair down and have some fun. They all knew what that meant and, sure enough, he had appeared with a tray full of brightly coloured shots: green, purple, and even some disgusting-looking concoction that he'd called 'brain haemorrhage'. And before long the drinking games had commenced.

Had it been Erica's idea to play Truth or Dare? Probably, she always did like to stir the pot. Anyway, it had definitely been Karla who had said they weren't teenagers at a sorority party, but she had been booed by Alex – he was always up for a dare, in defiance of his age. First had come the costume swapping, with Karla and Felicity challenged to strip off – to the men's delight – and swap costumes in under sixty seconds. They failed, and accepted the shot with a smile. All harmless fun – although Miranda's face had said otherwise. Felicity didn't know what her problem was, they saw more flesh on the beach.

Then the boys had been dared to kiss for six seconds – oh, hadn't they all thought that was hilarious! Marcus and Alex had seized the challenge – no tongues, mind you – and Jack and Peter had taken their shots.

That was when she'd done it – Erica. That was when she had turned to Peter, looked him square in the eye, and said, 'I dare you to kiss Felicity. A proper kiss.'

The room had fallen silent, everyone looking between Peter and Mary-Beth, all wondering who would speak first.

'I'll do it,' Alex had joked, putting his hand up.

'You bloody will not,' Miranda snapped, 'and neither will Peter. Don't be ridiculous, Erica.'

'It's fine,' Mary-Beth had replied, her shrug so nonchalant that Felicity had wondered what was going through her mind. *Did she know?* 'It's just a dare. Go on, Peter, these lot are your witnesses. I said you can play the game.'

Peter had looked at Erica as though he would like to kill her. She knew, as well, then. Did everyone? Not Karla, she would have just asked. That meant Marcus didn't know, either – they told one another everything.

'Don't be stupid,' Peter had scoffed. 'My life wouldn't be worth living when I got home.'

'I'm serious, Peter.' Mary-Beth's voice grew more insistent. 'It's fine. Play the game. Be a sport.'

'No,' Peter said, more firmly now. 'Stop it, Mary.'

'Why won't you just kiss her, Peter? It's no big deal.'

The two of them – Mary-Beth and her best friend, Erica – stood shoulder to shoulder now, and Felicity thought everyone in the room must realise that this was a stand-off. Felicity looked desperately at Karla for her to put an end to the awkwardness.

'Oh, for goodness' sake,' Karla snapped. She stepped forward, grabbed Felicity's face in her hands and pulled her in for a kiss, long enough not to be considered chaste but far from an erotic encounter. Although, if you judged it from the boys' reactions, it may as well have been a full-on porn film production. Alex, Marcus and Jack erupted into cheers and applause. Peter looked as if he was going to throw up, and Mary-Beth had tears in her eyes. Erica just smirked.

'Welcome to the family, Fliss,' Marcus laughed. 'Although you two could have let me join in.'

Mary-Beth slammed her wine glass down onto the table and stormed from the room. Erica followed.

'I don't know what her problem is.' Alex slapped Peter on the back. 'Damned if you do, damned if you don't, by the looks of it, mate.'

Felicity's cheeks burned at the memory. Not just at the situation Peter had been put in, but at being used as a pawn in Erica's game. Felicity – the poor, sad singleton who couldn't get a man of her own – she'd be happy to let another woman's husband kiss her just to get some action. God, Erica could be a bitch sometimes.

She was so deep in thought, so lost in the remembered humiliation, that she almost didn't notice that Peter's car had followed the police car through the gates. *This is it, then,* she thought, *they have found Mary-Beth. Peter will be arrested and I'll have to take the girls to visit him in prison.*

Some father he had turned out to be.

Taking a deep breath, she pushed open the front door and stepped out into the darkness. Peter was getting out of his car, fear etched onto his face.

'What's happened?' Felicity asked, watching the police officer pull up outside number seven.

'There's been a missing person report,' Peter said, his own gaze fixed to where DC Allan was approaching the door. 'Tristan Patterson.'

Felicity felt relief, then instant guilt. Another person was missing.

'The lad who lives there?' she asked. 'I don't think I've ever met him. I've seen him drive past in that yellow car of his, but I don't think I've ever seen his face. You?'

Peter nodded. 'He used to do some odd jobs for people on the street when he was younger, before he could get a proper job. Cutting grass and that sort of thing. Nice lad. I bet he's just out with his mates. You know what twenty-year-old boys are like.'

'Not really,' Felicity murmured, but Peter didn't hear her, or he didn't react if he did. Felicity spotted Karla, Marcus and Brandon coming down the driveway.

'What is it now?' Karla asked, nodding at the police car. 'Something to do with Miranda?'

Peter shook his head. 'Missing person reported. I think it's Tristan.'

Karla visibly shuddered. She looked at Brandon. 'I don't suppose you know where he might be?'

Brandon scowled. 'Yeah, I've got him locked in my room

194

with—' He stopped talking when he realised Peter was standing there.

Karla tutted and shook her head. 'I was only asking, Bran.'

DC Allan emerged from the house. When he saw the group gathered on the street he crossed the road to speak to them.

'I don't suppose any of you have seen Tristan recently, have you?'

'I don't even know what he looks like,' Felicity admitted. 'Although I could accurately describe his baseball cap and the noise his car makes at three a.m.'

'Here . . .' DC Allan pulled out a photo and handed it to her. 'Let us know if you remember when you last saw him.'

Felicity looked at the photo and felt her stomach drop. She hadn't seen Tristan in the last three weeks; the last time she'd seen him he'd been serving her a flat white at Starbucks. In fact, he'd been serving her for the last year. And never once mentioned that he lived only eight doors away.

46

'Mr and Mrs Patterson, you did the right thing calling us. If it's okay, I'm going to have to ask you a few questions?'

Janet Patterson nodded, unable to stop the tears from streaming down her cheeks. She sat on the sofa, flanked on either side by her husband, Mike, and the family liaison officer, Tracy Barker. 'Go on,' she whispered. 'Get it over with.'

DS Harvey looked at his notes. 'We have a list of Tristan's friends, people who might know where he is or have seen him in the last three weeks. It would be great if you could give us an idea of who to speak to first?'

'His mate John would be the best,' Janet sniffed. She gave her husband a sidelong look that DS Harvey couldn't quite work out.

'But he lives here, with you?'

Tristan's mum nodded. 'Of a fashion. He'll stay here a few nights, then he'll stay at John's, and then we might not see him for a couple of weeks, or he'll go to a festival and just come in when we're at work to pick up clothes and raid the fridge. He's a twenty-year-old lad – he gets annoyed if we ask too many questions.'

'Mrs Patterson,' DC Allan sighed. 'I know this is very hard for you, and we are here to help you, not to cast any judgement on your situation. But can you give us some idea why it's taken you three weeks to report your son missing?'

Janet looked wide-eyed at her husband, who held up a hand.

'Look,' he rubbed his wife's shoulder, 'we thought we were doing the right thing. But now I think we made a mistake, perhaps we should have done this weeks ago. It's just—' He took a deep breath. 'We thought Tristan had gone with our neighbour, the one who's been reported missing.'

'Mary-Beth King?' Allan and Harvey looked at one another. It wasn't that it hadn't crossed Harvey's mind that two missing people in the street was a huge coincidence, but no one they had spoken to had given any impression that the straight-laced Mary-Beth was involved with anyone, let alone anything as scandalous as an affair with a much younger man.

'Yes . . .' Janet's voice was quiet and her cheeks were red. 'He'd been acting quite shifty, going out at odd hours, then staying longer and longer at John's. Then he quit his job for no reason, and when we asked him about it he got really defensive. He was all over the place. Then Mary-Beth went missing and it made sense. All the sneaking around. Mike saw them hugging once.'

'At the end of her drive,' Mike offered. 'It was getting dark so I couldn't see her properly but it was definitely her. Her arms were pulled around her chest and I thought they were arguing. She looked like she might be crying, and he hugged her.'

'When was this?'

'Just after Erica died. But I've seen them together a few times, just stopping to talk in the street, and once he came out of her back garden. He doesn't do that with anyone else – he avoids our neighbours mostly. Then I found a picture of her in his room.'

'Okay, so you assumed they had gone together. Why didn't you tell us?'

'I didn't want us getting dragged into their scandals. They have so much drama going on – if it isn't those bloody Kaplans, it's this business with Erica and the podcast. We don't want any part of their drama, and we were a bit annoyed at Tristan for dragging us into it. We thought they would be back in a few days, bored of one another once the clandestine thrill of the affair had worn off.'

'So what's changed? Do you still think they are together? Why report him missing now?'

Janet sniffed. 'John called us. He hasn't heard from him – none of his friends have. And his phone is always off, we've all tried calling constantly. And all these things coming out on this podcast – it's clear we're surrounded by violent, deranged people. What if Peter King found out about their affair and hurt them both? It's been driving me crazy for days now, a week. But making the decision to call you seemed so . . . official, I suppose. He's a grown man – he doesn't have to tell any of us where he is, if he doesn't want us to know.'

Allan supposed he could see it – Patterson was a young, attractive lad and Mary-Beth was a bored, middle-aged housewife. She was only early forties, he'd seen stranger affairs.

'Okay, so let's go back to the last time you saw Tristan. When was it?'

'Sunday the 19th of August. He'd quit his job and we had a bit of a fight. He said he had a lot on, and Mike said he didn't know the meaning of responsibility and he had to grow up.'

Mike looked pained. Janet ploughed on.

'I assume he was here Monday morning, because he didn't have to go to work and his car was still here, but I didn't actually see him. Then when I got back, his car had gone and there was a note saying he was going to stay at John's for a while. At first I thought he was annoyed at us, then I found out Mrs King had gone missing and it seemed to add up.'

'Did you speak to John?'

'Yes, but he hadn't heard from Tristan. I said we knew about the affair and he said that he didn't know what I was talking about and Tristan probably just needed some time and space of his own. It was clear to me that he knew what was going on—'

'Only he didn't,' Mike interrupted. 'When he called us a couple of days ago he said he hadn't heard from Tristan since before we called him, and that he had no idea where he was.'

'Okay, we'll look into where Tristan might have gone after he left here on either Sunday evening or Monday. My colleague has taken down his registration number, plus the make and colour of the car. We'll try and locate it as soon as possible. If we could have your permission to access his phone records and bank statements? You can give those details to DC Allan, as well as any social media details you have of his. Have you looked through his room? Anything missing?'

'God only knows,' Janet groaned. 'It's such a mess. He has so many clothes, he could have taken a year's worth and I wouldn't know. Oh! His laptop is gone,' she remembered. 'He took that everywhere with him.'

'Right, we'll get cracking on this as a matter of urgency.'

'Will you be speaking to Peter King?'

'Not yet.' DS Harvey shook his head. 'And I'd appreciate

it if you kept your suspicions about your son and his wife to yourself. If there is a connection, I'd rather he thought we hadn't made it yet.'

47

'Sir, you asked for me?'

DS Harvey took a few steps into the DCI's office. DCI Barrow looked up and gave an insincere smile. He gestured for Harvey to come all the way in.

'Close the door, please, DS Harvey. Have a seat, and don't look so nervous. I can't reach you from here anyway, the size of this bloody desk.'

Harvey took a seat opposite the man he had once hoped would be his mentor, perhaps even a friend. How stupid and naive he'd been. All he'd ever been was a scapegoat, used to ensure that his DCI's hands stayed clean.

'You know I've asked you here to find out what's going on in Severn Oaks.'

No beating around the bush then.

'Yes, sir. As you know, we have two active missing persons reports; one is Mary-Beth King, which has been ongoing for three weeks.'

'And we have no concrete leads on that? Seems strange after all this time. Usually we would have some idea of what's happened by now.'

'We have a couple of lines of enquiry ongoing.'

Barrow knew all of this. He'd been present at the back of the room during a couple of the morning briefings and Harvey knew that, as much as he pretended not to be showing an individual preference for this case above any others, as soon as he'd heard the name Severn Oaks he'd been watching the developments with particular interest.

'The husband?'

'Yes, Peter King is of interest, of course. We're still trying to find someone who saw him at the training course he was booked on to. There's evidence he turned up but no one can remember seeing him on the second day at all.'

'Okay. Any evidence she left of her own accord?'

'Her bank cards haven't been used, and we can't find evidence of her siphoning off any money in the weeks prior to her disappearance. We have a possible sighting we are working to verify.'

'The taxi driver who says he dropped her off for a holiday at a campsite?'

'Yes, sir. DC Allan has checked with the owners of the campsite and we've knocked on the doors of the caravans and spoken to all the owners. We'd need a search warrant to go through the empty ones and at the moment we have no grounds – the driver says she got into his taxi of her own accord and was alone when she got out. So we have no evidence that anyone is in any harm, to start busting open doors.'

'And the latest misper?'

'A twenty-year-old boy, Tristan Patterson. Lives a few doors down from the Kings. The Pattersons keep to themselves for the most part, the other residents don't know a lot about them, and no one has seen Tristan. Apparently, his car comes and goes late at night so a few of them wouldn't be sure they knew him even if he passed them in the street.'

'I thought it was supposed to be a close community?'

'I get the impression that there are those who participate a lot – group messages on Facebook, street parties, kids at the same school. Those with older children, or no children at all, seem a bit less in the loop. It's an opt-in situation, and the Pattersons don't seem to have opted in all that often.'

'Right. Any leads on that one? He's not just staying with mates? Twenty-year-olds are rarely at home, in my experience.'

Harvey wondered what that experience might be. Unlike Harvey, whose son had just turned eighteen – and Harvey would have no clue if he was missing or not, half the time – DCI Barrow had no children, to Harvey's knowledge.

'His mum has checked with all the friends she knows of, and we've followed up. She, um . . . she feels there may have been a connection to Mary-Beth King in some way.'

'A connection how?'

'Like there may have been something going on between them. Tristan was last seen the night before Mary-Beth disappeared, and he hasn't been seen by any of his friends or by his parents since.'

'Right. Anything else linking them together?'

'Nothing, sir.'

'Fine. Anything else?'

The podcast sat between them like a clandestine affair.

'I don't think we can ignore the links to Erica Spencer, sir.'

'What links would those be, sergeant?'

His voice held a hint of steel. The last name DCI Barrow wanted to hear was Erica Spencer's. It was the same voice Harvey had heard his DCI use less than twelve months ago when he had encouraged – and that word was being generous – a keen trainee PC Harvey to submit an accidental death report to the coroner. *We don't need a scandal involving the Kaplans.*

'Erica Spencer pulled Tristan from a river three years ago – we are still looking into the circumstances as to how they were both by the river at the same time. Then there's the podcast—'

'Fuck the podcast,' DCI Barrow said, his voice even. 'It's just some idiot who knows nothing about the investigation that went on into the original incident. Have we got any actual evidence that Erica was pushed?'

'No, sir, but—'

'But what, DS Harvey?'

He had never heard his name spoken like a threat before.

'There were the inconsistencies at the time, if you remember, sir. The photograph that showed Erica wearing flat pumps when she was found in heels, the blood found in the tree house that matched Erica's—'

'A tiny amount of blood that was probably transferred there by the investigating officer,' Barrow said. The implication was clear – Harvey had been the investigating officer. 'And what woman do you know who doesn't change constantly? My wife changed outfits twice during our New Year's Eve party. Neither of those things on their own warrant a full criminal investigation, and the media circus that surrounds it. That was your conclusion, was it not?'

Harvey took a deep but unnoticeable breath. He knew that arguing was futile. And yet, if DC Allan had the courage to question every decision he made, why could he not do the same to his superior? Was Allan just ballsier than he had been?

'Under your instruction, sir. I now believe that we may have been too hasty in closing the case. I'm recommending that we open a new investigation into Erica Spencer's death.'

Barrow looked as though he'd just eaten something disgusting. 'Reopen the investigation? On the strength of some podcast? We'd be a fucking laughing stock, and you know it, you fucking idiot. Every dickhead with a computer and a microphone would be demanding we reopen cases from years back – and when I say *we* I mean the rest of the team, because none of us would be here to see it. I don't want,' DCI Barrow rose from his desk, 'to hear you so much as *think loudly* that we made a mistake on the Erica Spencer death, am I clear on that? Because if I do, you will be back in uniform faster than you could fall from a tree house.'

Argue back, a voice told him. *Make your case. Be a fucking man.*

'Yes, sir,' he heard himself say. 'I understand, sir.'

48

Peter stared at the phone in his hand. It felt warm, although he knew that was impossible – it hadn't been used in weeks. He was desperate to turn it on, he had been weighing up the pros and cons in his mind constantly all morning. He needed to know if his wife had left any links to Tristan Patterson, and her phone seemed like the only way to find out. He'd searched her office and come up with nothing, her social media equally as unyielding. They hadn't been friends – he'd never even seen them speak to one another, save for holding up a hand as the young lad drove by. Felicity had been genuinely shocked that she'd never made the connection between the young barista serving her every morning and their neighbour, although she had no reason to know him. Like typical teenagers, Tristan had avoided any get-together that involved spending time with his parents, and Felicity had moved into the community in the winter – a time when the sociability of the summer months was swapped in favour of early nights in front of the fire. She'd only spent one summer in Severn Oaks before this one, and had probably never been introduced to the boy who would turn their lives upside down.

Would the police be able to track it if Mary-Beth's phone was turned on, even for a second? He was fairly sure that they could only get a location if he actually made a call from it – he'd listened to *Serial*, so he knew about the unreliability of phone tower evidence. The problem was that his only experience of these kinds of things was from programmes like *CSI*, where they knew within seconds if the perpetrator made a mistake. He was fairly confident that, in real life, policing didn't work like that; it was a slow, arduous process without all the special effects. But not sure enough to risk his freedom. There was another option, of course.

He could feel the eyes of the street on him as he got into his car. The house at the end of the street was still cordoned off but no police presence remained there now. The curtains of Tristan Patterson's house were closed, the house shrouded by an air of grief.

Cameras flashed as he pulled out of Severn Oaks, viperous faces shoving themselves against the passenger windows, microphones held outstretched, their owners desperate for any comment from within the walls. Peter kept his eyes fixed ahead as he accelerated steadily until he was away from the prying eyes, then put his foot down.

He didn't know where he was going but as the car whipped past the Cheshire countryside, still a luscious green, he began to feel himself relax. The further he drove from Severn Oaks – those claustrophobic walls, the police cars and suspicious eyes – the more he felt the heavy sensation inside his chest dissolve. When all this was over, he decided, he was leaving Cheshire for good. Would Felicity come with him? Maybe not before all this – she wouldn't have wanted to uproot the girls from their school or leave the home and business she had worked so hard for. But now? Possibly. If they both came out of this unscathed and un-incarcerated, which was looking less likely by the day.

The ringing of his mobile cut in over the sound of the radio, making him jump. There was no name on the console – number withheld. The police. Peter cut the call off guiltily, as if DC Allan could see what he was doing right now.

He did feel bad about DC Allan. While DS Harvey seemed suspicious of everything he said, Allan seemed to actually believe him, and want to help.

He couldn't think about that now. He had to drive as far away as possible and turn on Mary-Beth's phone to find out what, if anything, there was to discover on it.

Peter drove for nearly forty minutes before pulling into the grounds of a disused garage off the main road. He felt certain there would be no CCTV here, the place was a wreck. The glass front was completely smashed, the paint almost completely peeled away from the rotting boards. The road had a 60mph speed limit, and traffic going past would be travelling too fast to notice anything about him.

Pulling the phone from under the passenger seat, Peter took a final glance around and pressed the power button. The Samsung logo appeared on the screen, then the excruciating wait while the phone loaded and scanned for a signal.

Within a couple of minutes the phone was beeping almost continuously. Messages from friends, missed-call alerts, emails, all flooded in. Peter opened the message folder and began scrolling through, careful not to open any of the new messages. He saw names he recognised: Karla, Felicity, Alina, Mum, Hannah. Nothing out of the ordinary. He wanted desperately to click on the messages from Hannah, intimate musings from daughter to mother that Peter imagined must have turned into desperate pleas for her mother to get in touch. That was the real reason why he had let Mary-Beth's mum look after the children – yes, he was constantly busy with the police, and home wasn't the best environment now – but the real reason was that he didn't want to see his children's faces, he didn't want to look into his daughter's eyes.

Peter wiped away a tear with the back of his hand and took a deep breath. He had to get this done quickly. He clicked on the contacts in his wife's phone and scrolled until he got to the T's. No Tristan there, although of course she could have saved his number under any of the names in there. Going back to the messages, he scrolled down to the 'read' ones from before Mary-Beth went missing. There were several texts from his wife to an unknown number.

I KNOW IT'S YOU.
YOU HAVE TO STOP.
WHY ARE YOU DOING THIS?

There was one reply.

WHAT ARE YOU AFRAID OF?

Then nothing more.

Peter clicked on Mary-Beth's emails but found nothing but work stuff and PTA nonsense. If any more exchanges between Mary-Beth and the unknown number existed, he couldn't find them. He turned off the phone and tossed it out of the window, started the car and drove over it – one, two, three times – until only pieces of his wife's phone remained on the tarmac.

49

'Any news on Patterson's car yet?' Harvey asked, not needing to look up to know that the shadow across his desk was DC Allan. Mainly because the man never seemed to go home.

'None, sir. We've had the email and bank record reports back – nothing on there that suggests where he might have gone. No hotel bookings or car hire, and his cards haven't been used since the Sunday he was last seen. It's not looking good, sir.'

'Sit down,' Harvey gestured to the seat opposite him, 'this is all good work, thanks, constable.'

'Thank you, sir.'

'No, I mean it.' Harvey cleared his throat. 'I realise I might have . . . well, I . . . perhaps I gave the impression that Mrs King's disappearance wasn't important. When of course it is. And what with the podcast, and Tristan Patterson disappearing, I suppose I'm just trying to say that I appreciate the time you're putting in.'

DC Allan looked like he might puke with pride and Harvey was glad he'd said it. As much as his tenacity frustrated Harvey sometimes, DC Allan was a good officer, and he still remembered how it felt at the start of your career, before you realised that police work was as much politics as it was actual investigation.

'Do you think he might be with Mary-Beth King?' Allan asked.

Harvey sighed. 'Honestly? Until we spoke to his mum and dad there was no indication from anyone that Mary-Beth was seeing anyone else – let alone a young lad. I find it hard to believe that they would have been able to carry on an affair, and none of their neighbours knew about it – not in a place like Severn Oaks. But I've seen it before, people carrying on with their brother- or sister-in-law, husband's best friend, and no one being any the wiser. Besides, the people in Severn Oaks have never been forthcoming with their information – they are the kind of people who would lie to your face to protect their own backs.'

'If Tristan and Mary-Beth were having an affair then Peter King would be the number one suspect in their disappearances, right?'

'Either that, or they've done a runner together. But in the real world people don't just get to disappear and start a new life without leaving a shred of evidence. They slip up, call their family – she has children, for Christ's sake – or use their bank cards. In the days or weeks leading up to the disappearance you'd usually find increasing withdrawals from bank accounts, and bookings for hotels or a ferry or whatever. If they have run away together, they are two of the cleverest runaways I've ever come across.'

'Do you think they just might be the cleverest runaways you've come across?'

DS Harvey shook his head. 'Between you and me? I think we'll be opening a murder inquiry by the end of the week.'

50

'The search continues for missing Severn Oaks resident, Tristan Patterson. Tristan was reported missing by his mother after he failed to return home from a friend's house where he was believed to be staying. Severn Oaks, home to celebrity couple—'

'Oh God, turn it off.' Miranda paced the room, stopping every few seconds to twitch the living-room curtains, which were still closed. She could only just see the corner of the street where a police car now sat outside the Patterson's house.

'Not going to go and confess to that one as well then?' Alex snapped, but he flicked off the TV as requested.

Miranda had been waiting for this. They had barely spoken two sentences to one another since Alex had picked her up from the police station nine days ago when she had been – shudder – released on bail. Following her confession, Miranda had been arrested for administration of a noxious substance and released pending charges. Her solicitor had advised that there was still a slight chance that she could be charged with manslaughter, but it looked unlikely. The police would have to prove that Erica had been entirely unaware that she was drinking alcohol, and that the alcohol given to her by Miranda specifically caused her to fall out of the tree house. At this point, he'd suggested, it was impossible to prove how much alcohol Erica had drunk of her own accord, as well as how much – if any – of the spiked drink Miranda had served her. He argued that it was entirely possible that Erica had known that Miranda had given her alcohol and drank it anyway, in which case all she was guilty of was serving a drink. Erica might even have thrown it away. All they had was an anonymous voice on a podcast to suggest that Erica had given up alcohol, and no evidence to support the claim. All in all, it was unlikely the police would press any charges at all.

She was relieved, in a way, that he had finally brought it up now. He'd been sullen, only speaking to her when the children were around, and it had been almost unbearable. She'd spent most of the time in her bedroom – the room that Alex hadn't been sharing since her arrest.

'Very funny. Are you going to stay mad at me for ever? It was stupid of me to spike her drink, I know that.'

Alex looked at her, his mouth half open. 'You think that's why I'm mad at you? Because you got someone drunk at a party?'

'Why else?'

Alex stood up. 'Perhaps because you went to the police to confess to murder without even talking to me first? They could have locked you up, Miranda, you thought they were going to charge you with murder. Didn't you think for a second what that would do to the kids? What it would do to me? To have you taken away from us and locked up for God knows how long? I would . . . I wouldn't . . .' He shook his head and made a strangled noise in his throat. 'And you didn't even bother to tell me.'

'Because you would have convinced me not to go,' Miranda said, her eyes filling with tears.

213

'Of course I bloody would!' Alex looked livid. 'What good does it do for you to tell the police after all this time? Did it bring Erica back? It didn't change anything for anyone other than us.'

'Not us,' Miranda whispered. '*You*. I went for you. I thought that once the police had my confession they would stop, the podcaster would stop.'

'And what difference would that make to—? Oh fuck, no, Miranda. You thought . . .' His handsome face creased in pain. 'You think I killed Erica? That's why you wanted the police to stop investigating, so they would stop looking for me?'

Miranda didn't speak, she didn't need to. This was it, Alex knew now why she'd done what she'd done. Her marriage was over.

'I don't know whether to be furious that you think I could push Erica out of a tree house, or flattered that you'd confess to murder to cover up for me.' He paced the floor. 'Why the hell would you think I'd do something so horrific? What was the motive you dreamed up for me?'

This was the bit Miranda had been dreading. Because the minute she told him the reason why she'd confessed, she'd have to see his face, and she'd know the truth – and he'd know that she knew Erica Spencer was carrying his baby. Right now they could still pretend – while it was unspoken – but not once it was out there. She'd have to demand to know how long it had been going on, and – however painful – if he'd loved her. If he'd been in love with the woman across the road who was pregnant with his baby. Then she'd have to forgive him, if he even wanted her forgiveness, but she would be left wondering if he was only with her because Erica was dead. Nothing would ever be the same.

She took a deep breath.

'Because of the baby,' she said, her words barely audible. 'Because of Erica's baby.'

'But what does Erica's baby have to do with . . . ?' Realisation dawned. 'You think it was mine?' He looked disgusted and heartbroken. 'Is that what you think of me?'

Miranda was stunned. She'd readied herself for a denial – of course she hadn't expected him to just come out and admit that the baby was his – but she hadn't expected his denial to be so convincing.

'Cynthia Elcock said . . . and I thought everyone knew . . .'

Alex crossed over to her and held out his arms. Miranda folded herself into him, too relieved to speak.

'I love you, Mim,' he said, using the special nickname only he had ever called her by. 'I might be working a lot to keep your nails looking perfect, and I might drink too much at parties and make jokes like I'm a stupid hormonal teenager, but I thought under all that exasperated tutting you liked me like that. I thought it was boyish charm.'

'You were listening to that podcast and I heard you, Alex – you were *crying!* And you came home early stinking of alcohol. Because you'd found out about the baby . . .'

'I lost my job, Miranda.' Alex let out a breath, and his face crumpled.

Miranda couldn't understand. 'You what? Don't be ridiculous, that was ages ago, and you've been going to work every day.'

'I've been out meeting potential clients. They told me they'd decided not to renew my contract that day – I finished at the end of that week. I'm pretty sure it was because of that podcast.'

Miranda let out a sob and Alex held her at arm's length, looked at her in a way he hadn't in years. 'I should have told you. I just didn't want to worry you, because there's nothing to worry about. I've had three possible offers anyway.

And I never touched Erica, or anyone else. I've never cheated on you, I love you.'

Miranda felt so, so stupid. She had confessed to wanting to hurt Erica in order to protect a man who she should never have doubted for a minute. He'd never given her a reason not to trust him, but that hadn't stopped her taking fucking Cynthia Elcock's word as gospel. Maybe she had just never believed that a man as good-looking and funny as Alex would only be hers, just hers. Next time she saw that woman . . .

'So the baby *was* Jack's then?' Miranda's entire body felt lighter as she and her husband lay on the sofa, their limbs intertwined, his hands stroking her hair.

Alex chuckled. 'Well, I didn't say that, did I?'

51

It was true what they said about rumours being like fire, without fuel they fizzled and died. They were still waiting to see if Miranda would be charged, the only remaining smudge on the horizon of an otherwise blue sky.

'So do you think Mary-Beth will come back now?' Karla asked, taking a chocolate from the box on the counter and popping it into her mouth.

'Now what?' Felicity asked. She held up a hand in a 'no thanks' to the box Karla offered her.

'Now that the podcast has gone away. That's why she left, right? Because she was scared of what might come out? Or do you think she had a breakdown?'

'I don't know, she really doesn't seem the type to have a breakdown, she's just so buttoned up.'

'She's a pushover, you mean,' Marcus said.

Karla scowled.

'That's an awful thing to say, Marcus Kaplan. We didn't push her around. She liked helping people.'

'Don't let the police hear you refer to her in the past tense,' Marcus mocked. 'You might be next on the suspect list.'

Karla's hand flew to her mouth. 'Oh God, you're right, I did do that. Jesus, I knew I'd be a crappy criminal.'

'Did you say Miranda was coming over?'

Karla nodded. 'I spoke to Alex. She's terrified of seeing us after what she said to the police but I said she was going to have to, sooner or later. I mean, unless they are going to move away. She may as well come tonight and face it.'

'What do you think, about what she did?'

'What, getting Erica drunk?' Karla shrugged. 'I don't believe Erica didn't know. Even if she thought she was drinking non-alcoholic wine – which I'm not sure she did – she must have felt herself getting drunk. Everyone pours bigger measures at a party, it's not a big deal. Erica knew she was drunk when she went into that tree house.'

'Well, thank God it's over now. I mean, I feel awful for Janet and Mike, obviously.' Felicity flushed beetroot red. 'I'm just glad we can go back to normal. I've even had a few new clients, so business isn't ruined.'

'What did I say about all publicity being good publicity?' Karla said.

'I'll get that,' Marcus said, in response to the doorbell.

'Is Peter okay?' Karla took the opportunity to hiss at Felicity as soon as her husband had left the room.

'How would I know?' Felicity whispered back. 'I . . . well, it sounds like you can ask him yourself.'

Peter, Marcus, Alex and Miranda entered the room one after the other, and Karla wasn't sure who looked more uncomfortable. She jumped to her feet to hug Peter as Felicity crossed the room to embrace Miranda.

'How are you holding up?' she asked Peter, regarding him at arm's length. 'How are the kids?'

Peter nodded. 'We're okay. The kids are coming home tomorrow, we have to start trying to get back to normal.

They've already missed too much school and I need to prepare them for what the other kids might be saying.'

'She'll come home, Peter, you know that, don't you?'

Peter sniffed. 'That's what I've got to keep believing.'

'The God's honest truth is that I was jealous,' Miranda was saying. 'And believe me, it costs me a lot to say this but I was jealous of Erica. She was always so in control, she *always* had the upper hand.'

Everyone in the room nodded.

'And I know it was a terrible thing to do. Just like I know I shouldn't park directly in front of the school and say horrible things about your gorgeous home-made cakes, Felicity. I'm sorry. It's like I just can't help but crave the feeling that people think I'm better than everyone else somehow. It's like a drug, you know? When just one person says, "Oh, Miranda, you're so organised." When really I have to drive to Asda at least three times a week before school to buy new bloody PE kit so no one will know I've forgotten it again.'

'Bloody hell, Miranda, I have to pay sixty quid an hour to get all that shit off my chest.'

Felicity hugged her again. 'Shut up, Marcus. I think it's brilliant of you to be so honest, Miranda. You know we're all just faking our way through it, don't you?'

'You liar,' Karla snorted. 'You've never faked it in your life. The only difference is that now Miranda's a fuck-up like the rest of us we have to start making fun of *you* behind your back.'

Miranda looked as though she was going to cry. 'I . . .' she sighed. 'I was petrified you'd all think I was a total idiot.'

'We thought that anyway,' Marcus said. 'At least now you're a flawed idiot. Always more likeable.'

'Gee, thanks, Marcus.'

'Well, I'm just glad it's all over.' Marcus pulled two bottles of beer from the fridge and handed them to Peter and Alex. 'Shit, sorry, Peter, not all over for you.'

'No. I keep hoping that now there's no more podcasts Mary will come back – perhaps she just couldn't bear last year being dredged up again. We know how hard she took Erica's death. I just can't make sense of her leaving without telling us – if she'd wanted to get away, we could have all gone.'

'She'll be back now,' Miranda said, placing a hand on Peter's knee. 'I'm sure she will.'

'And when she is, we'll have a massive party,' Alex added. 'A street party – although the weather's not getting any better. Maybe you should host that, Marcus, it could be themed. I know, Cluedo! We could each dress as a character and have to figure out whodunnit.'

He looked so ridiculously pleased with himself that no one wanted to tell him just how distasteful a Cluedo party would be. Besides, a party might be exactly what they needed – just one where they weren't all dressed as prospective murderers obviously.

'I just feel like I want to sleep for about ten years,' Karla groaned.

'I don't think it's over,' Felicity whispered, but no one was listening.

'Where's the champagne, Karla?' Marcus asked. 'The *Sunday Times* stuff my agent sent. I think we deserve it.'

'In the wine fridge. Right there, under your nose! Should I get strawberries? And I've got entrées in the freezer, I'll get them out.'

'I could go out for cake?' Marcus's phone rang. 'Bran, you okay?'

'There's been another one, Dad.' Brandon's voice was grave. 'Another podcast just went up.'

52

Welcome, listeners, to part four of The Truth About Erica.

Last time we talked about what happened at the party once the other guests had left. We pieced together from interviews with some of the guests left at the party that shots had been taken, games played. Then a body is found at the foot of the tree house, a heel caught in the top step of the children's hideout. Only, if those who were at the party were to cast their minds back they might remember a simple detail that sullies this picture of a tragic accident. Erica Spencer was dressed as an evil spirit girl, with white nightdress, long black hair falling in front of a pale face with black-ringed eyes. And **black ballet pumps**.

So let's look now at our suspects. Of the six, only four would have been wearing heels that night; Peter King and Marcus Kaplan wore boots. Does that rule them out? Perhaps not. But what we do know is that, at some point, either Erica changed into heels of her own accord – which has never been mentioned by anyone at the party – or someone planted one heel in the tree house and the other on the dead body of Erica Spencer.

While I leave you to digest this information, I want to play you an interview with Simon and Gilly Barker.

'It had only ever been Severn Oaks residents at Karla's Halloween parties – the Kaplans held get-togethers for outsiders all the time, but never usually at Halloween. Which is why I was surprised when Gilly said that she'd seen someone outside that she didn't recognise. A woman . . . right, Gill?'

Gilly nods her agreement.

'Yes, she was a pretty woman, I only saw her for a minute talking to Karla on the front driveway. She was blonde, she had no costume, she was wearing an expensive-looking jacket and lovely boots – I assumed she was one of their fancy friends, but Karla didn't look pleased to see her. Their voices were raised but I couldn't hear what they were saying. She got into a Range Rover and drove off, but when we walked home I'm certain her car was still parked around the corner.'

So, could this mystery woman have anything to do with Erica's death? Or is it a coincidence that the first year a stranger turns up to the Kaplans' Halloween party is the same night a tragedy occurs?

Well, my friends, I'm about to tell you.

Karla pressed the 'pause' button on the podcast player and turned to her husband, whose face was slack.

'Marcus, I'm so sorry.'

'What did you do, Karla?'

Felicity looked between the pair, bewildered, then at Peter who gave a small shrug.

'Why don't you put it back on?' Alex suggested. 'I want to hear what he's about to say.'

'Alex,' Miranda muttered. 'It looks like Karla wants to explain something to Marcus before he hears it from a random stranger through his computer.'

'Perhaps we should go,' Felicity said, standing up. 'Leave you two to talk.'

'No,' Marcus said, his voice firm. 'You're all going to hear it anyway – best we all listen together, not that it'll make the situation any better. I'm guessing, from my wife's horrified expression, that the woman she was talking to was my mother.'

'Your mother? But I thought . . . ?' Felicity looked at Karla, who avoided her best friend's eyes.

Marcus pressed 'play'.

As regular listeners know, I have managed to get hold of a diary kept by the late Erica Spencer, in which she goes into great detail about the 'Cult of Kaplan', as it is jokingly referred to by teenagers outside of the area. We've heard about Erica's thoughts on Karla – just to refresh: 'Had an interesting conversation with Jess a few months ago who questioned if Karla had even read her own books.'

'Jess' refers to Jess Tandy, a well-known celebrity ghostwriter. Now, while this may be difficult for Karla's legions of fans to hear, it is hardly a motive for murder – after all, plenty of celebrities hire ghostwriters for their book. And it's nothing compared to the revelation Erica had for Marcus Kaplan. Because it was Erica who invited the mystery woman to the party, the woman who Karla was so desperate to make leave. That woman was Marcus Kaplan's mother, Samantha Burgess.

Those of you familiar with Marcus Kaplan – and who isn't? – will know that he left his family home at the age of fifteen, after a horrifically abusive childhood. He doesn't go into great detail in his books but it is enough that we know that young Marcus was often forced to eat dog biscuits because his junkie mother refused to spend a penny of her drug money on feeding her son. Beaten at the hands of her many boyfriends, he fled after one threatened to sell him to a paedophile to assuage his

223

mother's drug debts. Young Marcus, forced into a life on the streets, turned to drugs himself to cope, and was on the brink of death after an overdose when a kindly stranger gave him a notepad and pen. It was then that Marcus discovered his passion – writing – and it was this passion and his on-the-brink experience that led to the empire we see today.

So, in Erica's words, it was an 'interesting day' when she found out the truth. Here's an extract from her diary.

'Interesting day today. Spotted a woman hanging around outside the gates and obviously, as Neighbourhood Watch co-ordinator, went to ask what she was doing. She looked upset, said she wasn't really sure. That she'd come to see Marcus but it was probably a bad idea. And that was when I noticed the uncanny resemblance to Marcus Kaplan and invited her in for coffee.'

And what Erica found out that day had the ability to blow the Cult of Kaplan wide open. Because Marcus Kaplan's real mother has never touched drugs in her life. Marcus Kaplan was brought up in a small village in Pembrokeshire, Wales, where he lived as Tommy Burgess until the age of seventeen when, unable to come to terms with his 'simple' life, he left home to live in London and attempt to make it big with several unsuccessful internet businesses. It was here that he met already wealthy Karla Kaplan outside a bar in East London, and, over the course of a drunken evening where the pair talked of their oversized ambitions, the Cult of Kaplan was born. Changing his name to Marcus Kaplan, growing out his teenage quiff and inventing a tragic past over which he had triumphed, Marcus's blog was picked up by the likes of Ricki Lake, Trisha and eventually Oprah, rocketing Marcus quickly to join the ranks of self-help gurus such as Tony Robbins and Stephen Covey. A life built on a lie.

So when Erica introduced her plus one on Halloween night as the one woman who could bring down the Kaplan enterprise, one can only imagine how Karla must have felt. Desperate to rid their lives of this woman, Karla offered to up the fifteen-hundred-pounds-a-month allowance the Kaplans had been paying Samantha Burgess to two thousand. Samantha reluctantly left – she had simply wanted to see her only son for a few minutes. That just left Erica to deal with. And deal with her she did.

Only Karla and Erica know exactly what happened when Karla confronted her neighbour that night – a neighbour who ended up dead. What I can tell you is there was one head injury that Erica Spencer didn't sustain in her fall from the tree house. One head injury that she described as 'nothing, just a scratch', despite it bleeding profusely. Erica attempted to stem the bleeding with a flannel, presumably from the Kaplans' bathroom. Where did that flannel go? And how greatly did the head injury Erica sustained – along with the alcohol she never intended to consume – contribute to her lying dead on the grass less than an hour later?

Stay tuned until next week, when we will find out why the other guests at the party had just as much reason to make sure Erica didn't reveal their secrets to the world.

Until then . . . stay honest.

53

'You hit her?' Marcus turned to his wife. 'Why didn't you tell me? What did you hit her with?'

Karla felt as though she was choking on her own guilt.

'How was I supposed to know she was going to climb into the bloody tree house? She was fine! It was just a scratch – you heard him say it!'

'He also said it was bleeding profusely,' Peter pointed out.

Karla wanted to hit him harder than she had Erica.

'It was a picture frame. The edge caught her temple. I don't know what made me do it – I'd never hit anyone before, I swear – but she looked so *smug* and—'

'And you just wanted her to shut up,' Felicity said quietly.

'Yes!' Karla breathed. 'She was standing there holding this picture of Marcus and his mum, she was shoving it at me like some kind of trophy. I was upset from seeing Samantha here and I just lashed out. That must be why she fell out of the tree house, it *must* be. It was me, I killed her.'

'It's probably not.' Felicity rubbed her friend's arm. 'I'm sure there were other factors.'

'Wait! He said there was a bloody flannel?' Alex asked.

Karla groaned and covered her eyes. 'Yes, well—'

'But how would he know that? Unless he—'

'Or she,' Miranda interjected.

'Or she, had seen Erica after you bashed her?'

Karla cringed at the word 'bashed'.

'He's right,' Marcus said slowly. 'How would he know about that? The fucker must have been in the house? Did anyone see anyone else in the house?'

No one replied.

'Maybe she told someone on the phone?'

'Why would she do that?'

'Why would she invite Marcus's mother to the bloody party?' Karla snapped. 'Because she loved to cause trouble, that's why. She literally had no motive except to piss everyone off for her own amusement.'

'But—'

'Is it true?' A voice cut through the discussion as Brandon's face appeared at the door of the kitchen, his younger brother at his side.

'We should go,' Felicity said, standing up and indicating for the others to do the same. 'Call me, Karla. Don't go through this on your own.' She hugged her best friend and tapped Peter on the arm. 'Come on.'

They moved past Brandon and Zachary one by one, none of them able to look the boys in the eye. When they were gone, Marcus spoke.

'It's true, Bran, every word. I'm so—'

'You lied to us! You told us—'

'I told you I'd fallen out with your grandmother. I never told you anything else – you read that yourself, in my book.'

Brandon stormed into the kitchen to face his father. 'Bullshit!'

Marcus didn't even attempt to tell him to watch his language in front of his brother.

'You knew I'd read that book – you knew what the people

at school were saying! And never once did you tell us the truth. Everything I know about you is a lie.'

'That's not true,' Karla said, tears spilling down her cheeks. 'Not everything, Brandon, just that one thing – just the past. The nights we spent taking turns at your bedside when you were sick, the day your dad spent six hours in the rain because you had a new bike and wanted to ride it until it was dark, the times you—'

'The time I got punched at school because my mum and dad thought they were better than everyone else? The day someone broke into my locker and swapped my lunch for dog food because that's what my dad used to have for lunch? All the times my bag has been searched at school because I'm a celebrity kid and therefore a junkie?' Brandon was shouting now, unable to contain years of emotion that Karla had no idea he'd been holding in.

'Oh, Bran,' she breathed. 'Why didn't you tell us?'

'So you could do what? Send your thousand-pounds-an-hour lawyer into the school? Or put it in Dad's next book?'

'We wouldn't have . . .' Karla trailed off, not knowing if Brandon's teenage struggles would have been turned into another interview, another chapter in a book like the rest of their lives. She turned to Zach. 'Have you had these problems?'

Zachary shrugged. 'No, my friends think it's cool that you go on TV. I just . . .'

'You just what, baby?'

'I just wanted a nan, the same as the other kids. Grayson's nan died, and he was really upset because she used to take him loads of places and buy him ice cream. Then I got upset, and he asked if my nan had died too, and I said no, I'd never had one.'

Marcus let out a breath and looked at Karla. She knew what he was thinking because it was the same as her. Was it all worth it? All the stuff they had, all the fancy holidays, was it all worth this moment? The moment when they realised they'd failed as parents?

She heard the buzz of Marcus's phone against the countertop and saw the number on the display. Marcus glanced at it and pressed 'decline'.

'Is it her?' Karla mouthed. His mother, back again, just like the night of the party.

Marcus nodded. 'She's been turning up at my gigs. I've been seeing her sometimes.'

'What, so you get to see her but we don't?' Brandon spat. 'Fucking brilliant.'

'I'm sorry,' Karla said, throwing her hands open. 'We both are.'

'Yeah, well, sorry doesn't change anything, does it? Answer your phone – it's probably more important.'

Before his parents could speak again, Brandon stormed from the room and up the stairs, slamming his bedroom door shut behind him.

54

With the complete lack of respect it often shows for people's personal situations, time moved on. The safe, self-contained weekend turned into another Monday morning, and not just any Monday, either. Harvest Festival.

Usually, Karla and Marcus would donate a reasonable sum to the local church at harvest, along with a huge basket of produce. They didn't go in for grand gestures often, but when it came to harvest Marcus was determined to feed the world. The food was donated to local food banks – to which Marcus donated hundreds of pounds a year anyway – but his reasoning was that big, visible donations via the school created competition, and the winner was the charity.

This year, though, Karla was conflicted. Marcus had barely spoken a word to anyone since the row on Friday night, instead holding crisis talks from morning until night with his agent in his office, and she had no intention of asking him how many tins of food they should donate to the school right now. She had ordered the usual £50 hamper from Waitrose but this morning, packing it into the car while Zachary sat in sullen silence in the back, it seemed a bit vulgar. Had they really ever thought that flaunting their ability to throw money at every situation was a good idea?

The entire drive to the school had been spent in silence – not for the want of trying on Karla's part.

'Are you looking forward to Harvest Festival?'

Grunt.

'Do you know all your lines?'

Silence.

'Zach, you can't stay mad at me and your dad for ever.'

'Why not?'

And then nothing.

When they pulled up outside the school Zach swung open his door and bolted towards the school without looking back at the car.

Karla looked down the street at the other parents walking their normal, chatty children into school. How was she going to get out and just pretend like everything was fine? After Friday night she was certain that all eyes would be on her, waiting to see the famous Karla Kaplan break down at the school harvest performance.

She couldn't get out of the car. One of them had always been there for their children's performances, but this time she didn't think she could do it. It was his last ever harvest performance – he would go to secondary school next year, and Karla would have no more babies to watch – but Zach didn't even want her there.

Frozen to the spot, Karla's chest began to tighten. She tried to take a deep breath in but her lungs betrayed her and it came out as a sob. She couldn't do this. She had to get away from this place, from the stares and whispers, real or imagined. She shoved her foot on the clutch and put the car into gear, when there was a banging on the window. Looking up, she saw Miranda Davenport leaning down to her window, Felicity at her side. Karla took the car out of gear and wound the window down.

'Get out,' Miranda instructed.

'I can't.' Karla's voice was practically a whisper. 'I can't do it. I need to go home.'

'Get out of the car, Karla.' Miranda pulled open the driver's door. 'Now. You're coming to this performance. Come on.'

Karla undid her seat belt and got out.

'How can I?' she said, looking around. 'What is everyone going to be saying about me, about Marcus? They're loving this, Miranda, you know that.'

Miranda reached down and took Karla's key, locked the car with a loud beep and put the keys in her pocket. Reaching down, she took Karla's hand in hers and Felicity did the same on the other side.

'We all make mistakes, Karla. You stood by me after mine, so now we're walking into that church with you. Hold your head high. We'll get through this, together.'

Karla nodded, tears of gratitude forming in her eyes.

Together they walked towards the church.

55

'Sir, we've got Tristan's phone records back.'

Harvey's head snapped up from the CCTV footage report. Allan was jabbing a finger at a piece of paper like it contained the Holy Grail.

'Well?'

'Two calls to Mary-Beth King on Sunday the 19th of August. Just seconds in call duration – maybe answerphone, or they literally spoke a couple of words to each other. Then a text message to her number on Monday the 20th. A few hours later, the calls and texts stop completely.'

'Same as her records then?' Harvey mused. 'Anything in the lead-up?'

'Nothing, sir. If they were having any kind of an affair they weren't using those phones to carry it on. I've checked three months back on both phones. Nothing suspicious at all on either. All her numbers match up to known contacts: Peter, the school, dentist, et cetera. Tristan's match his parents, friends and work.'

'They might have had pay-as-you-go phones.' Harvey had seen it before – a second phone that looked identical to their main phone, to avoid arousing suspicion. Nothing like that had been found in either of the houses, which meant either they didn't exist or Mary-Beth and Tristan had taken them wherever they had gone.

'If they had burner phones, why use their own phones on the days before they left? Seems sloppy, considering how careful they had been.'

'Yeah, I don't buy it. Until we find proof otherwise, we have to operate under the assumption that these were their only phones. Which means they might not have been having an affair, after all. But why the contact on the day they both disappeared?'

'I hate to say it, I mean I *really* hate to say it, but I think it has something to do with that podcast.'

56

Miranda eased the door of Charity's bedroom closed and let out a breath. She'd been convinced that her daughter would take forever to go off to sleep tonight, it was always the way when she was desperate for Charity to go to bed early – as if her daughter knew Mummy had somewhere else she'd rather be than reading three chapters of *Matilda*.

'Ready?' Alex raised his eyebrows as she entered the front room. He'd lit a fire – he knew she loved it when the fire was roaring – and had the laptop on the coffee table ready. He'd even poured her a glass of wine. Good, she was going to need it. Even though she knew her part in the story was over, she was still waiting for something to rip another hole in their existence.

'Is it there?' Miranda imagined what the others would be doing now, whether they even knew another podcast had been released. They were no longer a week apart any more, just four days had passed since the voice had exposed Karla and Marcus Kaplan as frauds. Had the others been waiting, as she and Alex had, for the next one to drop into iTunes?

Alex placed a hand on her arm, letting her know he was

there for her, whatever the voice on the laptop said next. 'It's here.'

'Karla, there's another one.'

Karla looked up from her book and uncurled her legs from her husband's lap. She shifted position so she could see what Marcus was looking at on the laptop balanced on the arm of the sofa.

'What, another episode?' She sank back into the sofa. 'Delete it. I don't want to hear what that bastard has to say.'

'We have to listen to it,' Marcus said with a sigh. 'We need to know if there are any more accusations against us.'

'Should I call Felicity? The others?'

Marcus shook his head. 'I don't want the kids to know about it, if they don't already. There are some Bluetooth headphones in the basket next to you, grab them, will you? I want to know what we're dealing with before the kids round on us again.'

'It's me. Can you come round? There's been another episode.'

Peter groaned. 'I've been with the police all evening, Felicity, do we have to do this tonight?'

'Yes,' Felicity's voice was urgent. 'Why do you think we've got away with it so far, Peter? I'm sure he's saving us until last. I think this might be about us.'

'Fine,' Peter sighed. 'I'm on my way.'

57

Hello, listeners, and welcome to The Truth About Erica, *where we aim to find out what really happened the night Severn Oaks resident Erica Spencer fell to her death at a Halloween Party at the Kaplan Residence on 28th October 2017.*

Last time we heard about how Marcus and Karla Kaplan built their brand on a bed of lies. I wonder what kind of week they have been having in Severn Oaks? Enjoying this new level of fame, guys?

Well, this week I promised you a closer look at our other suspects, so here we are. For a long time in Severn Oaks people have had the feeling that something is going on right under-neath their noses between Peter King and his next-door neighbour, Felicity Goldman. Felicity, as you may be aware by now, is a beautiful single mother who has managed to develop a business in marketing, specifically brand management. She moved to Severn Oaks two years ago with her three-year-old twins, who I won't be naming – I don't believe children should suffer because of the sins of their parents, although so many children do.

Erica herself had suspicions about this pair; her diary charts clandestine meetings in the back garden, an unusual amount of Peter's energy spent fixing things at the Goldman residence, and secret looks that would pass between the pair. Here's a couple of extracts – there's more on the blog.

'It's laughable that Peter and Felicity think they can hide their relationship from Mary-Beth for ever. He was at her house again earlier! When he saw me putting the bin out he made some excuse about her toilet seat needing tightening. ***Note to self – mention loose loo seat to FG and see what she says!'

And another . . .

'Wonder if Peter will get a Father's Day card from next door this year!!!'

So did she threaten to expose their secret? Did one of them arrange to meet her in the tree house to plead with her not to tell King's wife about the relationship between the pair?

And how did their relationship begin? Well, for her sins, Erica was nothing if not persistent when she wanted information. And Erica had found a new place to buy her jewellery. From a little studio in a back garden in Shropshire, from a woman who looked almost identical to her neighbour, Felicity Goldman.

The relationship begins with months of sexual tension, building slowly at first and then crashing into a crescendo of furious, passionate sex, made all the more exciting by the thrill of the illicitness of sex with a married man. Then, a mistake. A positive pregnancy test. And nine months later the twins, Felicity and her sister Melissa, are born. Their father, Peter King, has already moved away with his new wife, Mary-Beth, unaware of the lives he has created, and he will remain unaware until twenty-one years later, when his daughter Felicity contacts him out of the blue.

To his credit, Peter King was devastated when he discovered that he had been missing for such a huge chunk of his twin daughter's lives. Less forgiving than her sister, Melissa decides she will have nothing to do with him, but Felicity is thrilled to have a father at last and Peter throws himself into the role, even securing the house next door for his daughter to bring up his granddaughters close to him. He invests in her business, which turns out to be a shrewd move, and spends an inordinate amount of time with his grandchildren. There is one little snag. He can't be sure that, even after all this time, his wife will forgive the mistake he made twenty-plus years ago. So he lies to her, time and time again, until, one night, at a Halloween Party, Peter's secret is about to be exposed. Not only that, but Erica knows all about Felicity's life before Severn Oaks, and the controversy surrounding her children's father. Did Peter King kill to protect his secret? Or Felicity hers?

Last week we heard about the heels that Erica was wearing when her body was found at the bottom of the tree house. Peter King wasn't wearing heels that night, but his wife and his daughter were. As was your hostess.

So many guilty faces walk the streets of Severn Oaks, the place where your dreams come true and your family is safe. But is one of those faces a murderer? And if so, which one?

Next week, murder inside the gates: The Confession.

58

'Well,' Karla looked at Marcus as the episode came to a close, 'I wasn't expecting *that*. Explains a fair bit, though.'

'You're telling me you didn't know? All those times you were getting your nails done, or whatever you women do, she never told you anything?' Marcus slid the laptop onto the table. 'Want a drink?'

'No, thanks. Honestly, she's never said a word. I'm desperate to know who the twins' dad is, though. What do you reckon, a politician?'

'Ask her. You're her best friend, she'll tell you.'

'She won't. I've dropped so many hints, if she was going to tell me she'd have done it by now. Do you think I should call her? Or is that going to look like I'm being nosy?'

'Which you are.'

'Am not! I'm worried.'

Marcus raised his eyebrows and Karla raised her hands.

'Okay, and curious. I'll just text her.' She tapped out a text to Felicity and held it up for Marcus to see.

U okay, hun?

'There – not nosy. Just concerned.'

Marcus grinned. '"You okay, hun?" is basically code for "tell me everything", but okay.'

Karla stuck her tongue out and snatched up her phone as it beeped a reply.

Was going to happen sooner or later. Free tomorrow for chat?

'Looks like she's ready to spill the beans,' Marcus observed, reading the text over Karla's shoulder. 'If none of us have been arrested by then.'

59

'Thanks for coming down. You probably know why I've called you.'

'The podcast last night,' Peter said.

'Well, yes, obviously I've got to ask you about that – although you did tell us about your affair you didn't mention that your next-door neighbour was your daughter.'

'Mary-Beth didn't know about that. There didn't seem to be any need to tell you.'

'And if she'd found out? She might have been mad enough to leave.'

'Me, yes, but not the kids. What happened last night changes nothing. Mary-Beth wouldn't leave without contacting the children. I thought we'd dismissed the runaway idea.'

'We have. Tell me, what was Felicity Goldman's relationship with Mary-Beth like?'

Peter shrugged. 'They were neighbours. Friends, I suppose. Our kids went to the same school, different years, but it's such a small school that they still played together.'

'Did Felicity ever put pressure on you to tell Mary-Beth about her?'

'Yeah, sometimes. Although – sorry, where is this going? I hope you're not about to suggest that Felicity—'

'Your daughter.'

'Yes, although it feels weird to hear someone say that out loud. It's been a secret for so long that I never thought I'd be able to tell anyone.'

'But now you can.'

'Yes, no, *we* can.'

'Because your wife is gone and this podcaster made sure that everyone knew your secret.'

'I suppose you could say that. Although we were going to tell Mary-Beth, then Erica died and she was so upset. It was just the wrong time.'

'Ah,' DC Allan said, closing the folder in front of him. 'It very often is the wrong time to tell someone you've lied to them, cheated on them. Not that it would matter if Mary-Beth didn't come back. Maybe, with her gone, Felicity could have her dad all to herself?'

'I see what you're getting at but Felicity and I had nothing to do with Mary-Beth going missing! It's hardly the way I wanted things to turn out.' Peter wanted to get out of there, the walls were closing in on him, Allan's questioning harsher than it had been before. This was all wrong.

'But if Felicity knew that podcast was going to come out, that your secrets were no longer safe . . .'

Peter stood up. 'We're done here,' he announced, waving a hand at DC Allan. 'And if you want to speak to my daughter, you'll need to contact my lawyer.'

60

'How are you feeling?' Karla asked, passing Felicity a mug of tea.

Her friend sighed. 'Okay, I mean we both know it could have been worse. But I don't suppose it makes things any easier for Peter. He was furious last night, I've never seen him so angry. It scared me a bit.'

'Does he know who the podcaster is?'

Felicity shrugged. 'If he does, he hasn't told me. But I'm starting to think there's a lot he isn't telling me.'

'Funny,' Karla mused, wrapping her hands around her own mug. 'Because I thought the same about you last night.'

Felicity groaned. 'I'm so sorry, Karla. I wanted to tell you of all people, but it wasn't just my secret. Peter didn't want anyone else knowing before Mary-Beth. He really was going to tell her, I think, and he thought it would be twice as hurtful if other people knew before her.'

'Erica knew, though. How do you think she found out?'

Felicity shook her head. 'That woman watched *everything*. I caught her hiding behind my bins once – she said she'd dropped something. If Mary-Beth even so much as hinted

244

she thought Peter was hiding something, Erica would have wanted to know what it was. She was relentless.'

'I know,' Karla scowled. 'Of all the people to find out about Marcus's mother it had to be her. If it had been anyone else, they would have assumed she was a friend or business associate – but Erica wasn't happy until she knew everything about everyone, was she? Although it seems like there's perhaps something even she didn't know.'

'What?'

Karla gestured her head towards the hallway, where Mollie and Amalie were colouring in the playroom. 'He never gave away who their dad is. Perhaps Erica didn't know.'

'I think she did,' Felicity admitted. 'But I think she'd only just started her investigations, maybe she hadn't had time to put it all in her disgusting burn book.'

'What makes you think she knew?' Karla sat up a bit straighter. If she played this right, she might just be about to find out the answer to the question that had been bugging her for two years.

'Something she said about my age. Oh, don't look like that, Karla, I'm going to tell you it all now, aren't I? The thing is, I'm not twenty-nine, like I said. In fact, I'm not even close. I'm twenty-three.'

Karla nearly dropped her mug. Of all the things she'd been expecting, it wasn't that.

'Why the hell would you lie about that? Most women around here lie to make themselves younger not – oh, wait, twenty-three? Which means you had the twins when you were—'

'Eighteen,' Felicity confirmed. 'But I was still seventeen when I got pregnant.'

'And their father?'

'Wasn't. He was a long way off seventeen, actually. Closer to thirty. He was married.'

'I see . . .' Karla didn't really see. What difference did it make that Felicity had been a teenage mum?

'You don't look like you see. Maybe because you've never been looked at with disgust in the street, or in the doctor's surgery. Maybe your babies have never been mistaken for your siblings. When we moved away, I started learning how to dress older, how to wear my make-up so that I looked mature not trashy. I put on as much weight as my frame could take. And when I first met people here – Erica, as it would happen – she seemed so ready to look down on me that I lied and said I was twenty-seven. Still a young mum, but no younger than she was when she'd had Max. Once I'd lied about my age once, it was easy to do it again.'

'And the girls' father?'

'Had nothing to do with any of us. I think he might have wanted to, had the circumstances been different. He wasn't a bad guy, but no one could ever know he'd got me pregnant.'

'Why didn't he just leave his wife? If he loved you? You were legally old enough, he wouldn't have been in trouble.'

'Well,' Felicity looked down into her mug. 'He would have really. He was my teacher.'

'Holy fuck!' Karla spat, then looked quickly at the door to the kitchen. No tiny faces appeared. 'Sorry. I just – your teacher?'

'I was in sixth form, he wasn't my school teacher. Although he had been. I went to one of those schools where the upper sixth is just part of the secondary school, so he'd been teaching our PE lessons – yes, I know, cliché alert – since I started. But he never even so much as looked at me sideways, or any of the girls, until I was seventeen. I was one of the oldest in my year so I was coming up eighteen. If he hadn't been my teacher, no one would have been bothered.'

'But he was, Fliss. He massively overstepped the mark. I'm pretty sure he could have gone to prison.'

'That's what my mum said. It's why we moved. I didn't want him to get into trouble – my mum wanted to go to the police but I told her if she did I'd leave and she'd never see me or the twins again. She wasn't happy, but she also didn't want her teenage daughter's name dragged through the press. So we left.'

'You just let him off the hook?'

'Not exactly. He sends me money every month – I'm not sure if his wife knows about that but I wasn't so proud that I could afford to turn it down. A few years ago I decided that if the twins weren't going to have a father, I wanted them to at least have a grandad. So I set out to find Peter.'

'And you found him here.'

'Yep. And look where that got us all.'

61

There was no point in trying to sleep. Too many thoughts crowded Karla's mind, too many images of Erica falling through the air, hearing the sickening crunch as she hit the ground. What was going on in Severn Oaks? Where were Mary-Beth and Tristan?

To make matters worse, her husband was periodically omitting grunts and snorts so ferocious that Karla was certain she felt the bed shudder with each one. With a sigh, she pushed herself out of bed and lifted a jumper from the clean washing pile on the chair. Pulling on some tracksuit bottoms, she gave a low whistle to Gigi who lifted her head, gave an almost amused snort and flopped back on her pillow. 'Come on, you,' Karla muttered, scooping the pup into her arms. 'Don't you know misery loves company?'

The night was cold and crisp, so Karla pulled Marcus's walking jacket from the cupboard and slipped it over her small frame. Fixing Gigi's lead to her, Karla gave a sharp tug. 'Come on, dopey. Let's take a walk. Clears the head. Not that your head is full of anything but chasing rabbits anyhow.'

A flat, round moon lit up the street. Security beams from the houses flicked on one by one as Karla passed by. The houses themselves were cloaked in darkness, all except the Pattersons', where their twenty-year-old son was missing from his bed. Karla shivered at the thought of Tristan's mother and father sitting side-by-side on the sofa, waiting for their son to come home. A picture of Brandon and Zachary, snuggled up in their own beds, flitted through her mind, panic rising as she imagined Brandon's bed crumpled and empty. Her husband and boys were her life, she couldn't conceive of not knowing where any of them might be, not knowing if they were alive or dead.

Gigi gave a tug at the lead, desperate to stretch her little legs now that she had been dragged unceremoniously from her bed. Karla reached down to unclip the lead from her collar. Gigi was allowed to run free, Karla was confident that she wouldn't go too far – she knew which side her bread was buttered.

Tonight she skittered ahead, bolting off to sniff at fallen leaves and then returning to Karla's side. They rounded the corner together, but the moon wasn't as bright at the far end of Severn Oaks, and Karla's chest tightened at the sudden darkness that seeped in around her.

'Come on, Gigi,' Karla called. 'Let's go and get some more milk and watch trash TV. Hopefully that will put me back to sleep.'

Gigi glanced back and gave a snort. She trotted towards the gate of number seven and began to sniff at the post.

'Fine,' Karla muttered, shaking her head. 'You do your business, I'll wait here.'

Karla shoved her hands deep into the pockets of Marcus's coat, her eyes straying to the window of the Pattersons' house, to the bedroom windows where the curtains remained open. No one would sleep in that house tonight.

A twitch of the downstairs curtains made Karla snap her head back to where Gigi had been sniffing around.

Gigi was gone.

'Oh, for goodness' sake,' Karla muttered, sorely regretting her decision to get some air. Even lying in the darkness listening to Marcus's impression of a freight train was better than trespassing in her neighbours' gardens looking for her dog. Not that she had seen the old woman who lived next door to the Pattersons for a while, now she thought of it. Brenda had hardly been the most sociable of the residents of Severn Oaks, but she had sometimes bumped into her walking her own dog, a jumpy Dalmatian called Edwin.

'Gigi,' Karla hissed, leaning over the fence. 'Gigi Kaplan, get here right now.'

The house was in darkness, no car in the drive, but still Karla felt reluctant to open the gate and go into the garden. Six months ago, she'd have thought nothing of it – everyone had been so open and friendly that you knew that if someone was in your garden at midnight they would have a good reason for it. And of course the estate was gated. They were safe behind the gates. That was before the secrets, the lies and the disappearances. Before Erica began exposing them all, even from beyond the grave.

Still, she had to retrieve Gigi somehow, and the dog wasn't responding to any of her low, urgent calls, so she leaned over the gate and flipped open the latch.

'Right, you.' Karla marched over to where Gigi was sniffing. She leaned down to clip on the lead and spotted something silver lying on the grass. A phone. Karla reached out automatically, then withdrew her hand. She stared at it for a second, not knowing what to do. She shouldn't touch it, not if it might be evidence. But evidence of what? Could this be Tristan's phone? Probably not – more likely to be Brenda's – it was in her garden, after all. And she was old, she probably didn't know anything about Find My iPhone. She nudged it with her foot. It was a new iPhone in a silver case, a black skull on the back. Not exactly Brenda's style.

There was only one way to know if this was Tristan's phone, and it was the last thing Karla wanted to do. Or, she supposed, there was secret option two – she could take Gigi home, crawl into bed beside her snoring husband and try to get back to sleep until morning came, when she could knock on Brenda's door and let her deal with it. If it wasn't her phone, she should be the one to decide whether or not to call the police.

Karla looked up at number seven, at the single lit window in the street, and imagined how Tristan's parents would be sitting, waiting for any information about their son. What's the worst thing that could happen? They were clearly awake. She would have to go and speak to them.

God, she wished Miranda was here. She would love to get involved, insert herself into the drama any way she could. She'd be banging on every house in the street, waving the phone at them, demanding to know who the owner was.

Dragging Gigi reluctantly behind her, Karla approached number seven. How was she going to bang on the door, knowing that, for even the tiniest second, Janet was going to think her son was home? Or perhaps she would be expecting it to be the police, bearing bad news. Good God.

'Karla?'

While Karla had been staring at the door, the living-room window had opened a crack.

'Janet. I'm so sorry, I just . . .'

'Wait there.' The window closed, and Karla waited. A few seconds later the front door opened.

'What time is it?'

Tristan's mum looked awful. Angry red bags under her eyes stood out on her pasty white face and her hair hung limply around her cheeks.

251

'It's late, Janet. I didn't know whether or not to come over but I thought you should know.'

'Know what?' Janet looked confused. 'Do you know where Tristan is? Did Brandon tell you something?'

'What?' Karla started at hearing her son's name. 'No, sorry. I found a phone in Brenda's garden. It's probably Brenda's but it's an iPhone and—'

'Show me,' Janet said. She stepped out of the house and pushed the door almost all the way closed. 'Mike has fallen asleep on the sofa. He is, we're both . . .'

'Exhausted,' Karla finished. 'I'm so sorry, I shouldn't have disturbed you.'

'No, I want to come and have a look. Show me.' She followed Karla down the path, not seeming to notice that she hadn't put any shoes on.

'It's there, see? I didn't touch it.' Karla pointed at the grass where the phone still lay.

Tristan's mum drew in a breath.

'It's his,' she said, a hand to her mouth. 'That's Tristan's phone.'

62

It started with one police car turning into Severn Oaks slowly, as if they had all the time in the world. It had been nearly an hour since Karla had first spotted the mobile phone in Brenda's garden. Janet had woken her husband immediately and he had insisted they call the station, there and then, glad that Karla had managed to convince Janet to leave the phone where it was until the police arrived. She'd hung around nervously on the front doorstep until Janet had roused her husband and then, feeling like a gratuitous voyeur, she had taken Gigi back home and woken Marcus.

'What is it?' he'd asked, his eyes snapping open instantly. 'Bran?'

'No,' Karla had soothed, 'the boys are fine.' She sat on the end of the bed and told him what Gigi had found in the garden next door to number seven.

'Your hands are freezing,' he said, taking her hands in his and rubbing them. 'What were you doing in Brenda's garden anyway? Why were you out at this time?'

'I couldn't sleep, so I took Gigi for a walk. Look . . .' She pointed out of the window to where the two police officers were knocking on the door of Brenda's house to no avail. 'No one's answering.'

'Well, they're not going to, are they?' Marcus replied, pulling himself out of bed and shrugging on his dressing gown. 'Brenda's ill. She moved in with her daughter about a month ago. That house is empty.'

63

DS Harvey stood by the body sprawled on the floor below the balcony, dried blood pooled beneath the head. There were thirteen houses in Severn Oaks and there had been two deaths here in eleven months, both falls. Coincidence? Harvey knew the old cliché, cops in films who said, 'I don't believe in coincidences.' But he'd seen plenty of them in his time on the force, and read about some of the most interesting co-incidences in history. Mark Twain's birth and death both occurring on the same day as sightings of Halley's comet, Edgar Allan Poe predicting the cannibalism of poor Richard Parker and – perhaps the most startling – the Simpsons predicting Donald Trump's rise to President of the United States. If it hadn't been for everything else they had found in this house, he might believe this was a coincidence – after all, it was hardly the sinking of the *Titanic* written years before it happened, or the accidental absence of the Twin Towers put down to terrorism in a video game.

But a young man was dead here, a young man not much older than his own son. And as much as DS Harvey wanted to believe that Tristan Patterson had fallen from that balcony, the way he had determined eleven months ago that Erica

Spencer had fallen from that tree house, he couldn't make the same mistakes this time around.

'Sir, the coroner is here.'

'Thank you, Allan. The family?'

'Have been taken back to the house. Family liaison are with them. There is a unit at the gates keeping the press back, but we are going to have to give them something.'

'I'm not issuing anything until the morning. Show Thomas through, then start knocking on every door in this bloody place. Let's find out what happened to this lad.'

64

The Severn Oaks Six all watched as the SOCO units and the blue lights descended on their once peaceful, tranquil world. Felicity stood alone on her doorstep, jigging from foot to foot, her giant fluffy dressing gown wrapped around her. She still couldn't believe that the man – boy? Tristan was barely in his twenties – who had been serving her coffee every morning for God knows how long had lied to her about living in Severn Oaks, or that she hadn't recognised him. Although he *was* on the other side of the curve – the street behind them was quieter, less social and no one could take the time to meet absolutely everyone – she'd only been there two years. She thought back to the day when he'd told her his 'friend' Tristan lived there. Had he been testing the waters? Seeing if she'd recognise him? He obviously knew who she was, she just couldn't figure out why he would pretend he didn't live half a street away. What was he trying to hide?

Peter, the man she had counted on for two years to be there for her, couldn't face going outside to comfort her – instead, he watched from the window of his missing wife's office, waiting to see what the police brought out of the empty house at the end of the road.

Eight-year-old Emily Spencer sobbed into the chest of her father while her older brother slept soundly upstairs.

Miranda watched from her window, her husband's arms wrapped around her shoulders. Where would this all end?

65

'Okay, what have we got?'

DS Harvey surveyed the items on the table in front of him. They were all bagged in evidence bags, the seals scribbled on with the signature of the scene of crime officer and the date.

'The laptop was in the satchel found in the front room. It's a Mac Air, currently in with tech for analysis. Wallet, keys, coat, gloves.'

'Has the mother identified the coat and the gloves?'

The SOCO nodded again. 'We're pretty sure it's all his. All except this.' The SOCO motioned towards a woman's handbag lying on the table. Individual bags containing its contents were scattered on the table next to it. 'These are clearly a woman's, and the wallet inside has been identified as Mary-Beth King's.'

'Have we spoken to Mr King?'

DC Allan nodded. 'We spoke to him last night, at the same time as we did our door to doors, although we didn't know the bag had been recovered at that time. He doesn't know that yet either. Our questions were the same as we asked everyone else, they weren't specifically relating to his wife.'

DS Harvey nodded, satisfied. 'Don't tell him yet, I don't want him knowing about this. What else?'

The SOCO indicated Mary-Beth King's wallet. 'There was blood, only a small amount, found on the wallet itself. That's been swabbed and sent to DNA. There was a larger amount of blood inside the bag itself, but only enough for a small cut maybe on someone's hand.'

'Anything in the bag to tell us where she might be?'

The SOCO shook his head. 'There's nothing else of hers in the house – no evidence she was ever actually in there in person. There are a ton of fingerprints; we'll need some control prints from the owner and also anyone she knows has definitely been inside.'

'There was no damage to any of the doors,' Harvey mused. 'Did you find any keys?'

'His house keys were in his coat pocket, one of them fits the front door.'

'Right, so we need to find out if he or his parents knew Brenda well. Perhaps he did odd jobs for her or they checked on her cat while she was on holiday or something. Any reason why he might have had a spare key.'

'I've got a possible answer for that, boss,' Allan said. 'I spoke to the daughter this morning. Apparently, they were preparing to have the house put on the market – the mother is too old to live by herself now and has early-onset dementia. They had been in talks with an estate agent to get a team of cleaners to go in and to have photographs taken before they emptied the house. The estate agent—'

'Let me guess – Tonks?' The estate agency where Mary-Beth had worked before she went missing.

DC Allan nodded. 'Bang on. Mary-Beth had the key so that she could check the place out and decide what needed doing.'

'So even if we find her prints in there, we have no idea

if they are from before or after she went missing. Brilliant. Okay, here's what we need to do. Find out if there's any link between this lad and Mary-Beth King. We need to establish if he had any reason to hurt her and steal her handbag. And did he have the means? He was only young, I know, but we've seen kids much younger than him abduct fully grown women. Were her keys in the handbag?'

'Her house keys and car keys. No spare key for Brenda Fitzgerald's house.'

'So it's possible Tristan stole Mary-Beth's handbag and took the spare key to the Fitzgerald house off to put on his own key ring. But when?'

'We've got two options,' WPC Lewis spoke up. 'Either it was after the car was dumped, or he's the one who dumped the car – which probably means he's done something to Mary-Beth King. She couldn't have dumped the car if her keys had been stolen.'

'There's a third scenario we have to consider,' Harvey said, noting all three points on the gigantic whiteboard on the wall of the briefing room. On the wall he'd written 'PETER KING DUMPS CAR'. 'It's likely King would have keys to his wife's car, so he could have moved the car without needing her handbag.'

'Nothing about that makes sense, though,' Lewis said. She looked down at her notes. 'If he dumped her car then he must have had a reason, so that means he's the one who killed her – assuming in this scenario she's dead, which I think we're all coming round to. So . . . what? Tristan robs her, and then her husband kills her in the same day? Pretty unlucky.'

'Maybe he sees what's happened to her. Maybe Peter drops her bag on the driveway while he's dumping the car and the body. It's late, dark, he doesn't see it. Maybe Tristan sees this and steals the bag.'

'Why wouldn't he tell anyone that his neighbour murdered his wife? Seems a pretty big secret for a lad to keep.'

'He was bribing King. Says he'll keep quiet but he wants cash or something. King gets fed up of it and – bang! – Tristan takes a fall.'

'Are we discounting that this had anything to do with what happened to Erica Spencer, then? Seeing as they disappeared the day the podcast was first mentioned.'

'We're not discounting anything. At this moment we haven't processed enough evidence, and the last thing I want to do is make the evidence fit a theory. Let's get the answers to our questions first, then see where that gets us.'

'Guv, one last thing?' Allan asked as they turned to leave.

'Yes?'

'Are we planning to officially reopen the Erica Spencer case in light of all this?'

DS Harvey sighed. Why wouldn't this man give up? He felt a burning knot of shame pulsing inside him – perhaps if he'd been as insistent eleven months ago, that young man would still be alive. He couldn't think like that now, though – it wasn't helping anybody.

'Not today. Get tech on that computer and see what they find. I want to know that all this is connected before I open that can of worms.'

66

The door to flat 11a was opened by a mop of dark hair and a grunt.

'John Lucas? My name is DC Allan. Can I?' He inclined his head and the young lad stepped aside without a word.

In the twenty minutes since Allan had called, John had gone to the effort of getting rid of any illegal substances and spraying the place with aftershave but the sickly smell of weed still hung around him like piss on an old dog's bed. The surfaces had all been cleared off in as much of a hurry, and Allan would place bets that if he opened any of the cupboards they would be full of magazines with rectangles ripped from the covers and week-old plates crusted with blobs of tomato ketchup.

'Thanks for agreeing to talk to me. It must have been quite a shock to hear what happened to Tristan.'

John was long and scrawny, pale-faced and incapable of sitting up straight. He nodded.

'Yeah, it seems like I was only speaking to him a few days ago, you know? It's crazy that he's not here any more. Like I can't just call him up and go for a . . . drink or whatever.'

'Did you hang out often? His mum put you down as his

closest friend.' DC Allan had to admit, the contrast between the two boys and where they lived was unexpected. Although John had no criminal record, he still lived like a student, whereas Tristan's house was – well, Tristan still lived with Mummy and Daddy in one of Cheshire's gated communities. That was some difference.

'Yeah, I suppose I probably was. He had workmates he saw every day but I don't think he ever hung out with them outside of work. Didn't see him much in the week – he did early shifts, like – but most weekends he'd stay here and we'd get some drinks, watch some Netflix, whatever.'

'Did he ever talk about home?'

John shook his head and sniffed. 'Not much. He didn't really like that place. That's why he was always here. Said it felt more like home than home did.'

'That place being Severn Oaks?' Allan made a note, his eyes not leaving John.

'Yeah, said they were all stuck-up cunts. Sorry, but that was what he said.'

'No worries, I'd rather you were accurate, I've heard bad language before. Spent three years in uniform.' Allan went with what he hoped was an encouraging 'I'm cool' grin.

John didn't look impressed. 'Right, yeah.'

'So he didn't like his neighbours. Did he mention anyone in particular?'

'Nah, well, maybe sometimes he'd say like one of them had pissed him off but I can't remember names. He didn't talk much after Erica bit it. Sorry, died.'

This was what he'd come for, and DC Allan had to force himself not to sound too keen. Mates were the best sources of information, but that didn't mean they would want to get their friends in trouble, even if they were dead.

'Right, that's Erica Spencer. Tristan's mum said they were close at one point – they were in a relationship, right?' Allan lied. He had a hunch that he hadn't shared with the DS yet and he wanted it confirmed.

John looked surprised at this, obviously he was under the impression Tristan's parents had no idea about the nature of Tristan's 'friendship' with Erica Spencer. They probably didn't, they thought their son was involved with Mary-Beth King. Allan didn't.

'Yeah, but Tris didn't want anyone to know. He said they had to be careful cos of the kids, like.'

'Erica's kids?'

'Yeah – she was worried her husband would take them away if she left him. So Tris said they had to keep it all quiet. Then she was . . . she fell, didn't she? And he just wouldn't talk about it any more.'

Then she was . . . was he about to say she was pushed?

'Did Tristan think there was more to Erica's death than the official reports? He thought she was pushed?'

Spots of pink appeared on John's pale cheeks. He pushed the dark hair from his face. 'Nah, I don't know nothing about that.'

Allan sighed. 'Look, I get it, you don't want to get him in trouble, even now. But we already know Tristan made the podcast, you're not grassing on him. We have all that evidence. All I'm looking for is to understand him a bit better, find out why he was so invested in what happened to Erica. You're not telling me anything that will incriminate him.'

'Right.' John leaned forward, his elbows on his knees. 'I just, he told me stuff in confidence sometimes, when we were drinking. I don't think he'd want me talking about it.'

'I get it. But right now it's looking like Tristan was going a little bit mental – maybe too much . . . drinking . . . if you know what I mean? A bit paranoid. If you can help me understand, maybe we can get him a bit of justice. Help people understand why he did it. And there's still a woman missing, you know . . .'

'Tris wouldn't have had anything to do with that,' John said quickly. 'He loved Erica – you already know that. He was in love with her and he got a bit . . . I don't want to say obsessed, that sounds bad, but a bit – keen? I don't know about this podcast thing, and getting Erica justice, but he wouldn't kidnap anyone.'

'I don't think he did either, but some people will. That's why I need your help.' DC Allan leaned closer to the boy. 'You said he loved her – but their relationship finished years ago, right? When she pulled him out of the river.'

That was what Erica's diary had said – there was barely any mention of Tristan after that – but John shook his head.

'Nah, that was a misunderstanding. He said she didn't mean to shove him – and she got him straight out. They didn't break up. If anything, it got more intense. I thought you knew that?' He looked panicked now.

'I think I might have misunderstood the evidence we have. So, to your knowledge, when did their relationship actually end?'

'When she died. They were still together the night she fell. That's why he was so cut up about it.'

'Right, but he didn't talk about what he thought really happened?'

'Look, we didn't exactly have deep and meaningfuls – we're not girls, like. He'd just mention it sometimes when he got agitated, he'd say about how the truth was going to come out. I thought he was just messing, he could be a bit of a conspiracy theorist, you know? Like the moon landing was a fake, Lee Harvey Oswald was innocent – that sort of shit. He'd go off spouting all sorts of shit when he was s— I mean, when he was drunk. I never took him seriously. Not until I heard about the podcast, anyway.'

'And did you ask him about it?'

'Not straight out, but I thought it might be him. He asked if I'd heard it and he had this look in his eye, all smug and proud. I said yeah, but I didn't know how this Andy guy could know what had happened unless he was there. He just said maybe he was.'

'And that was all he said about it?'

John screwed up his nose. 'I think so – I don't remember everything we talked about. It would be pretty late, sometimes we'd stay up watching films until, like, three or four, and I'd have forgotten the plot the next day.'

'Fair enough. If you do think of anything else, anything you think might clear up Tristan's state of mind before he died . . .'

John let out a chuckle.

'What?'

'There was one thing – this Andy Noon.'

'Yes?'

'I asked him what kind of name Andy Noon was – he was still pretending it wasn't him, even though we both knew it was. He just grinned and said, "Oh, I don't know, probably just a no one."'

'What's funny about that?'

'It's his name, isn't it? Andy Noon, initial A. Noon, no one. There was this one time when we were out once, we were about eighteen and we were in town. We bumped into Erica and some mates and Tristan went over to her – I don't know what he expected, he knew they weren't allowed to be seen together. She kind of brushed him off and he sloped off, tail between his legs. When we walked off, someone asked Erica who he was and she said, "Oh, a no one." Not just "no one", but "A no one". It was like the ultimate brush-off. I took the piss out of him constantly about it – that's why he was so pleased with himself when he said "probably just a no one". He was telling me it was definitely him, wasn't he?'

'I think he probably was,' DC Allan replied. *I just wish he'd told you what the hell he'd done with Mary-Beth King.*

67

The final podcast, when it dropped, was given a two-word title. The Confession.

Felicity was the first to see it. They'd listened to the last one separately and it had been awful, not knowing what the others were thinking, not knowing what might be said next. Which is why the minute her phone notified her that *The Truth About Erica* had one new episode, she flipped through her phone and called Peter.

'I know. Marcus just called. I've got somewhere to be, I'll try and meet you at theirs.'

Peter hung up without a goodbye. It occurred to Felicity that he didn't want them walking in together, but she shook that thought out of her head. Everyone knew now – what would be the point in being cagey? But he'd been off with her this afternoon after he'd got back from identifying his wife's handbag at the police station. Where was he going at this time? And what was going to be in this fucking podcast?

And Peter knew it wasn't as simple as 'I'll meet you at theirs'. It was 8.30 p.m. – she had two five-year-olds!

Predictably, Amalie was still awake.

'Come on, sweetheart, we're going for a midnight adventure.'

'In my jammies?'

'Yes, baby, in your jammies and with your quilt . . . look, pull it here. Don't forget Benji. I'll get Molls.'

'Where are we going?' Amalie asked.

'To Aunty Karla's.'

'Yay! Can I play in Zach's room?'

'If he's still awake. It is very late.'

Mollie was fast asleep and confused when Felicity tried to rouse her. In the end she gave up and picked up her sleepy daughter, still wrapped in her blanket, and leaned down.

'Jump on, baby.' She tilted her shoulder and Amalie wrapped herself around. Felicity had never imagined that her life would go like this. If someone had told her that at the age of twenty-three she would be a dab hand at carrying five-year-old twins around on her hips, and under suspicion of murder, she'd have laughed in their face. Still, she had also built up a business, had a beautiful home – yes, the deposit had been financed by Peter, but she still had to meet the mortgage payments, didn't she? And they were higher than any of the others around here would be paying out because which high-street lender would give a mortgage to a twenty-one-year-old girl with less than three years' business accounts? Even with a hefty deposit and a guarantor.

Karla opened the door before she had time to kick it. Felicity shoved Mollie at her.

'Come on, everyone's here except Peter. I'll put Molls down in the princess room, shall I?' The princess room was what the twins called the guest room that Karla had had decorated in pink, with miniature four-poster beds just for them. 'Don't start it without me.'

68

Good evening, listeners, I'm Andy Noon, host of The Truth About Erica, *and you're listening to our final ever episode: The Confession.*

Let me set the scene. It is one a.m. on the 28th of October 2017, the tail end of a fairly standard Halloween party. Most of the guests have left, only the core Severn Oaks residents remain. Miranda Davenport is listing all her year's achievements to anyone who will listen – I wonder why it is so important to her that people think she's wonderful? Her husband looks bored to tears – wouldn't we all assume he'd be the one with wandering hands, and yet even Erica couldn't find evidence that he'd done any worse than mentally undress every woman he came in contact with. Alex certainly took the 'looking but not touching' adage seriously. Felicity is chatting with Marcus, still wearing Karla's costume from earlier, while Karla herself has donned an oversized jumper and is tidying the kitchen. She doesn't notice but there is a smear of blood across her right wrist.

Marcus pressed 'pause' on the laptop and turned to Karla. 'What is he about to say?'

The only sound in the room was of Felicity's gentle sobbing, Miranda's arm around her shoulders.

Karla's eyes filled with tears. 'I couldn't have saved her, there was nothing I could have done. She was dead.'

'What did you do, Karla? What are we about to hear?'

'You already know I found Erica's body, I was the first one to find her. She was dead, I swear.'

'So why is he talking about you again?'

Karla took a deep breath.

'I ran over to her body, I looked up but I didn't see anyone there. I panicked – it was my house, my tree house. I thought about what health and safety would say – I saw that Erica had brought non-alcoholic wine with her and I didn't know that it had been swapped.' She said the last bit without looking at Miranda, not wanting to seem accusatory. She needed them on her side, needed them to believe her.

'What. Did. You. Do?'

Karla's face paled. She looked at Felicity imploringly. 'I had to make it look like it was her fault, not ours. I thought it was an accident, I just quickly swapped her shoes with mine, flung one up onto the top rung. I had Marcus's hoodie on, his cigarettes were in the pocket, so I shoved them into her bag – it was at the foot of the tree house, like she'd left it there before she climbed up, so I put the strap round her ankle. I just wanted it to look like she'd been smoking and got her heel caught. I didn't kill her.'

'Put the podcast back on.'

'I can't listen to this any more.' Felicity stood up sharply and swayed.

Marcus grabbed her arm. 'We have to hear this. Put it on, Karla.'

Karla shook her head so Marcus turned and clicked 'play'.

Karla rushes out to find the body of her friend, her neighbour – and the only person who knew the truth about the lies she and her husband had been telling – lying crumpled on the floor. Was she dead at that moment? Only Karla Kaplan knows that, and she will have to live with that knowledge. And upon finding, presumably, the first dead body she'd ever seen, Karla Kaplan does what Karla Kaplan does best. She calmly and coldly takes off her friend's heels and tosses one onto the top step of the tree house. Then she places the other by Erica's foot, to look as though it has fallen off. She plants cigarettes in Erica's bag and removes her phone. Scrolling through a phone that Erica should have known better than to leave unlocked, Karla deletes the messages between Erica and Samantha Burgess, replaces the phone and composes herself. Then, she lets out a blood-curdling scream and runs back into the house.

So, how did Erica end up at the foot of the tree house?

69

It was eleven thirty on the evening of the 28th of October, 2017.

Felicity gasped. 'That's him! That's Tristan.'

'How is that even possible?' Miranda whispered. 'He's dead.'

'He scheduled the podcast,' Felicity replied. 'That's why there was never anything about Mary-Beth's disappearance – he'd already recorded them all.'

'Ssshh!' Karla hissed. 'We're missing it. Rewind it.'

It was eleven thirty on the evening of the 28th of October, 2017.

I was at home in my bedroom, trying to find anything I could do to stop myself crossing the road and joining the Kaplans' Halloween party. The invitation had been open, after all, to everyone in Severn Oaks – why should that exclude me? I'll tell you why – Erica.

I know how most of you feel about Erica. Did you know that she knew too? She would tell me about how you would laugh when you thought she wasn't listening, make sarcastic comments about her involvement in the school and the

274

community. None of you minded her taking the responsibility off your shoulders, though, did you? If any of you had bothered to get to know her properly, you would know that the real Erica was wickedly funny, caring and deeply insecure – not that any of you bothered to find that out. That was how our relationship started, three years ago, when I found her clearing up rubbish from the street party after the rest of you had all sloped off to bed. And from there our relationship deepened.

They say that you always hurt the ones you love, and my relationship with Erica was no different. There were times when she denied how much she loved me, but she would always come back – you can't separate true lovers. We were 'until death do us part'.

By the time of the Kaplans' Halloween party our relationship was at an impasse. Erica told me to stay away and I was respecting her wishes – even if I was sitting on my hands to stop myself calling her.

Across the street I could just make out the platform that led to the Kaplans' infamous tree house. Infamous before the party because of the cost – afterwards, for other reasons.

I wonder what would have happened if I hadn't seen Erica on the platform of the tree house that night? If I'd just popped to the toilet or gone to get myself a drink? If I'd gone out with my mates instead of staying in sulking because I knew she was there with her husband? Doesn't matter, I can't turn back time. And I can't forget seeing Felicity Goldman follow her up there.

'You went up there?' Karla moved towards Felicity. 'Are you going to need a lawyer after we listen to this? Should I call him now?'

Felicity buried her head in her hands. 'I don't know,' she whispered. 'I don't know. I'm so sorry.'

'What happened?'

'Mary-Beth was so upset by that game of Truth or Dare. I just wanted to make her feel sorry.' Felicity looked up at the group imploringly. 'I just wanted her to stop being such a bitch.'

'So you dropped her fifteen feet over the edge? That stopped her,' Alex remarked.

Miranda shot him a warning look.

'I didn't push her.'

'Screw this!' Alex reached over and pressed 'play'. 'I want to know what *he's* got to say about what happened.'

70

I admit I was curious. What were Felicity and Erica doing in there? Was it some kind of game? We already know Erica had sustained a head injury thanks to her hostess – although I didn't know that at the time. So I watched. I waited ten minutes to see Felicity emerge from the tree house alone. She started down the steps and hesitated. Bending down, she ripped the loose plank of wood from the top of the stairs and rammed it under the door of the tree house, effectively locking Erica in.

'Why did you lock her in there?'

No one had taken their eyes off Felicity as the man they now knew to be Tristan had spoken.

Felicity tried to look defiant.

'She was drunk. She was being unreasonable, she wouldn't listen! I was just going to get Mary-Beth, or Jack maybe, to take her home. I didn't think she'd . . .'

'Bullshit,' Alex countered. 'You were teaching her a lesson.'

'Fine! Maybe, yes,' Felicity looked around at them all, 'but you have to realise I didn't know she was going to run at the door, I didn't know she was going to fall. But she did, and it was my fault.'

Karla wrapped her arms around her best friend as Felicity said the words she'd been trying to say for nearly a year.

She had killed Erica Spencer.

71

At this point I was worried, of course I was. Erica was locked inside the tree house and, for all I knew, Felicity was going to set fire to it. I know Erica had told me to stay away – but surely she didn't mean it now, when her life was in danger?

The Kaplans' back gate was unlocked – this is Severn Oaks, after all – and when I opened the door of the tree house I expected her to at least be grateful.

'What are you doing here?' she hissed. 'I thought I told you to stay away tonight. What if Jack sees you?'

'The door was jammed,' I stuttered. 'I came to see if you were okay.'

Erica let out a laugh. 'Fucking Felicity,' she said. 'Doesn't want me getting to Mary-Beth before the party's over. Doesn't want Peter's little secret coming out.'

'What secret?'

'Never mind.' She was still smiling, but it wasn't her usual smile. It was sly and secretive and I didn't like it.

'You're drunk,' I said.

'Am not!' Erica tried to get to her feet and stumbled. 'Whoops! I'm not even drinking.' She put a hand to her head, where I saw blood.

'What's happened? Are you okay?'

She snorted unattractively. 'Karla Kaplan, that's what happened. Wants the whole world to know her business, as long as it's the bits she chooses. I just invited an extra guest and she went mad. Clobbered me with a picture frame! I bet the papers would have a field day with that information. Maybe that's why my head is spinning.'

She touched a hand to the drying blood on her temple, smearing it across her forehead, then grabbed onto the wall to steady herself. 'You have to get out of here. I can't risk Jack seeing you and asking questions.'

Bloody Jack again. Always so concerned about Jack finding out.

'Why don't you just tell him about us, Erica? What are you so afraid of?'

She looked at me then like she was seeing me clearly for the first time. Then she said the words that sealed her fate.

'There is no us, Tristan.' She pushed past me to the door. 'You're being ridiculous. Did you really think I was going to leave my husband and family for you? What, am I going to come and live down the road in the bedroom of your parents' house? Me, you and the baby – a proper family in your mum and dad's spare room.'

She laughed to herself but I could only hear her words 'me, you and the baby'.

'You're pregnant? Is it mine?'

I won't ever forget the horrified look on her face. She'd said too much.

'No,' she said quickly. 'Of course it isn't yours. It's Jack's, my husband's. Do you honestly think I'd be so stupid as to have your baby, Tristan? You're just a baby yourself.'

'But you said—'

'Forget what I said,' she snapped. 'Forget it all. I told you, it's over. Leave me alone.'

She turned to walk out of the door, not realising that the top step Felicity had used to jam the door was missing. I'd like to say I reached out to grab her to stop her falling – I'm sure that's what it was. But she tried to push me away, she didn't even want me to touch her.

'Look at you,' she said, disgust dripping from her lips. 'So desperate. Just like that day at the river, begging me not to leave you, threatening to kill yourself if I walked away. I should have left you in the river, I should have let you drown. You're pathetic.'

And that's when I pushed her.

72

Everyone sat in absolute silence until those words.

And that's when I pushed her.

Karla let out a gasp and covered her mouth with her hand as though she was going to be sick. Small, silent tears fell down Felicity's cheeks. Miranda stared at the laptop as though it might blow up.

'Did any of you know?' Marcus asked, looking between the three women. 'About Erica and Tristan? That she was using that, that *kid*?'

'He wasn't a kid,' Alex interjected before Miranda could reply. 'He was old enough to know what he was doing, what he'd done.'

'He was vulnerable,' Marcus snapped. 'You heard him, he tried to kill himself because of her! Did you know?'

'I did,' Karla admitted quietly. 'At the time, when she pulled him out of the river. I heard her and Jack arguing about it at the time – he was asking her what she was doing down there with him in the first place – he basically accused her of having an affair.'

'And you didn't tell me? I thought we told each other everything.'

Karla shrugged. 'I thought I did.'

'Well, you didn't! Don't you think someone should have put a stop to it – someone should have done something? He's dead, for God's sake!'

'Oh yeah . . .' Karla raised her voice – something the others had never heard her do to her husband. 'Because I knew he was going to push her out of our tree house and then kill himself! It was none of my business.'

'I suspected,' Miranda whispered. 'Alex too. They weren't always exactly discreet. But I didn't know he'd tried to kill himself in the river – I thought it was an accident. Honestly, I don't see what we could have done.'

'Don't any of you get it?' Marcus looked between them. 'We are supposed to be friends. All these bloody picnics and street parties – what do they even mean if none of us are willing to actually look out for one another? To get to know each other properly?'

'That's what he's been saying all along,' Felicity agreed quietly. 'We all put on a show of being a safe community but when put to the test we all just looked after number one.'

'Didn't you hear what he actually said?' Alex looked confused. '*He* killed Erica. Not Miranda with the alcohol or Karla with the picture frame or Felicity jamming that door. None of us killed Erica.'

'He wasn't saying that at all,' Felicity whispered. 'He's been saying it all along. We were all responsible in some way. We all killed her.'

73

'Sir, we've had a strange call to the hotline. About five minutes ago. They said Mary-Beth King can be found where she was left.'

'Mary-Beth can be found where she was left. What does that mean?' DS Harvey looked around at his team, his eyes falling on DC Allan who was staring at him, a hardness in his face. Damn the bloody trainee who had been right all along, who had pushed and pushed at him to reopen the Erica Spencer case, who had had the audacity to question his judgement, knowing that in his position he would have done the same. In fact, he had done the same, hadn't he? But under pressure from a senior officer he had shoved his suspicions to one side, done as he was told. It was all any of them could do.

But DC Allan hadn't changed his mind completely. In fact, he'd increased the pressure, if anything – okay, so he hadn't gone over Harvey's head, but in his own quiet way he'd stuck to his guns. Which was more than could be said for Harvey.

'The campsite,' Allan said, as though it was the most obvious answer in the world. Heads around him began to nod. 'That was the last place she was seen – the taxi driver said he dropped her there.'

'We don't know that was her. We searched the campsite – there was no sign of her.'

'We were looking for a runaway woman, not an abductee,' Allan argued. 'We could have spoken to Patterson using a different name, for all we know – Mary-Beth could have been tied up in the bedroom.'

'If I send all my resources down there and we're looking in completely the wrong place . . .' Harvey let his words trail off. He knew that the campsite was the only lead they had, he just didn't want to admit it. Because he knew the truth: if he hadn't been so bloody-minded, so desperate not to connect Erica Spencer's death and the podcast to Mary-Beth's disappearance, they might not have been treating the missing woman like a runaway when they searched the campsite. They might have found her back then – Tristan Patterson might still be alive.

'Okay,' he sighed. 'Get every available unit down there and search the whole place. Every caravan and building. And pray to God that you're right, and we find her in time.'

74

The thick, guilty silence was broken by a hammering on the front door.

'Where have you been? Did you hear it?'

Peter nodded. 'I had it on my phone in the car. The police called me as soon as it finished.' He walked straight through to the Kaplans' kitchen and spoke directly to Felicity. 'They've had a tip-off, they're going back to the campsite, I'm going to meet them there.'

'I'll come,' Felicity offered, standing up. Her knees buckled. *What if she . . . ?*

'You stay here,' Peter instructed sharply.

Karla wondered why she hadn't seen the parental relationship between them sooner. The way he had been with her, always so worried, always upset when the twins were ill, the protective father – just Felicity's father, not Mollie and Amalie's.

'I'll let you know as soon as she's safe. It's a good job that bastard is dead, otherwise I'd kill him myself.'

He stalked from the room, followed by the remaining voices of the Severn Oaks Six and Alex telling him to drive safely, they hoped Mary-Beth was okay. Karla crossed the room to Marcus, who took her in his arms. She couldn't believe what she'd just heard.

'He was just a kid,' she whispered.

'Mum!' Brandon practically ran into the kitchen and into his mother's arms. 'Are you okay?'

Karla nodded. 'Is your brother okay up there with the twins? Did he hear any of it?'

'I had my headphones in. What's going on with Peter? He almost knocked me over.'

'The police have had a tip-off. They're going back to the campsite. I hope to God they're right.'

'Do you think she's going to be okay?' Felicity looked at each of them in turn, but no one was able to meet her eye. 'I mean . . .' She took a huge sniff and Miranda grabbed a box of tissues from the kitchen counter and pushed them towards her. 'Thanks. God knows how long Tristan's been dead for. He can't have been keeping her safe or fed in that time. She might have starved to death.'

'We have to try not to think about that. It might not have anything to do with Tristan, we don't know. She still might have run away.'

'But he *killed* Erica.'

A flash lit up the street behind the back fence.

'Wait – did anyone else just see that?'

Alex nodded. 'Like lightning.'

Karla and Marcus both sprang into action. Karla rattled the patio door handles. 'Locked,' she confirmed. Marcus pressed a switch and all the blinds inside the windows closed. He stalked through the utility room while Karla checked the front door.

'What the hell is going on?' Miranda demanded.

'Photographers,' Marcus shouted. He appeared back in the kitchen. 'Come on, through here.'

'How did they get in?' Miranda shrilled. 'They aren't supposed to be able to get in!'

No one replied but Felicity knew exactly how she was feeling. A few weeks ago they'd thought Severn Oaks was a safe haven, impenetrable and protective. How easy it had been to breach their safety all along – and not just physically.

Marcus led Felicity, Miranda and Alex into the snug, Karla following behind, with Zachary, Brandon and the twins in tow.

'Why have I never seen this room?' Felicity asked, looking around in wonder.

'It's the secret room, Mummy,' Amalie told her knowingly. 'Sometimes Zach lets us watch films in here with hot chocolate. It's his favourite room.'

Karla looked at her son. 'Is that true, Zach?'

Zach's cheeks flushed and he nodded. Marcus and Brandon were deep in conversation, their voices low while they discussed the severity of the situation. Alex was on the phone to his own father who was at their house, sitting up with Logan and Charity. Karla could hear him instructing the army veteran to check the doors and side gates were locked and close all the curtains, not to scare the children.

'God only knows what Jack and the kids are going through,' Felicity was muttering to herself.

Mollie handed her a miniature bag of Skittles to open. She pulled the top apart and handed it back. Mollie looked as though she'd won the lottery and started shoving Amalie, encouraging her to try the same trick.

'Maybe he wasn't listening. Maybe he decided it was too painful.'

'He'll find out, though, in the papers tomorrow,' Karla said. 'And the police will have to tell him, won't they?'

'He'll hardly be able to miss you all being locked up for obstruction of justice,' Brandon said.

Karla frowned at him and gestured her head towards the younger children.

'Will we all be charged?' Miranda groaned. 'This is awful, just not knowing.'

'Max said his dad had been to see an estate agent,' Brandon said. 'They're selling up anyway.'

'I don't blame him. I don't see how anything's going to be the same around here now.'

'Will you get in trouble, Mum? For, you know, tampering with evidence or whatever?'

Karla nodded. 'Probably, Bran, yes. But I'm still glad it all came out. I'm glad all of it came out. Perhaps now we can move forward.'

They sat in silence, Felicity and Karla holding hands, Brandon's arm around his mum, and Felicity holding onto Amalie with her other arm for dear life.

Zach sat in the corner of the snug, colouring with Mollie on his lap, while Miranda looked to be sleeping on Alex – although they knew she wasn't, because every now and then a small sob would come from the direction of his chest.

Marcus got to his feet several times to pace, always sitting back down with a defeated look on his face.

No one spoke for what seemed like hours, until the beeping of a text message broke the stillness.

'It's Mary-Beth,' Felicity said. 'They've found her.'

75

The campsite was lit up like a fairground, full of flashing blue and red lights from police cars and ambulances. This was no cursory check now, no simple knocking on doors and showing Mary-Beth's photo. The police officers attending had been briefed: be ready to find a body.

Tristan Patterson had been dead for over three weeks. If he had left Mary-Beth King tied up in one of these caravans it was possible she was already dead, dehydration taking around a week to kill someone. And that was if he'd kept her alive in the first place.

DC Allan shuddered against the cold, the image of Mary-Beth King's decomposing body contributing to the chill inside his thick, lined police jacket.

'Okay, everybody.' DS Harvey's booming voice pulled Allan back to the search. 'We're going to do this in quadrants. The occupants of every caravan are to be taken to the club, which the owners have very kindly heated up, and where hot drinks are being provided. Let's not ruffle any feathers here, it's highly unlikely – given that our only suspect is dead – that any of these holidaymakers are involved, so let them get their warm clothes on before chucking them out of their vans. It makes sense to do any empty vans first. The owners have given us a list of those that should be unoccupied and I've highlighted the ones in each quadrant.'

'Don't suppose you've got a van registered to Tristan Patterson on that list, guv?' someone shouted.

'Bloody hell, Stuart, I hadn't thought to check that. Good job you're here, isn't it?' Harvey retorted sarcastically, and feeling thankful he'd already checked there was no van registered to Tristan, Janet or Mike Patterson. 'No, there's no Patterson caravan. Team five – you're scouring the surrounding areas and undergrowth. There's no guarantee she's even in a caravan – or alive. And don't assume we're looking for a woman here, we could be looking at nearly four-week-old remains. Off you go.'

DC Allan was on team five, checking the undergrowth surrounding the campsite. Harvey had made him team leader, given all his work on the case. He stood now at the back of the incident van with a large map of the area in front of him.

'What's this?' he asked, pointing at a square on the map, located in the far corner of the site grounds.

'Looks like some kind of storage shed,' one of his team remarked.

'Go and get the owners for me,' Allan replied, his heart beginning to thump. 'I want this checked out first.'

The owner, a ruddy-faced woman named Caroline, was at his side in minutes. 'That's where we used to store the kitchen equipment, before we had B block built,' she confirmed immediately. 'It's derelict and locked up. You can't get in there. Well, I mean, I can – you couldn't. I have the keys here.'

'Can you take us there?' Allan asked. 'We need to check it out.'

'I'd almost forgotten it existed,' Caroline remarked as she lead them through the field. 'It's been over a year since we stored anything we needed access to in it. It's just full of junk now.'

'Can it be accessed through the back field?' Allan asked.

Caroline nodded. 'If you wanted to, yes.'

Allan was certain now that they were on to something. 'I'm guessing Patterson would want to.'

'There, see it?'

He almost didn't. This area of the field was on the edge of the site, with trees to the back, and in the darkness the cabin was almost invisible. As they approached Allan could see that the huge bolt locking the door was still in place, and his heart sank. How would Tristan have had keys to this?

'Any spare keys?' he asked as Caroline searched her bunch for the right one.

She shook her head. 'Lucky we've still got this one. Like I said, we don't really use it any more.'

She struggled with the key in the rusted lock. Allan tried not to show his impatience but his earlier elation was wearing off quickly. When the lock finally gave way, he indicated for two of his team to join him and for Caroline to stand back. He pushed open the door and swung his torch around.

The storage cabin was, as described, full of junk. An old gas cooker sat rusted and untouched in the corner, piled high with boxes on top. There was a broken lawnmower and a wheelbarrow missing its wheel, a bag of what had once been clothes but was now rotting rags, and one of the bouncy sit-on toys from a playground.

No Mary-Beth.

'Nothing,' Allan said, his voice dripping with disappointment.

'Oh God, wait.' Caroline flung a hand to her mouth. 'Come with me. There's more.'

The three officers trotted to keep up with the woman as she took long, hurried strides out of the door and around to the back of the cabin. Allan couldn't see what she was getting at until she pointed at the ground to reveal steel doors set into the floor.

'It was some kind of bunker originally. The underground bit was used to store rations during some war or other. It's why we weren't sure if we could tear it down – you know, history.'

'And is it usually locked?' Allan asked, shining his torch over the top. There was no lock on it now.

'Bolted, like the front, usually. We didn't want any kids going in and getting trapped.'

DC Allan fired up his radio. 'Sir, team five at a storage unit on the far east side of the grounds. There's nothing inside but there is an underground section which is supposed to be padlocked. There's no lock on there now. Permission to go in?'

Harvey's voice came loud and clear down the radio. 'I'm on my way. Wait for me.'

76

Harvey left his team and ran east towards where Allan had described the unit. Part of him had expected this to be a wild goose chase, a final game played by Tristan Patterson to get them running all over the campsite in the middle of the night. He was twenty years old – could he really have kidnapped a woman and held her for weeks without anyone noticing? But Harvey knew what kids were capable of, he'd been in the job long enough, which was why he'd mounted a full-scale manhunt the minute the tip had come in. It remained to be seen what would happen to his career now that Erica Spencer's death had been revealed to be more than an accident. Was there any clue that Tristan had been in that tree house? Should he have pushed further? He had no idea, and no head-space to think about that now. For now he wanted Mary-Beth found before he had even more blood on his hands.

The torch lights and high-vis jackets lit his way to the cabin, where Allan had followed orders and kept his team outside.

'Good work,' Harvey said to him, shining his own torch at the hatch. 'I guess we'd better open it up.'

*   *   *

SOMEONE IS LYING

The one thing that hit him as he lowered the ladder into the hole was the absolute darkness of the pit he was descending into. Even a day in here alone would surely drive you mad. A week and you'd, well, you'd be confessing to murder.

He swung his torch around the basement, the beam touching on barrels, more boxes . . .

Then a foot . . .

A leg . . .

A body.

'I've got her!' he shouted up to the team above ground. 'Get the paramedics here, we've found Mrs King!'

77

Karla tiptoed around the kitchen, trying not to wake anyone. Marcus and the boys were still comatose in their own beds, Felicity on the blow-up bed in the princess room. Despite Karla insisting that there were plenty of beds for her to use, she'd wanted to be close to the girls in case they woke up in the night and wondered how they'd got there. Alex and Miranda had fallen asleep on the sofa in the snug at around 2 a.m. as they had all waited for news of Mary-Beth. When Peter had eventually texted Felicity to say she was in hospital, but alive and stable, Karla had thrown blankets over the sleeping pair and Marcus had dug out the airbed to put in the girls' room. They had finally passed out around three, but unfortunately Karla's body clock didn't seem to understand that and had woken her at 6:30 a.m. on the dot.

'You couldn't sleep either, then?' Felicity's whispered voice came from the doorway.

'Not a problem for the boys, of course.'

Felicity smiled. 'I don't suppose Peter got much sleep.'

'Aren't you going to call him Dad now?' Karla teased.

Felicity laughed. 'I don't think so. Do you think it's all over now?'

Karla shrugged. 'I guess so. Poor Mary-Beth. Do you think Tristan kept her there the whole time? It seems crazy to think he could have done that, he was just a kid.'

'He was only three years younger than me,' Felicity reminded her.

'God, yeah, sorry. I can't get used to you being a child.'

'Piss off.'

'Such language in one so young!'

'Funny. So what happens now?'

Karla handed Felicity a mug of coffee. 'God knows. I'm still waiting for the police to show up and arrest me for assault. You for . . . I don't know, kidnapping? I mean, you did lock her in there against her will.'

Felicity scowled. 'It's not funny, Karla. I spent eleven months thinking she'd died because of what I did. If we hadn't all been so busy covering our own backs we could have convinced the police to investigate properly. None of this would have happened.'

'If Marcus hadn't sent his lawyer to put pressure on DCI Barrow, you mean. Don't think I don't know that, Fliss. I have no idea what happens next. To be honest, I just want to take my family somewhere far away and never hear the words Severn Oaks or Erica Spencer again.'

'At least Brandon is speaking to you again.'

'True. Although I think we have a lot of bridges to build before we can claim to be a "model family" again.'

'Have Marcus's publishers said what will happen?'

'They're still talking things through with his agent, but the feeling is that the books that mention his childhood will have to be pulled. To be honest, it's a bit of a relief. Keeping that kind of lie going is exhausting.' She looked away from her best friend before speaking again. 'We've been talking about selling up, moving on. The house is all paid off, we could downsize and live on the equity and our savings. We don't need any of it any more.'

Felicity sighed. 'You know I'd hate to see you leave, but I get it. Things aren't the same around here any more. I don't think they ever will be again.'

'Maybe that's a good thing,' Karla said, as she heard low voices coming from the snug. 'The way they were before was all just smoke and mirrors anyway.'

Mary-Beth King was alive. The relief that emanated from DS Harvey had been palpable, another dead body would have been the final nail in the coffin of his career. She had been taken straight to the hospital where she would be looked after, nursed back to health and questioned about everything that had happened in the last few weeks. Perhaps then they would get the truth.

'Harvey, come in.' The door to DCI Barrow's office stood open and Harvey made the sign of the cross before entering, an old joke that had turned into a habit.

'Sir.'

'Good work today, Harvey.' DCI Fred Barrow stood up and leaned over his desk to shake Harvey's hand.

Harvey managed to stop himself from wiping it on his trousers afterwards but it burned, feeling unclean.

'It was actually DC Allan's quick thinking that led to the recovery of Mrs King,' Harvey found himself saying. 'He remembered where the taxi driver claimed to have dropped her off, and found the cellar.'

'So all's well that ends well,' Barrow said, a nauseating smile on his face.

Harvey wanted to punch him.

'Hardly *well*, sir, a young man is dead.'

Barrow's eyebrows rose. 'A young man responsible for the kidnapping of Mary-Beth King, though, yes?'

'Possibly, yes.'

Harvey knew what he was saying. They had their case wrapped up. Tristan Patterson kidnapped Mary-Beth King because she threatened to reveal he was the person behind the podcasts. Then, realising that the only way to silence her for ever was to kill her, he left her there in the underground chamber to die, and killed himself. Patterson was the bad guy. Except Harvey believed Allan when he said that not everything added up. Only this time he wasn't going to go straight to his superior without evidence.

'Any idea how he got her there?'

'He had a notebook belonging to Erica Spencer in his possession when he died. We believe he used the information in the book to lure Mary-Beth to the campsite. We know she got a taxi there and didn't tell anyone where she was going.'

'That's that, then. What condition is King in?'

Harvey recalled the dirty, stinking woman they had pulled from the bunker beneath the abandoned shed on the campsite grounds. The hospital reported that she was having nightmares, afraid to let the male doctors near her, but there was no sign of sexual abuse – no sign of any abuse at all, for that matter. The basement of the shed had been damp and below freezing, yet Mary-Beth King showed no sign of hypothermia. There had been water bottles and wrappers from cereal bars scattered around the floor, and the stench of urine and faeces had been overpowering, but she was physically unharmed.

'She's doing better than can be expected. Any news on the Spencer case?' asked Harvey.

'The CPS are still considering the case, but without Patterson alive – and only that podcast thing as evidence –

it's going to be hard to overturn the original findings. As far as I'm concerned, we don't have any proof that Erica's death was anything other than an accident – just like you concluded in the initial investigation.'

'We,' Harvey countered.

'Pardon?'

'*We* concluded in the initial investigation, sir. If I remember rightly, it was you who suggested that we advise that Mrs Spencer's death was an accident.'

'If you remember rightly,' DCI Barrow's voice had an edge to it now, one that Harvey had heard before, 'and if I remember rightly – and believe me, I do – it is your name on those reports, Harvey.'

'That's right, sir. I was a trainee DC and I followed the recommendations of my superior. I regret that now, and I believe the initial investigation should be reopened in light of Tristan Patterson's confession and a full enquiry into the manner of his death—'

'I appreciate your input, DS Harvey. I'll be recommending that the original death remain classified as an accident and Patterson's death be recorded as a suicide, but unfortunately it is out of both of our hands now. You can go now.'

'Thank you, sir,' Harvey muttered.

'Oh, and Harvey?'

'Yes, sir?'

'If the Spencer investigation *is* reopened, I'll deny any accusations that you were pressured into your conclusions. Understood?'

'Yes, sir.'

78

Felicity took in three deep breaths, in through the nose, out through the mouth.

I breathe in calm, I breathe out stress.

I breathe in success, I breathe out failure.

I breathe in the truth, I breathe out lies.

She pushed open the door with the palm of her hand and gave a smile to the woman lying in the hospital bed.

'Felicity, it was good of you to come. Peter not with you?' Mary-Beth looked around as though Peter might be hiding somewhere ready to jump out and shout 'surprise', and when he didn't her face fell in disappointment.

'He wanted to come,' Felicity assured her. 'I asked if perhaps I could come and speak to you alone this time, I hope you don't mind?'

Mary-Beth smiled slightly. 'We had to talk sooner or later. I thought you'd have waited until I got out of hospital.'

'Oh, is this a hospital?' Felicity pretended to look around in surprise. 'It looks more like a four-star hotel.'

Mary-Beth rolled her eyes. 'You know Peter.'

'Yes,' Felicity said quietly. 'I do.'

They sat in silence for a moment, neither knowing where to begin.

Eventually Mary-Beth said, 'I suppose I'm the evil step-mother now then?'

The words rang closer to the truth than Felicity was supposed to know.

'When did you find out about me and Peter?' she asked.

Mary-Beth looked momentarily shocked but recovered quickly. Because that's what she did, Felicity thought. She recovered quickly and made snap decisions. Mary-Beth looked as though she was considering lying, then thought better of it.

'From the beginning,' she said.

Felicity felt the shock reverberate through her chest.

'I knew about you before Peter did, actually. Your Aunty Laura told me that your mum and Peter had slept together a few times – we were having a drink together in the pub, and I don't think she meant to. Anyway, she said that your mum was four months pregnant with twins.'

'She—'

Mary-Beth ignored Felicity's attempt to cut in. 'I made a vow to myself that we would be gone before those babies were ever born, and if your mother didn't tell him then neither would I. We moved away from the area before she even started to show. Peter, like a typical man, had no clue. I took my fiancé and ran, never thinking about the young single mother he was responsible for, or the twin girls growing up without a father. It was my fault you grew up without your dad. I could have insisted he took responsibility for his actions but I chose to ignore your existence.'

Felicity bit her lips, poking at her feelings to test what they were telling her. Did she hate Mary-Beth now? For so long she'd felt guilty that she and Peter had kept this secret from her, when all the time it was Mary-Beth who was keeping secrets.

'Did you know who I was when I moved here?'

'Of course I did. I always thought that Peter was a bit rubbish at keeping secrets, he would make up stupid excuses to pop out for ten minutes – not long enough to have any kind of an affair, but long enough to spend some time catching up with you. At least, that's what I thought he was doing.'

'When did you find out the rest?'

'The same time as you. I was there, the night she fell. I heard everything.'

Felicity closed her eyes and took a deep breath in. She could still picture it so clearly, spotting Erica climbing into the tree house and making the split-second decision to confront her about what she had been playing at, daring Peter and her to kiss. She had been so angry. It was obvious she knew at that point that Peter was her father – why did she get such a kick out of being a bitch?

Felicity pulled herself up onto the platform, feeling a thrill of satisfaction at the surprise on Erica's face. She'd been expecting someone different to follow her out of the party. But who?

'I don't know what it is that you think you're playing at,' Felicity started. 'But you can just stop it, Erica. This isn't some kind of game. It's only Mary-Beth you're going to hurt.'

Erica raised her eyebrows. 'Who I'm going to hurt? And how do you think she's going to feel when she realises her husband's secret daughter has been living next door for the last two years? Not to mention that Daddy funded the empire she's built for herself.'

'I paid Peter back every penny he put into my business. And he's going to tell her about me, just when the time is right.'

'Which will be sooner than expected, I dare say,' Erica smirked.

'What's that supposed to mean?'

'Well, let's just say your mother wasn't Peter's last, erm, indiscretion.'

Felicity watched in horror as Erica's hand slid to her stomach.

'You're lying.'

'Afraid not. How many does that make, five? He's very virile, your dad. Although your inheritance will be somewhat diluted.'

Felicity could barely make sense of the thoughts that smashed through her mind as she processed the implications of Erica being pregnant with her father's baby. If Erica told Mary-Beth, there was no way she would forgive him for getting her best friend pregnant. They had convinced themselves she would forgive a mistake made twenty years ago – but only three months? And so close to home . . . no, she would leave, take the kids, or . . . she would kick him out. Either one or, most likely, both of them would leave and her father would do exactly what he'd done the first time, he'd disappear. She'd be alone again. And poor Mary-Beth . . . Peter loved her, Felicity was sure he did. How could he be so stupid?

But he had always been weak – her own mother had told her that. 'Your father was a weak man who loved his wife, just never quite enough not to dabble elsewhere.' And Felicity had been furious, not at him but at her, at her mum for getting involved with a married man and denying them a father – which was ironic, given how her own life had turned out.

'You can't tell her,' Felicity had said. 'And why would you want to? It would end your own marriage, devastate your children. You would ruin everything for everyone.'

'It's going to anyway,' Erica replied simply. 'Jack had a vasectomy after Emily was born. The minute I tell him about the baby, he'll know.'

'So don't tell him. Get rid of it.' Felicity heard herself say *the words and she was disgusted at herself. How many people had told her she needed to get rid of the twins when she fell pregnant at seventeen? Her lover, his wife, her own mother, and she'd never known how they could so callously tell another person to kill their own child. Yet here she was, trying to save her father's marriage by doing the same thing.*

Erica blinked twice.

'You don't do unfeeling well, Felicity. I'm guessing you don't want to be here when I tell her?'

'I'm asking you not to tell her, Erica. You can sort things out with Jack, tell him he's a medical miracle, whatever. Just don't ruin your best friend's marriage.'

'I'll think about your concerns, thank you, Felicity. Do fuck off now.'

Felicity couldn't remember ever being so angry. Erica sat on the floor, swaying slightly, her eyes drooping. She had clearly drunk too much and wasn't used to the consequences. Well, let her stay in there and stew a bit. As she left, Felicity kicked at the loose top step, the wood splintering under her heel. When it came free she shoved it under the door of the tree house with all her strength. There, at least now she could warn Mary-Beth before Erica came and made her announcement.

'But I couldn't find you,' Felicity said. 'I wanted to warn you what she'd said about Peter, but you were nowhere to be seen.'

'I was in the garden. I heard every word she said to you. I watched you jam that step underneath the door. I thought about confronting her myself after you'd gone but I wanted to compose myself. I went to get a drink. I never saw Tristan go up there. I thought she fell.'

'I didn't see him go up either,' Felicity whispered. She could still remember the confusion and relief when she'd realised that Erica hadn't fallen from the tree house trying to slam into the jammed door. That someone else was to blame for the death she'd taken on her own shoulders all this time. 'I went to look for you in the house. I went upstairs. I was in the back bedroom when I heard her scream. The steps to the tree house were hidden from view, Tristan must have run straight home.'

Mary-Beth looked at her sharply. 'You heard Erica scream?'

Felicity nodded. 'I heard her scream. The music wasn't as loud upstairs, and I was looking in that direction. I saw her hit the floor.'

'So you saw . . . ?'

'I saw.' Felicity swallowed. This was what she'd come here to say. 'I saw you go out there, just seconds after she'd fallen. I expected everyone to go running out but no one else had heard her. They were all on the other side of the house. You looked at her lying there on the ground. She put up her hand to you. You walked away. You let her die.'

79

'Peter!'

Peter saw DC Allan get out of the car and pretended not to have heard him. He broke into a jog. Did this man never give up? What happened to the incompetent police officers the media were always moaning about?

'Peter, wait!'

Peter swung around, his face etched in a scowl. 'This is harassment, do you know that? If you have any more accusations – sorry, I mean *questions* – you can direct them to my lawyer or arrest me.'

'There's no need to be like that.'

Peter picked up his pace towards the entrance to the hospital, but Allan matched him step for step.

'I just wanted to know how Mary-Beth was doing. I'm the one who found her, you know that?'

Peter stopped. Perhaps he was being paranoid. As annoying as it had been, Allan had only tried his best to help Mary-Beth. It wasn't his fault they'd never wanted his help. 'I do, and I'm grateful, of course. DS Harvey said if it wasn't for you she might have starved to death.'

'Oh, I don't think that would have happened, do you?' Allan cocked his head to one side.

'Obviously it would have. She couldn't have survived any longer on those scraps of food that boy left her.'

'No, you're right. Convenient really, that she had just the right amount of food left when we found her. You know what else is convenient?'

Peter's eyes narrowed. He didn't like where this was headed. He should have just kept walking. 'What?'

'Well, for one thing, it was awfully convenient that Mary-Beth had been in that basement for weeks, and yet she had no lasting physical effects. In fact, I've spoken to the hospital and once the observation period is over she will be cleared to leave. No hypothermia, no malnutrition, nothing.'

'Something to be glad of, that she was so lucky.'

'Yes, very lucky. You know what else is lucky?'

Peter's teeth clenched. 'I'm sure you're going to tell me.'

'I will. It's another one of those pesky coincidences, like Tristan Patterson being found the exact evening the last podcast aired. You see, there's a row of static caravans on that site. You know who manages the empty caravans for them? Tonks – I know, the estate agents your wife works for. What are the chances?'

'Quite high, actually.' Peter sucked his bottom lip. 'Tonks manages over a thousand properties in this area. You'll find a house in every street they are selling or renting.'

'Including your street.'

'Yes, including mine.'

'Mary-Beth told us that Tristan arranged a viewing of a house the afternoon of the picnic. She parked across the road and was getting out of her car when he took her hostage.'

'Then that's what happened.'

'Yes, of course. Just strange that the taxi driver said he

picked her up in town later that evening and then dropped her at the exact place we found her.'

'He must have been wrong. '

'Lucky guess? And the name she used, Erica Spencer? That was another lucky guess, was it? I still can't figure out why she'd do that. Maybe she was just trying to get caught. Stopped before it went too far. Maybe she was getting cold feet.'

'Or the taxi driver saw the name on TV and came up with a story that matched the news. Why don't you just say what we both know you're trying to say?'

DC Allan grinned. 'Okay, I've been waiting to share this theory with someone. You see, I think that Mary-Beth suspected that Tristan was behind the podcast, knowing of his relationship with Erica, and that he planned to name you all as suspects, just like she claims. But rather than him arranging a fake viewing in order to kidnap her to keep her quiet, I think – correct me if I'm wrong – that your wife confronted Tristan in the empty house he was using and something happened. Maybe it was an accident. Maybe she didn't mean to hurt him but she did. So she pushes him off the balcony to make it look as though he couldn't go on living without Erica, and then runs.'

'This is—' Peter started. His heart was thumping so fast he thought he might have a heart attack on the street. That would shut Allan up, at least.

'I haven't finished. She checks her handbag and runs to the only place she had keys for – an empty caravan on Dalton campsite. I'm guessing we'll find evidence of Mary-Beth being there.'

'You probably will. Like you just said, she manages those vans – she's in them all the time.'

'How convenient. You didn't mention that, when I told you the taxi driver dropped her off there.'

'I didn't know Tonks managed those empty vans until you just said. It's not like she gave me a list of all the thousand-odd properties on their books.'

'Shame. We might have found her sooner.'

'Except she wasn't in the caravan – she was in that horrible hole.'

'So she says.'

'Okay, let me check I'm understanding you. Mary-Beth – my murderous wife, who lets spiders outside rather than step on them – kills Tristan, goes on the run and is hiding in a static caravan half an hour away. How is it that you found her locked in a basement?'

'Well, that's the thing.' DC Allan's eyes narrowed. 'She wasn't locked in, as such. Okay, the ladder to the hatch had been pulled up, and the door was heavy. It's true she probably couldn't have got out by herself. But she could have got in. All it would take is for her to lower herself down and pull the hatch closed. Then wait until we find her.'

'And if you didn't find her? Do you think my wife would be stupid enough to trap herself in a basement on the off chance you lot did your job properly? Because you were so competent when Erica died!'

Allan ignored the jibe.

'We didn't just find her on the off chance, Peter. Didn't anyone tell you? We had an anonymous tip-off. Except Tristan was supposed to be the only person who knew she was in there, and Tristan was already dead.'

'Maybe someone heard her shouting.'

'Why wouldn't they just come forward? Someone finds a missing woman, they're a hero. Seems strange not to wait for the police to show up.'

'So Patterson told one of his mates what he'd done.'

'If he did, we can't find them.'

'Look . . .' Peter felt his patience snapping. How had he

thought they would get away with this? 'My wife has been through a traumatic ordeal at the hands of an obsessed young man who I'm not sorry is dead. I realise it would be a much better story for you if Mary-Beth and I had planned the whole thing for our own twisted amusement, but you're wrong. You can't expect me to explain the actions of a crazy man. And if you keep harassing me, I will have no choice but to go to your boss, DCI Barrow, is it? And tell him your ludicrous theories.'

DC Allan held up his hands. 'Okay, I get the point. I've just got one more question for you and I'll leave.'

'What now?'

'I was wondering if you could tell me.' DC Allan leaned in so close that Peter wondered if he could smell the faint vestige of alcohol that hung around him. 'I've been trying to get my head around it but I can't. If Tristan was dead by the 21st of September, and Mary-Beth was locked in that basement, how do you think the PTA's WhatsApp message was delivered to her phone? It wasn't read,' he added, watching the colour flush through Peter's face, 'but it was delivered. Yet by the time Cynthia Elcock called me to report it, just ten minutes later, the phone was off again.'

Peter's mouth dropped open slightly. DC Allan held up a hand. 'Of course you're not a detective – I don't expect you to have all the answers. I'm sure the tech team at CID will give us all the answers we need. Send my regards to Mary-Beth.'

80

'I let the baby die,' Mary-Beth corrected. 'My husband's baby. Erica was collateral damage.'

Felicity had seen Mary-Beth walk away from her best friend, dying on the grass, and yet this coldness was still shocking to hear.

'Do you really think I could have risked Erica living? The baby living? I'd kept hold of Peter once, when he got your mother pregnant, but there was no way I'd be able to deny this one. When she told everyone, my life would be over. I'd made the decision that I could live with the evidence of a twenty-year-old infidelity living right next door, but to have a fresh humiliation living the other side? Sandwiched between the proof that my husband wasn't just fucking around but fucking around with my best friend? At that moment I hated her. And I didn't kill her, I just let her die. I let them both die.'

'And Tristan?'

She hadn't thought Mary-Beth could look any whiter, but she seemed to pale at the boy's name. 'That was an accident. He knew – or I thought he knew.'

'You thought he'd seen you?'

'I didn't know he'd pushed her out of the tree house. When I saw her fall I didn't even think to look up, I thought she was in there on her own. The steps were on the other side, I didn't see Tristan at all. When those Facebook posts appeared saying someone had murdered her, well, I assumed he meant me. As far as I knew, I was the only one anywhere near her when she died.'

'Did you know it was Tristan?'

'Straight away. Something he said in the first post, something about her being a "local hero". No one of us would describe her like that. I already knew they were having an affair, I knew he was obsessed with her. And when I asked him he didn't deny it, but he refused to tell me what he knew.'

'And then he kidnapped you and put you in a cellar?'

Mary-Beth looked around her as though the walls could absorb their words. 'Don't be ridiculous. Do you really think Tristan Patterson was capable of kidnapping anyone?'

'Then what . . . ?'

'He wasn't listening. I had to shut him up and make him listen. I lunged at him . . . he was leaning over the balcony, he was off balance. I just, it was just a push.'

Felicity's eyes widened. 'You killed him? They said he jumped.'

'It was an accident. I never meant for him to actually fall! His computer was there, awake. I tried to get into his hosting to stop the podcasts but they were password protected and if I'd guessed the wrong password it would be on record that someone tried to get in. I typed out a note saying I couldn't go on without Erica, and ran.'

'Did Peter know where you were?'

Mary-Beth's eyes dropped to study the table in front of them.

'Yes,' she replied quietly. 'But don't be mad at him. I didn't know what I was going to do. When the podcast went out anyway, without Tristan alive to upload it, we realised they must be pre-recorded and scheduled to upload at certain times. Without knowing Tristan's hosting details all I could do was listen, horrified. Peter brought me food when he could – he almost got caught trying to warn me that the taxi driver had identified me. So stupid to use Erica's name but I was in a state and it was the only one in my head. It was too risky to move but all the police did was shine a light in and bang on the door.'

'So you were there the whole time?'

'Until the last podcast aired. Peter called me to say that Tristan had confessed to pushing Erica.' For the first time, tears began to form in the corners of Mary-Beth's eyes. 'He never even mentioned me. Anyone could see it was going to end badly – I just didn't think this badly. He died for nothing.'

Felicity stared at the wall in silence. It was too much to take in. Mary-Beth had let Erica die, she'd known that much when she'd gone there. But this was different, wasn't it? Or was letting someone die any worse than killing them by accident? Was what Mary-Beth had done to Tristan worse than what she'd done to Erica?

'Was it Peter who tipped off the police?'

'Yes. He said it was okay, Tristan hadn't told everyone the truth and that he was going to ring in a tip-off of where I was. He'd found a bunker, I needed to climb in, and make it look like I'd been there a while. It wasn't hard – I'd barely eaten anything since Tristan . . .' Mary-Beth sighed. 'He hated every single one of us, you know. He blamed me for Erica not wanting to be with him, he hated the way we were all so selfish, all lying to preserve ourselves. No one came forward after she died to tell the truth about what they had done. We all just kept lying to protect ourselves, and pretended we all loved Erica. Except I *did* love Erica. Right until the moment she threatened to rip apart my whole family.'

'I still wonder how he knew so much about us,' Felicity whispered. 'It was like he could see through our very skins.'

'Maybe he could,' Mary-Beth replied. 'May God forgive us for what he saw under there.'

Epilogue

Erica

It's been two years since my death, a year since *The Truth About Erica* first aired. Severn Oaks has taken some re-adjusting. Jack and my children have moved away from Cheshire entirely, moving on in the only way he knows how. Karla and Marcus have moved as well, not because of the financial hit the revelations took on them – they were still more than wealthy enough – but because Karla insisted that she wanted to start again, to put right some of the mistakes they had made with their children. Brandon went away to college, using the name 'Burgess', and has managed to slip quite seamlessly and anonymously into normal student life. He visits his parents every few weeks but they have been instructed that under no circumstances should they ever set foot in his flat.

In the wake of the revelations about Miranda spiking my drink, she quit the PTA, the Parish Council and the Planning Committee. All of her resignations were declined. It seems that everyone likes her a lot more when she's not pretending to be perfect. She even has a group of friends of her own now, although Cynthia Elcock isn't one of them.

DS Allan – yes, a promotion and a commendation! –

remains unconvinced by Mary-Beth's story, only no one wants to listen to him. Everyone is more than happy to accept the gift-wrapped version that they were presented with. Tristan killed Erica, then killed himself, leaving Mary-Beth to die in a cellar. Everyone except DS Harvey, that is. The pair of them are quite the detective duo these days, and I don't think they're far off putting together the pieces.

Peter and Mary-Beth still live in Severn Oaks, next door to Felicity. Far from being the evil stepmother, they get on like anyone would expect two people harbouring a killer secret would. Felicity and the girls go over for dinner at least twice a week, and Mary-Beth cooks her famous soda bread for Mollie and Amalie to take to school. None of them have told Peter they know about his affair with me. Maybe if they had been honest with him, they would know by now that everything that happened on the night of my death, and everything since, was based on a lie.

Someone was lying that night and it caused my death. That someone was me.

In hindsight I never should have told Felicity that Peter was the father of my unborn child, but what's a little white lie between neighbours? I didn't think for a second that she'd believe that Peter would cheat on his beloved Mary-Beth a second time, and how was I to know that Mary-Beth could hear every word? I wanted to tell her the truth, as I lay there dying – that Peter would never have slept with me, nor I with him. We both loved her so much. I just wanted to hurt Felicity – beautiful, clever Felicity whose very existence caused Mary-Beth so much pain. I wanted her to feel like she wasn't so special after all, that she wasn't the product of forbidden love but a tawdry affair that her father would have with anyone. Even me. And yet it was that one lie that turned my best friend against me, one simple lie.

Only it's not always that easy, is it? You see, I have it on good authority that someone in Severn Oaks isn't happy with the verdict of suicide given to Tristan Patterson. Someone who has been doing a bit of digging of their own. And I wouldn't be surprised if, in a few days' time, Severndale Primary School's Facebook page receives a mysterious posting. Because although people know some of the goings-on in Severn Oaks, only you know the truth. All of it.

Until next time . . . stay honest.

Acknowledgements:

As always my first thank you goes to my agent and friend, Laetitia Rutherford. It's been over five years since we first met and you have changed my life in ways I only dreamed of, you are always there to encourage and support me. Also to Megan, Rachel and the whole team at Watson Little.

To the wonderful team at Headline, firstly Jess Whitlum-Cooper who is everything you could ask for in an editor and more. Thank you for your unwavering support and brilliant advice. Thanks also to the rest of my Headline family, namely Jo Liddiard, Jenni Leech, Jen Doyle, my copyeditor Shan Morley Jones and everyone behind the scenes who make a book a success.

Over the last five books there have been so many other people who have kept me going in this writing game – too many to thank and I'd be terrified of forgetting anyone but please be assured that if you have ever sent me a message, tweet, email or carrier pigeon to tell me you've loved one of my books then this thank you is aimed at you. If you have left me a lovely review or included my book on your blog, spent any of your free time recommending me to friends and family – this thank you is for you. You keep us going on the hard days.

To my crime writing family, without whom I could probably write four books a year – thanks for the procrastination. You know who you are.

And through all this there are the people who have to put up with me In Real Life. The people I can't edit my comments to before I press send, the people who know when my deadline is from my CWPS (cuss words per sentence) and the ones who bite their lip if my jeans are on back to front. Thank you to mum, dad and Jen for everything you do for us, my Farrs family and Vicky for all the impromptu deadline week childcare and both my nan and gran who listen to every radio show, still call me to tell me they've seen me in magazines and still read my books even after the awkward sex scene incident.

And mostly thank you to my boys, Ash, Connor and Finlay for still living with me, still loving me and for pretending you don't know where I hide my chocolate.

THRILLINGLY GOOD BOOKS
FROM CRIMINALLY
GOOD WRITERS

CRIME FILES BRINGS YOU THE LATEST RELEASES FROM
TOP CRIME AND THRILLER AUTHORS.

SIGN UP ONLINE FOR OUR MONTHLY NEWSLETTER AND BE THE FIRST
TO KNOW ABOUT OUR COMPETITIONS, NEW BOOKS AND MORE.